Contents

Faces

The plant labors all the year, green and growing and undistinguished. At last, in its season, it blooms, and all the folk remark on the beauty of the flower. Yet that bloom is only the product of the plant. It is wrong to see the flower as the only important thing, for it is the plant that makes it—yet it is the aspect of the plant designed to receive attention, and should be judged as such.

Similarly the writer labors to produce his narrative, and if it is wrong to treat that narrative as if it had no genesis, still it is the aspect the writer chooses to be represented by. Judge the writer by his narrative rather than his picture—but do not scorn the picture any more than the green foliage of the plant, for these may be alternative avenues to comprehension of the whole.

Alien Plot

I need to make a distinction: The title of this story refers to a plot of ground, while the title of this collection refers to a dastardly conspiracy. It is the conspiracy by editors to frustrate writers, and a number of the entries in this volume will harp on that theme. This present novelette is the major piece of the volume, and the major example.

It started in Mayhem 1990, when I received a solicitation from an editor to contribute a story to a volume titled *After the King: Stories in Honor of J.R.R. Tolkien,* to be published in mid-1992, the 100th anniversary of Professor Tolkien's birth. The guidelines were simple: stories that were true to the spirit of Tolkien's great accomplishments, or stories that his work made possible. "Please note," the letter said, "that you *cannot* use Professor Tolkien's characters and settings . . ."

Well, that seemed simple enough. Tolkien made possible the entire modern fantasy genre; virtually all current fantasy fits under that broad umbrella. As for the spirit of his accomplishments, let me make this plain: I was a Tolkien fan from the 1940's when I read *The Hobbit,* which I considered to be the greatest fantasy adventure ever. I see few influences by others on my manner of writing, but surely Tolkien had a significant effect. I didn't like THE LORD OF THE RINGS as well, finding it too long and diffuse, but it was still great fantasy. It would be hard for me to avoid the spirit of Tolkien in my own fantasy.

But I was jammed for time, because I was answering an average of 150 letters a month that year and had contracts for half a dozen novels. I couldn't just dash off a token entry; to do justice to the spirit of Tolkien I would have to make a significant effort. That was apt to put me behind schedule on my existing projects. So I wrote back, demurring because of the press of business. But the editor insisted, saying that he really had to have me in that volume. So, reluctantly, I agreed. I finished the novel I was then in, the 108,000-word *MerCycle,* and delayed the next, the 141,000-word *Fractal Mode,* so as to make space for the 16,000-word "Alien Plot."

I was not allowed to use any Tolkien setting or character, but was supposed to be true to the spirit of his fantasy. I pondered, and decided to go whole hog: I made a setting and characters that were nothing at all like his, but a spirit that was exactly his: that of an ordinary man getting gradually into something quite alien to the contemporary world, and finding fulfillment there. The original hobbit really wasn't looking for adventure; he was a quiet homebody. But before he was through, he had had the greatest adventure of them all. So I started with an ordinary, undistinguished contemporary man, who longed for the realms of fantasy, but never expected to experience them. Then, by an unexpected and strange route, he found himself in just such a realm, and managed to acquit himself honorably by its odd rules. Just as the original hobbit did. The person was unprepossessing, but underneath he had character that was to be respected. The spirit, the essence, without the form, just as the editor required.

I completed the story and shipped it off. The editor sent a brief scrawled acknowledgment, and didn't mention the matter again. But I saw a note on the volume in a newsletter which listed Anthony as among the contributors, so I figured that was set.

I heard from my agent: Another editor was offering me

more than ten times as much for the story. Now this was surprising in more than one respect. First, I hadn't used the agent on this story; I had dealt directly with the editor. The agent was handling my novels, but stories were really not worth his while. Second, the amount: I was being offered more than I got from some novels. What prompted such interest, which I hadn't solicited? It was a resounding endorsement of the story, but an odd proceeding.

I pondered, but concluded that it would not be right to pull my entry from the Tolkien memorial edition for which it had been written. My sympathy for editors is small, as this collection will document abundantly; I try not to miss an opportunity to make a snide remark about editors. But I try to hold myself to a higher standard than that practiced by editors, and to honor all commitments I make, whether express or implied. Though I had not yet received the contract for the story, so was not legally bound, I was ethically bound. So, with regret, I turned down the far richer sale.

Time passed. When, a year after sending in the story, I still had not received a contract for it, I realized that there had been a slipup somewhere. So I queried the editor, gently: Wasn't it time for a report on my story?

He didn't answer. Instead I heard from the other editor: "Alien Plot" had been rejected. The first editor hadn't bothered to inform me. I had never received notice, and I never got my manuscript back, but it seemed he had decided that my story wasn't right for the volume. Maybe I should have ignored the editorial instructions and done a clone of Tolkien, as I readily could have. That was, it seemed, why the second editor had felt free to make the richer offer. I had turned it down in favor of a sale I never had.

I mentioned editorial ethics. Well . . .

In this manner this story came to join my collection of rejects, so was available for this volume. I submit it as Exhibit A in my case against editors, who can treat seasoned pros as shabbily as hopeful unsold writers.

I do believe in my story. There are things here that I

subscribe to, such as protection of the environment and a longing for a better world. It is an editor's right to reject what doesn't suit his taste. But it is a writer's right to make his own case. Here is mine.

Alien Plot

It was a desolate region. What pollution hadn't stunted, the drought had wilted. Duff turned his eyes away from the dreary scene and snoozed as the taxi carried him on.

He imagined a melange of the great realms of fantasy, where magic worked and fantastic creatures roamed and swords were the state of the art in weaponry. Where wizards cast horrendous spells, and maidens were not only beautiful but innocent. He had used fantasy settings in role-playing games, and had tried many fantasy computer games, but none of them were quite enough. Mostly he just read and reread the wonderful adventures; they were his main escape from dullness.

For Duff had long since resigned himself to the fact that though he had the aspirations of an adventurer, he had the body and mind of a nonentity. He wasn't handsome or brilliant; about all he could claim was decency, and decency didn't carry much weight in the military life. Or the civilian life, he knew. So he longed for the realms where magic could supply what he lacked.

Soon he achieved his desire: He dreamed he was in such a land. He didn't have a quest; he was just walking through a world he knew was magic. He was sure that if he walked far enough, he would encounter both dragons and sweet maidens. He didn't even want to hurt the dragons; he just wanted to be in the same world with them. For in such a place, he would have some kind of magic ability that would make him a person of note. Not of great reputation, just someone to be respected for himself, that one woman would find intriguing.

He woke as the car slowed, approaching the project

grounds. Here, at least, there was greenery, and the main building looked like an old hotel. It probably was just that, converted to military use. Behind it was a tall wire fence with the top angled, the kind used to contain dangerous men or animals. But all that was visible within that compound was a forest, with a hill in the background.

A portly man in civilian clothing was waiting as the taxi stopped. Duff climbed out, and hesitated. "Sir?" he inquired.

"Colonel Clelland, but don't salute," the man said, proffering his hand.

"Sergeant Duff Van Dyke, sir," Duff said, taking the hand.

"Come in. Leave your things; you won't be using them." The Colonel drew him on into the lobby.

"Sir?"

"We have less than an hour to get you into action," the Colonel said. "Keep your mouth shut and listen while we get you ready."

Duff obeyed, knowing better than to argue with an officer. But he was beginning to doubt his wisdom in accepting this mysterious assignment. He had admitted to being bored with military life, and to the consideration of letting his hitch lapse so he could return to civilian life. But he still had three months to go, and his commander had made him an offer he couldn't refuse: finish out his hitch with this special assignment, and if thereafter he wished to re-enlist he would receive a jump promotion. If he elected to leave the service, he would be given an equivalent civilian job in any region he chose. The commander was a man of honor; Duff could trust the deal. So he agreed, without knowing anything about it. In fact, he had been flattered that his re-enlistment was so strongly sought; he had been no more than a quiet, hardworking paper-pusher. He hadn't figured they would miss him.

He still did not know the nature of his assignment. It was evidently secret. But strange.

The Colonel brought him to a private chamber. A middle-aged woman was there. "Dress him," the Colonel told her.

She approached Duff immediately and began to remove his clothing. "Sir—" Duff protested, surprised.

"Stand still; there's no time for that." The Colonel flashed a momentary glare that showed that he had indeed had decades of command, and Duff was cowed. He tuned out the woman as well as he could, and listened.

"As you know, we have been exploring alternate aspects of reality," the Colonel continued after a pause. Duff hadn't known that, but masked his surprise. The military cult of secrecy was one of the things that had made him yearn for civilian life. Evidently the Colonel assumed he had been briefed. "Most of the alternates we have discovered are similar to our own culture, with distressingly similar problems of overpopulation, depletion of resources, and fouled-up political systems. There really is no point in establishing relations with them; they can't help us and we can't help them. We have been looking for rich wilderness worlds to colonize and exploit; we could solve all our problems with a few of those."

"Yes, sir," Duff said. But he remembered how the Western Hemisphere had represented such a solution for crowded Europe. He was something of a fan of medieval Europe, because that was the implied setting for much of heroic fantasy. It was even said that Middle Earth was merely a map of Europe turned sideways. But in real life, Europe had destroyed most of its heroic natural resources. All too soon the New World had been fully colonized and exploited, and now had problems just like the old ones. Was it really good to have man laying waste pristine lands for short-term benefits?

Meanwhile, the woman was undressing him. She was perfectly businesslike, but it was hard to tune it out completely.

"A year ago, we discovered an ideal world," the Colonel said. "Phenomenal resources of wood, coal, oil, gold, diamonds, pure water—everything this Earth of ours ever had, because it *is* this world, but with all its assets untouched. There are people there, but they do not use these things. They do not seem to amass wealth. They do not practice war. They seem to live in absolute peace and harmony with nature. It's uncanny, and of course suspicious."

"Of course, sir," Duff agreed. Oh, to live in such a culture! He was tired of the rat race that was daily existence. He had enlisted in the military life because of the security of money, housing and health care it offered, but felt stultified by its lack of adventure. It would not be better in war time, he knew; then there would be excitement of a sort, but it could kill him. He wanted ultimate security and ultimate freedom, and it didn't seem to exist.

Which reminded him: He was now standing naked, the woman having stripped him completely. The Colonel didn't seem to notice.

"So we sent in an armed party to subdue them, naturally. And it disappeared. So we sent in planes and tanks—and they disappeared. Obviously the natives have some kind of weapon we don't know about. We don't dare try to colonize and exploit that world until we have pacified those dangerous aliens. But we can't pacify them until we nullify their weapon, and we can't do that until we know what it is."

"That makes sense, sir," Duff said. But in his private heart, he was rooting for the folk of the other world. Let them remain undespoiled!

Now the woman was dressing him in odd clothing. Strange thick underwear, and a winding around the waist. The dress of the otherworld folk?

"So six months ago we set up a special project," the Colonel said. "We constructed a village just like one we had photographed in the alternate world, and made costumes like those of the natives, and instituted a life-style just like theirs. It is medieval, actually; it most resembles our society of a thousand or so years ago. But patterned on what we know of the aliens. We copied their icons and their architecture, as far as we know it. We managed to get one of their books, and translate it; it's a book of spells and rituals. So these are required of the inhabitants. Then we populated it with volunteers. We gave them drugs and electroshocks to disorient them and erase their recent memories, and put them into that model village. Fifty-two people, evenly divided in sex, ranging in age from ten to fifty. We made an instant functioning alien community. People who believe in magic, and think they are in a land of dragons and sorcerers."

"That must have been quite a trick, sir." In fact, Duff doubted that it would work; strangers could not simply be dumped into a setting and made to operate like clockwork dolls. He himself longed to be in just such a world, but he would not be fooled for a moment. He did know the difference between reality and fantasy. But the military mind didn't know that people weren't automatons. Nevertheless his interest was intensifying. This was a fantasy setting!

The clothing, too, was fantastic. Now he was being garbed in a robelike wrapping with an attached hood, bright green.

"Of course we have pickups throughout the village. We can see and hear everything that goes on. We have everything on tape: every conversation, every bodily function, every sexual encounter. The idea is that by watching this community, we may learn how the aliens think. Then we hope to introduce our villagers into that other world, after teaching them as much as we can of the other language, and with luck they will get along well enough to find out where and what that secret weapon is."

"Smart ploy, sir." Trust the military mind to care nothing about any of the other culture; all it wanted was to nullify a weapon, so the conquest could proceed. And how much of a thrill were the voyeurs getting, watching the villagers have sex?

Meanwhile, the woman had finished the job of dressing him. All that remained was the shoes, which turned out to be soft green slippers with pointed toes that tapered into lengths of cord which flopped as he moved his feet. They were comfortable, but he would hate to be seen in public in them.

"But there's a problem. We can see that the members of this community are honoring the prescribed rituals. They make obeisance to the symbolic statues we installed. They seem to be truly accepting the life-style established for them. They have, to a remarkable extent, become aliens. But in the process, they have become too strange for us to fathom. That's why we need to send in a normal man to investigate."

Now it came clear. "Me. Because I read fantasy and am available for something unusual." It hadn't been his record or his dedication, it had been his weirdness. He should have known.

The Colonel nodded. "You. For those reasons. And because you're not one of our regular personnel. They wouldn't accept one of us; they know who we are, somehow, even when our number changes. But it takes at least an hour for them to pick up on a new member, so we must move you through within that time." He paused for a deep breath. "All the volunteers were fantasy addicts; we felt we would succeed better if they had a predisposition. The aliens seem to believe in magic, so our community believes in magic. We fear the people will not accept a person who isn't sympathetic."

"I'm not volunteering to be given shock treatments and memory loss!" Duff protested.

"No, of course not. You must remain one of us. That is the point. You must pass as one of them, but retain your objectivity."

Thus the costume: evidently what the members of this artificial community wore. He surely looked the part, now! "But sir, I am perplexed. If you have visual and sonic monitors throughout the village, surely you already know what's going on there."

"We thought we did. But the villagers seem to have developed types of communication we aren't aware of. They act with an uncanny unity we can't fathom. They have make-believe children that they evidently believe in—and when a 'child' goes from one family to another, the second family greets it though there has been no communication between the two families. They go up a hill to placate a dragon-god. We do have a mock-dragon there, but they—" The Colonel shook his head. "Sometimes I think I'm going crazy myself."

"Why should I see anything the sensors don't?"

"I don't know. But it seems that *they* see what the sensors don't, and we hope they will show you what that is. When you find that out, you will return to report to us. We expect it to take two weeks or a month; you will need that long to be accepted by them. A lot depends on the woman."

"Woman?"

"You are single. All of the villagers have paired. That was one of the earliest surprises."

"Well, sir, isn't it natural for men and women to get together?" He spoke as if this was routine, but it wasn't; he had spent his adult life longing for a woman who would love him. She wouldn't have to be beautiful, just adequate. Just so long as she cared.

"I must explain that for convenience we named them alphabetically. The men were given names beginning, in turn, with A, B, C and so on through the letter Z. The women were similarly named. It was patently artificial, but we were in a hurry. We never thought—" The man shook his head.

"What is the problem, sir? Names are just names." Actually, in fantasy, names were things to conjure with, literally, but there was no point in trying to clarify that.

"Arthur matched with Angela; Bradford with Belinda; Charles with Carla. We didn't do that; we named them randomly by computer. *They* did it. It seems that there is magical significance in names, so they believed they were destined for each other. Hundred per cent alignment."

"But you said some were children!"

"Down to age ten. Didn't matter. Todd is thirty, Tara is ten. They are a couple."

"Maybe like father and daughter—" Duff protested.

The Colonel merely looked at him.

They spied on every act of the colony. Evidently it was a complete union. This was apt to be more of an assignment than he had anticipated!

"Victor died, so Violet is alone," the Colonel said. "That

was the one remaining thing that brought you to the head of the list of availables."

"My name. Van Dyke."

"Yes. You will be Van, there."

"But Violet may not—"

"Don't be concerned. She will come to you."

"But to be assigned a woman, just because—I never agreed—"

"Sergeant, you have a mission to perform."

Duff saw the way of it. "How did Victor die, sir?"

"He was slain by the dragon."

"But there *is* no dragon! Not a real one!"

"Precisely." The Colonel took him by the elbow. "I regret that we lack time to brief you on the nuances of the culture, but all you have to do is say you can't remember, and act disoriented. If they accept you, you'll pick up on it quickly enough. When you discover how they do what they do, return here to the building and we will take you in. After your report, you will be done, and can return to your regular unit."

"Just like that, sir? In and out?"

"That's it, Sergeant. But it may not be easy to fathom what they are doing. They baffle us now in much the way the aliens do. In fact, they have become eerily like the aliens. So our problem may also be our success: If we can understand what has happened here, we may have the key to dealing with the aliens. That's why we have come to call their reservation the Alien Plot."

"Plot, sir? As in conspiracy or as in land?"

"Both." They had come to a door in the back. "Out you go, and good luck, Van. We are depending on you."

The door opened and Van stepped out. He heard it close behind him. He turned to glance back, and saw that it was a weathered stone wall without sign of an aperture. Excellent camouflage, that.

"I beg you—what is your name?" It was a dulcet woman's voice.

Duff turned. There stood an unattractive woman of perhaps thirty, wearing what he took to be the feminine equivalent of his own costume. It was green, like his, with the pointed slippers.

"Van," he said. Then he remembered to act confused. "I—where am I? I don't remember—"

"I am Violet. I knew you would come, Van, for I have need of you. I will take you home."

His heart sank. This was the single woman matching his initial. He had not had time to think about it, but given any choice he would have hoped for a beautiful creature, and settled for average. This woman had straight, hard facial features and dark brown hair tied into a severe bun. She was somewhat heavyset.

Well, duty was duty, and at least he wouldn't have to flounder around the countryside. The Colonel's notion that it took the villagers a while to catch on to the identity of new people had been proven false already; the woman had been expecting him. "Thank you, Violet. I—are we—I don't remember you—"

"We have not met, but we are destined for each other," she said, taking his arm much as the Colonel had.

"But why?" he asked, not having to pretend confusion.

"Because of the way of the name. Had you been any other letter, I would have known you were not for me. But you match, therefore it is ordained. We will be lovers tonight, and tomorrow I will begin to teach you the Way."

"But—"

"You do not feel it?"

"I don't feel anything! I don't know you, and as for being lovers, I'm certainly not ready for that!"

"You will be ready tonight," she said confidently.

Duff stopped arguing. He had a mission to accomplish, whatever sacrifice he had to make.

They came to the village. There were, he was sure without counting, twenty-six crude structures, each occupied by a couple. They were fashioned from local materials: stone, sod, branches, mud and grass. No trees had been cut, and the landscape remained wild except for the paths to the houses. This was truly a natural community, and he liked that.

Violet's hut was green, which at this point did not surprise him. It was open and neat inside, more attractive than he had expected. He hoped there would not be bugs.

"First we must address the hearth," Violet said. "I know this is new to you, so I will explain to V. I'm sure he will understand."

"Vee?"

"The patron spirit of this house. You must have his approval if you are to stay here, and you must stay here."

Duff remembered the Colonel's remark about rituals. Well, that was what he was here to understand. He knew that the monitors were recording them; in fact the Colonel himself was probably watching personally, to be sure Duff was settling in. So he would join the ritual, so that Violet and the others would accept him.

The patron spirit was unmistakable. It was a figurine in the shape of the letter V, with an eye and ear on each side and a mouth below, making a distorted face whose nose was formed by the hollow center of the V. It sat on the mantel above the fireplace, and its eyes stared into the main chamber.

Violet fetched a cushion and set it on the packed-earth floor before the hearth. "Kneel here. Bow your head. Do not gaze at V until I tell you. I will guide you through it."

Obediently, Duff knelt and focused on the floor. Violet set a similar cushion down beside him, and knelt on it herself.

Violet looked at the fireplace. Suddenly the coals blazed up, making a warm fire.

"Oh V, master of this house," she intoned. "I bring to you a new man, and I plead for your favor toward him." She paused. "Yes, he is of your clan. His name is Van." She paused again. "What?"

Then she turned to Duff. "As you value your life, tell me your real name!"

Startled, he answered before thinking. "Duff Van Dyke."

She turned back to the statue. "Oh V, I did not know! I thought he was—" Again she paused, as if interrupted by another person. As if she were having a dialogue on the phone, and he could hear only her words.

"Victor was true," she said after a moment. "But he found disfavor with the dragon, and the dragon killed him. I knew there would be another, and I hope the dragon accepts him, because I must not be alone when we go home. So I went daily to the wall, and today this man came out from it, and I asked his name, and he said Van, and I knew he was mine. I will teach him our way, and he will love me and be by my side when we go. I beg you, V, make it all right, for time grows short and there may not be another man for me."

She paused once more, then turned to Duff. "V will address you now. Lift your face and meet his gaze. Do not look away until he gives you leave."

Duff tilted his head up. He looked at the statue.

The face seemed larger and more lifelike. He stared at the eyes. They stared back at him.

"Say your name," Violet told him.

"My name is—" But somehow he couldn't speak it as he had before. He wanted to be accepted by this group, and he realized that it had been a mistake to give his full name. It really was irrelevant, because all the members of this planned community had been randomly renamed. So it would be consistent for him to adopt a new name too. Part of his own name was fine. So it wasn't even wrong to say it; it was appropriate. Especially since he would fail in his mission if he did not. "Van."

Only then did those penetrating eyes release him. Van looked down, relieved.

Violet reached across and hugged him. "V accepted you!" she exclaimed. "Now it's all right!"

They got up and returned the cushions to the chairs. Van felt somewhat light-headed, though that might be because he had stood suddenly after kneeling for a while.

"You must be hungry," she said. "I have nuts and fruit."

Indeed she did. Van was unfamiliar with the varieties, but satisfied to eat them. There was some kind of berry juice too, just at the edge of fermenting. It was a delicious drink.

"Uh, that trick with the fire," he said, remembering. "I could have sworn you just looked at it, and it blazed up."

"Yes, of course. I did a firemaking spell. It's not nice to address V without a fire, because fire makes him strong. If his fire ever went out completely, he would dissipate."

"You made it burn, just like that? How?"

"I thought the spell. I just focused on it and thought 'Fire, fire, light my hearth,' and it responded. Of course there has to be fuel."

"Of course," he agreed weakly.

There was a knock on the door. Violet opened it. A child of about four stood there. "Is it all right?" he asked.

"It is all right, Keith," Violet said. "The spirit of the hearth has accepted my new man. I will mother his children."

Van opened his mouth to protest. But he remembered that there were no children younger than ten here. Where had this younger child come from?

Violet closed the door as the child departed. "Keith will spread the word," she said. "It is all right, now. Except for the dragon. I hope he doesn't reject you!"

"I hope so too," Van agreed. "Uh—the child—Keith—"

"Kane and Kay's son," she said. "He's a good boy. You and I can't keep a child until the dragon approves you, but we can choose one if we wish. Tonight we can make love. In fact we had better, because the dragon may inquire whether we are sexually compatible. Go ahead and strip and use the sanitary closet while I get ready." She indicated a curtained alcove.

The woman was serious. She had accepted him the moment she verified his name, and in her view they were much the same as married already. How was he going to dissuade her, without risking the success of his mission? Because he realized now that it was all very well to dream of a nondescript woman, but this was real, and she did not turn him on.

For want of an answer, he went to the curtained alcove.

There was what was evidently a small composting toilet, probably installed by the project personnel, and a basin and pitcher with water. A furry towel and small sponge were on the counter.

He used the toilet. What now? She expected him to remove his clothes, preparing for a sexual encounter. He would have to tell her no. But would she accept that?

He stalled for time by undressing and washing up. It took a while to figure out exactly how the clothing attached, because he had not donned it himself. The robe seemed to hook into the underwrapping so that it would not slide around. It was comfortable enough, just odd. He poured some water into the basin, dipped the sponge into it, and sponged off his body. That worked well.

All too soon he was clean. He could stall no more.

He reached for his clothes—and they were gone. He stared at the place on the counter where they had been. No one had come in here, but somehow the clothes had been taken.

He poked his head out of the alcove, holding the curtain so that his body was concealed. "Uh, Violet, did you—?"

"I am ready, Van," she said. She had changed too, and now was in an opaque nightie. The material flattered her contours, but she remained by any standard an ordinary woman. "Come and make love with me."

"But—"

"Oh, I forgot!" she exclaimed. "I haven't used the love spell!"

This was proceeding in the wrong direction! "I really don't—" He was not being gallant, just desperate.

"Now watch," she said. She turned toward the statue on the mantel. "Oh V, help me bind the man to me in love, and bind me to him, so that we may enjoy this night and have a good report for the dragon two days hence!"

She paused for a moment. Then she fetched a small candle and lit it from a coal in the fireplace. She set it on the table, so that its musky smoke spread into the room. It was incense, he realized. She began to dance. Van watched, wishing for a way out of this. If he could spot his clothing, he could get it while she was distracted by her dancing.

She moved well, making intricate little steps. As she moved, she unbound her hair, and it dropped to her shoulders and then below them, swirling about her head. Van had never understood what was supposed to be so sexy about undone hair, but had to admit that this was doing something for her. The lines of her face softened and her eyes seemed larger.

As she danced, she stroked her nightie, and with each stroke it became lighter, turning translucent. Van saw that her body was not as chunky as he had thought; indeed, it was manifesting as voluptuous. The nightie seemed to disappear after a while, and she was dancing naked, and it was a sight to madden a man's mind. His mind—and body—were responding; he was changing his attitude about her.

She made one more turn, then glided close to him. "How do you like me now, Van?" she breathed, her breasts heaving.

He let go of the curtain and stepped out to embrace her.

He woke beside her in the morning, appalled. He must have been drunk! That berry drink, that incense—what a night it had been! And all being recorded by the hidden cameras. How could he have forgotten about that?

He got up and went to the curtained alcove, where he discovered his clothing. What a relief! He cleaned up and dressed. It took time, but he was getting the hang of the costume. He had to admit that it fit him well, and gave him that otherworldly look he liked.

He returned to the main chamber. Violet still slept. Well, that simplified things. He couldn't blame her for what had happened last night; she obviously wanted a man, and he was it, and she had used what she had to seduce him. But he was going to be wary of that berry drink after this!

"Van."

He jumped. The voice had not come from the bed. He went to the door, but no one was there.

"Not there, Van. Here."

He looked toward the sound. There was the V statue.

Oh. One of the monitors would be there. It must have a speaker. Someone from Project HQ was trying to contact him.

"No. We allow the men of science to see only what we choose for them to see. Kneel before me. Bow your head. Honor the ritual. You do not need to speak; I can hear what is in your mind."

Bemused, Van did as he was bid. Obviously someone had made a shrewd guess about his reaction.

"Enhance my fire."

Van concentrated. *Fire, fire, light my hearth,* he thought, remembering the spell.

The flames rose in the hearth. He had done it!

"Thank you, Van," V said, his voice stronger. But why didn't the voice wake Violet?

"I have put a sleep spell on her. There is something I must clarify for you, because time is short. You are correct about her; she feared becoming a pariah when she lost her man, and she is desperate to make this house whole again. Her discretion can not be trusted; her need overwhelms her judgment. But she is a good woman, and will make you a good wife; when you are one of us, she will always appear to you as she did last night, and will need no love spell. The question is whether you will make her a good husband."

If this was not a speaker in the statue—if it really could read his mind—it would know when his thoughts took a different tack. *Green monkeys and purple slime,* he thought.

"I will indulge you, Van. You are testing me. You are thinking 'Green monkeys and purple slime.' While I deplore such artificial mechanisms, the press of time requires that I satisfy you quickly, so that you will heed my warning. Try another test."

Either this thing really could read minds, or he was suffering a hallucination. The Colonel had said nothing about this! But since he was supposed to find out exactly what was happening here, he would play the game. *I am a spy from the outside world. Tell me what's going on here.*

"Now that's direct! But it is no news to me. Of course you are a spy; we knew that the outsiders would realize that their sensors are not doing the job. You are the only one sent in; by elimination, you have to be their agent. Try me on something else. Then I will tell you what is happening here, and deliver my warning."

Brother! Could he trust any of this? He could at least make it difficult. *Have Violet wake, and come to kiss my hand, and return to sleep without a word.* If that happened, either V had the powers it claimed, or he, Van, was hopelessly lost to reality.

Behind him, Violet stirred. Van did not move. She walked sleepily across the chamber and knelt before him. She was lovely. She leaned forward, took his right hand, brought it to her lips and kissed it. In the process her nightie, which had reappeared opaque, fell low, so that he saw her fine breasts. He experienced an involuntary thrill of passion.

"Already you are seeing her as you want to," V remarked.

Violet got up and returned to the bed.

Phew! Hallucination or no, Van had the urge to go and resume their activity of the night.

"You may do that in a moment. She will welcome your attention. I should clarify that in her prior life she was as you first saw her, unattractive to men. The love spell is a blessing to her. She will love you truly, if you become one of us. This is one of the things we offer you."

But you are suggesting that magic works!

"Magic does work, here in this colony and in the world it emulates. It is your science that is foreign to us. We must come to understand it, for it is dangerous. This colony will be the mechanism by which we learn. But for you, who are new to magic, there are formidable dangers. We can not let you go loose in our world. Even here in the colony we must protect you. That is why the spirits of the hearth are in every home. We advise our families so that they can survive and prosper. You must heed me not from any subservience, for you are the master here, but because I know the ways of magic you do not. I will keep you safe."

"You can control my mind?" Van asked, no longer bothering to focus thoughts instead of words.

"Only to the extent you wish. I caused you to adopt your V name as your identity, so that you could come under my protection. You can reject it, but then I will be unable to help you."

That was right! He had been Duff, until his first session with V. Then he had been Van, and he hadn't even noticed the change. "I am Duff," he said firmly.

There was no response from V. The statue was merely a statue.

Violet woke. "Something's wrong!" she exclaimed. She walked unsteadily across to Van.

He looked at her. She was in her nightie, but in other respects she had changed. Her hair hung in lank tangles across harsh features, and her body was pear shaped with breasts that sagged without a bra. The spell was off.

"Oh, Van!" she cried. "You've reverted!"

He realized that he himself was not any great prize as far as appearances went. He had dated, but women had not taken him seriously. He was not tall, handsome or muscular, and he did not scintillate with social wit. That was why he preferred the worlds he found in the great fantasy sagas. There, at least, he could pretend.

He was not sure how she saw him, but if last night was an indication, he was as attractive for a man as she had been for a woman. That had been one potent combination!

To hell with reality! He preferred the illusion.

"I am Van!" he said, and willed it so.

"You can indeed nullify my power," V said. "You must be of my clan, or I can have no effect on you. But it is not kind to do this to Violet, who wants only what is best for this house and family, as well as love."

Van stood and took Violet in his arms. She was beautiful

again. "I'm sorry," he murmured to her. "I had to know. I will join you in a moment, after I finish talking with V."

"Oh, I'm so relieved!" Then she kissed him, and he felt the magic of her passion.

She returned to the bed, and he knelt again before V. "I am sorry I doubted you. Tell me what you want me to know."

"Be silent. Do not speak aloud what I tell you, for this must be private from the devices of this world. They can not hear me, for they are not attuned to magic."

Van nodded. This might be his hallucination, but it made sense not to blurt out his craziness for the recorders.

"I can read what is in your mind, when you are here and when you wish it. I can make your home life nice for you, and for all members of the household. But my power does not extend to others, who will see you as your world does. When you go out of this house I can enable you and Violet to see each other as you wish, but you are the only ones who will. It is similar with the hearth spirits of the other houses. Outside you will have to speak in voices to others, and they will seem comparatively drab. But all of them understand about this, and are tolerant. All know that there would be no home life at all without acceptance of the hearth spirits. So your bond with Violet is your guarantee of your commitment to this community. You will not have any interest in the women of other homes, except as associates in the colony, and no other man will have interest in Violet. There is no marital discord here, and there is no conflict between members of the colony. This is what our magic provides for you."

I love it, Van thought. A woman who seemed beautiful only to him, while other women seemed beautiful only to their men. What a way to eliminate temptation!

"But you must settle with the dragon. The dragon will know what is in your heart, as I do not. If you fail the dragon's test, I can not protect you."

Victor! He was killed by the dragon!

"Yes, you are right to be concerned about this. Victor's heart was wrong. He had within him the seed of violence toward his woman and children. He would have destroyed this family and harmed the community. This quality was too subtle for me to grasp at this stage, for I am a limited spirit. The dragon knew, though Victor himself did not, and the dragon destroyed him. All of us were saddened, but it was necessary."

So he had the explanation for the death. But it was not one the Colonel would accept.

"Now you come to take the place that Victor forfeited, and we must know your heart, for we can not accept you otherwise. I want you to pass the dragon's test, for there may not be time to find another man for this house if you are wrong. Explore in your heart: Do you bear any animosity toward women or children? Do you harbor suppressed anger that might be expressed against them?"

Van pondered. He had always been disgusted by wife beaters and child molesters, but how could he be sure he was not one himself, potentially? *I have little experience with women and children. I don't think I hate them. My family life was normal. I just—longed for some other kind of life. A life like this. I—I know Violet is not exactly what she seems to me, and that I am not exactly what I seem to her, but I love that seeming. I think my heart is pure, in that respect.*

"The dragon will know. Beware his test. If you have any doubt about this, do not face the dragon. Leave this colony and ask the outsiders to send in another spy."

No! I don't want to leave! Van was surprised at his own vehemence, but it was from the heart.

"Then you must take the risk. Your life depends on your heart. Today you can come to know the village and the land. Tomorrow you must face the dragon."

Van waited, but V was silent. "Thank you, spirit of my hearth," he said, and got up. He replaced the cushion, then went to join Violet. She was eager for him, her need for love as great as his own. He realized that she was very like him, in this respect. Now the two of them were each other's fulfillment.

* * *

In the afternoon, their amours exhausted, they went out together. Now the villagers were in evidence, as they had not been before. Violet introduced him to any they encountered, but there were too many for him to assimilate all at once. They were at work on their various tasks: Some conjured foods, others conjured beverages, and others were magically fashioning materials for clothing and housing. All this was unnecessary, Van realized, because food, clothing and shelter were provided by the project. Probably the project supplies were being changed in appearance by illusion.

However, some were working on weapons. The spells seemed more complicated for these, and Van wasn't sure what the reality was underlying the swords and staffs and knives. If the culture this village emulated was so peaceful, so in harmony with nature, what was the point of weapons?

"You must find your natural ability," Violet told him. "Then you will be able to contribute your skill to the community. Perhaps the dragon will know."

The dragon. He felt a chill. Tomorrow he would have to face that dragon. But he suspected that no sword would help him there.

"This one's for you," a stout sword-maker said as they approached.

"This is Todd," Violet said. "And Tara." She did not need to say they were a couple; the matching letters made that obvious.

"Hello, Todd," Van said. He turned to the woman. "Hello, Tara." But as he focused on her, he saw that she was no woman but a towheaded girl of about ten. He controlled his surprise, remembering what the Colonel had said. No doubt she looked like a grown woman to Todd.

"And Tess," Violet said, as a child of about three appeared at the door of the house.

There it was again: a small child, where there should be none. Doubly so, in this case: a child with a child. Perhaps a ten-year-old girl could have a romance of a sort with a man, presuming that the dragon didn't consider it abuse. But she couldn't have a baby—and how could there be a three-year-old in a colony which had existed only six months? There hadn't been time for any children to be born, let alone to grow to age three or four. So any way this was figured, it didn't make sense.

"I see you are perplexed," Todd said.

Van reoriented. "Well, I don't know anything about swords."

"About my family. No, don't try to dissemble; you're new here, and it takes a while to get into the way of it. But T told me you were coming. This sword's for you, and my wife will show you where to go with it." He glanced at the three-year-old. "Honey, fetch the harness for him; it's hanging by the mantel."

The child disappeared into the house. "It's too big for her, Todd," Tara said. "I'll do it." She turned to Van. "Come on; I'll put it on you."

Van hesitated. "Go ahead," Violet told him. "You may enter a house at the invitation of its family."

Bemused, he went to the door, following Tara. "I really don't—"

He had to stop, because inside stood a slender but quite mature young woman with silken tresses. She looked like Tara, twice as old. Beside her was Tess, unchanged, but now he saw that she was much like the woman, with similar facial features and almost white hair. Mother and daughter, obviously.

The woman smiled. "Yes, I am the same person, Van," she said, her voice half an octave lower than before. "Forgive me my vanity; I wanted you to see the real me, so I asked T to show you. After this, you will know me for what I am."

Van lifted his hands in surrender. "A beautiful woman and mother," he said.

She smiled brilliantly and approached him. "Soon you will believe, Van." She reached around him, holding the straps of the harness. Her light perfume made him think of a field of perfect flowers.

Van stood quite still, not daring to do otherwise. It was a back harness, with straps crossing his chest, and her breasts pressed against him as she reached, and her fine hair tickled his nose. She tugged at a strap, tightening it, and he lost his balance and grabbed for her involuntarily, his hands falling on her solid hips and buttocks. She was about six inches shorter than he, though outside she had seemed much smaller, and she was definitely all woman. She was beautiful to the senses of sight, sound, touch and smell. "Uh, sorry," he said, recovering his footing.

"Now you know," she breathed.

"Now I know," he agreed, dazed.

"Mommy did that on purpose," Tess said, giggling.

"I knew that too," he confessed, having to smile. He understood that Tara was not trying to vamp him; she was just making her point. She was absolutely no child, where it counted.

They stepped out of the house—and Tara was the girl again, the top of her short-haired head well below the level of his shoulder. She glanced at him obliquely, and smiled mischievously. Todd and Violet, facing the house, both laughed. They knew what had happened.

Todd stepped up and lifted the sword. He passed it over Van's ear and set it into the scabbard within the harness on his back. Now the sword was angling from his left shoulder to his right hip. It felt surprisingly comfortable, as did the harness.

Todd stepped back. "Now draw it," he said.

"But I don't—I'd only slice off my own ear, trying," Van protested.

"I don't think so. Pretend there's a griffin coming at you. No time to think. Now!" He tossed something into the air, and suddenly a huge bird-headed tiger appeared. It screeched ear-splittingly and launched itself at Van.

Van's right hand whipped up across his chest to his shoulder, where the handle of the sword projected near his left ear. It closed on the hilt and tilted it forward and then down. The sword slid down and out across his chest as the scabbard pointed up behind him. Suddenly he was standing with the gleaming blade at the ready.

The griffin squawked with surprise, then dissipated in smoke. It had been illusion. But Van's newfound expertise with the sword wasn't; he had drawn it expertly, and knew he could use it well.

"It's magic," Tess explained. "Daddy makes good swords."

Evidently so. Van lifted the blade and tucked the point into the scabbard. He slid it on in, all two feet. This was some weapon!

"Okay, c'mon," Tara said. "I'll show you the enchanted forest."

Van looked helplessly at Violet. "Go ahead," she said. "She knows the magic better than any of us."

So Van followed the girl out of the village and down a winding path. The trees seemed larger and more exotic than they had the day before, and odd birds flitted through their foliage.

"See, this is what Todd calls our practice zone," Tara explained brightly. "To get the feel of the magic, you know. I'm the youngest of the originals, so I adapted quicker." She smiled impishly. "In fact, this was easier than sex, the first time. I mean, my body was there, but I had no experience at all, 'cause I hadn't had years to get into it. Todd was nice about it, though, and now we've got Tess. But out here it's just magic, and I'm closer to it, with less to unlearn. It's fun."

"I've had one day to get into it," Van said.

"Yeah, 'cause you came in late. Gee, I hope the dragon doesn't fry you!"

"Well, I do have your fa—your husband's good sword to defend me."

"It's no good against the dragon. But out here it's fine. That's the idea: Maybe we'll see something you can use it on."

"But I understood everything was peaceful, here," he protested. "That you don't even kill animals to eat, or cut down trees."

"Sure. We conjure all the food we need. But some animals are mean, so we have to know how to fend them off. Like that griffin Todd conjured. When we go home, griffins will be real."

Van was beginning to appreciate the need for weapons.

They circled around a huge tree, and stopped. There was a little boy sitting in the path.

The boy jumped up. He was about Tess's age, but there was a pugnacious jut to his jaw and mischief in his eyes. "So you're the new lout," he said boldly to Van.

"Go away, Nothing," Tara said. "I'm just showing him the forest."

"Well, he's new, ain't he?" the boy retorted. "The dragon ain't seen him yet, right? So he can't make me go away."

"Just ignore him," Tara advised Van. "He's just a pest." She walked on along the path, suiting action to word.

But the boy danced around her and returned to the path to block Van. "You don't look like much to me, crap-stuff," he said. "You come to feel up the woman of that freak who got toasted? Dragon'll toast *you*, tomorrow, for sure!"

"Don't even speak to him," Tara said. "He's nothing but trouble. That's why nobody took him."

"Took him?"

"For their child," she said impatiently. "Like I took Tess. I sure wasn't going to have a daughter the outside way!" She grimaced.

So the children weren't born, they were taken. From the forest, evidently. Adoption was much easier to explain than natural birth. But where had they come from originally? Surely they weren't strays from the normal world!

"You couldn't take anything anyway," the boy said to Van, dancing before him, impeding his progress. "You couldn't take a joke if it bit you in the rear!" He lunged as if to do exactly that.

Van put out a hand to stop him. So the boy bit his left hand instead. Right on the center finger.

Van's breath hissed between his teeth as the pain lanced through his hand. He tried to pull it away, but the boy's little jaws remained clamped. Van couldn't get his finger clear without losing skin.

"You let go of him!" Tara cried. "Leave us alone!" But her plea was ineffective.

Van put the thumb and fingers of his right hand against the sides of the boy's mouth, back far enough to get beyond the teeth. He squeezed, slowly, and the mouth had to open. His finger finally got free.

"Aw, you don't taste good anyway," the boy said. Then he kicked Van in the shin.

Again the pain surged. Van hopped back, grabbing his leg—and the boy rammed a finger at his nose.

But Van was already getting smarter. He ducked his head, dropped his leg, and caught the boy under the shoulders with both hands. He lifted the small body up. "What's the matter with you?" he demanded.

The boy spat at him. The spittle scored on Van's chin. "You're crap!" he cried. "Dumb stupid ugly ol' crap!"

Van was furious, but didn't know what to do. So he set the boy down. "Get out of here," he said.

The boy picked up a handful of dirt and flung it in Van's face.

"That's it!" Tara exclaimed. "I'm going to thump you, Nothing!"

The boy retreated, dancing backward. "Nyaa, nyaa, can't catch meee!" he chanted, putting his thumb to his nose and waggling his fingers at her. "You think you're a woman, but you're just an underaged slut! Just kiddie-porn! I bet that man feels real good, when he—"

Tara lunged at him, but the boy managed to elude her grasp. He turned and darted around a tree whose foliage reached thickly to the ground, forming a kind of hedge.

Tara pulled up short of the curve. "C'mon, we'll take another route," she said. "I'm acting violent, and I shouldn't. T will reprove me. After tomorrow, you'll be able to drive him off too. He's such a pest."

Van had to agree. His finger and shin still hurt, and the

spittle remained on his chin. He wiped it off with his fingers. What possessed the boy to be so obnoxious?

They started back along the path, the way they had come. Then there was a scream, coming from the direction they were not following.

"Something's happened to that boy!" Van said.

"Oh, darn," Tara agreed. "We'd better look."

They reversed course and went around the bend. There was the boy, standing terrified before a monstrous dog. The dog had his teeth locked onto the boy's robe, holding him with one head, while the other head licked its jaws and sniffed the best place to bite first.

Van drew his sword. "Turn loose that boy," he said.

"What is this brat to you?" the free head inquired growlingly. "Many times has he teased me, and now I have caught him, and I shall make a messy end of him."

"It's wrong to eat a human being," Van said, somehow not surprised that the creature could talk. He had already seen other magic as surprising as this.

"It may be wrong by your definition, but not by mine," the dog said. "This place will be better off without this obnoxious cub." The other head hauled on the cloth, drawing the boy back a step with a frightened cry.

"Let him go," Van said evenly, "or you and I will find out exactly who is the better creature."

"You annoy me," the dog said. His right head jerked up and back, and the boy went flying through the air, to land in a cage Van hadn't seen before. He seemed unhurt, but could not climb out. "Since I see you too are fair game, I will deal with you also, now." Both heads faced Van, snarling.

"Don't try to fight him!" Tara cried. "I forgot that you aren't safe until you have seen the dragon."

"I have this good sword Todd gave me," Van said. "It is magically competent. I should be able to dispatch this animal."

"But the dog is magic too," she said. "He can counter the sword."

Van experienced a chill. He had been trained for combat, and could control fear, but he didn't like going into action against a creature of unknown potential. Yet he didn't seem to have much choice. "I'll just have to risk it." He advanced on the dog.

"Well, it has foolish courage," the left head said. "But it will avail him nothing," the right one said.

Van decided not to wait for the dog to make the first move. He charged, his blade swinging at the left head.

The dog dodged aside, spun, and leaped at Van from the left. Van's blade swung quickly back to intercept the creature's body as he ducked down. But the body dodged in air, avoiding the cut.

It was magic, again. This creature was more formidable than he had thought. Maybe it was unkillable. But he was in this fight, and he had to finish it.

Van stalked the monster, stabbing repeatedly at the heads, first one, then the other, and swinging at both when he had the chance. The body and both heads maneuvered with marvelous cunning, avoiding every attack. But Van refused to quit, fearing that he would be finished if he did. He drove the dog steadily back from the cage. If he could get it far enough away so that he could lift out the boy—

Then the dog disappeared. Van whirled—and spied the animal behind him. Beside the cage. So that stragegy was no good either.

How could he defeat an animal that used magic to get around him, literally? Van stalked the creature again, not with any real hope of success, but giving himself time to ponder. He had had dog-training at one point, and knew how to defend himself from an ordinary canine. It involved padding for an arm to block the dog's teeth, and less polite techniques, depending on whether the dog was to be discouraged, captured, disabled, or killed. All he wanted to do was the first, so that he could rescue the boy. But the dog showed no sign of being liable to discouragement.

Then Van had a bright notion. This was a magic scene.

He had nulled the magic before simply by changing his name in his mind. If he could do the same thing here, the scene would revert to reality as this world knew it. Then he should be dealing with an ordinary dog, and that one he could handle.

Duff, he thought. *I am Duff. This is reality.*

It worked. The spell on him faded. He saw things as they were. The great odd trees became relatively small mundane trees. The dog was an ordinary mongrel. Behind the dog was a crude cage, and in the cage was—nothing.

He was fighting over an empty cage?

Duff looked across at Tara. She remained as she was, towheaded ten. But she was startled. "It changed!" she cried, alarmed. It seemed that his change had overwhelmed her illusion too.

"This is reality," Duff told her. But he kept a wary eye on the dog. Now he realized that he was carrying a stick. Some sword!

It didn't matter. He threw away the stick and grabbed at his clothing, which was unchanged. He tore off his robe and wrapped it around his left arm. "Okay, doggie," he said. "Let's settle this my way."

"But you mustn't do that!" Tara protested.

"I'm not going to give way to a dog," Duff said. "I'm going to get him out of here one way or another." He advanced on the dog, who retreated, growling.

"But it only counts if it's magic!" the girl cried.

"Counts for what?"

"For the dragon."

Duff was perplexed. "You mean this is supposed to be some kind of a game, and I have to follow the rules to get points?"

"It's no game," she said. "Please, Van, do it right!"

Duff shook his head, bemused again. He was here to understand these people, so it was indeed better to play by their rules. Without rules, no game worked. So be it.

Van, he thought. *I am Van. This is fantasy.*

The magic returned. The dog grew larger, and developed

two heads. The boy reappeared in the cage. The trees became exotic. And his sword lay where he had thrown the stick, gleaming on the ground.

The dog leaped for the sword. He stood over it. "Now you have lost your weapon, fool," he growled.

Van's robe remained wrapped around his arm. "I don't need it, animal," he replied. "I am going to put you in a headlock and strangle you until you quit." He advanced, his padded arm in front.

"But I have two heads," the dog said. "While you strangle one, the other will bite your face off."

"So it's a fair fight," Van said. "I'll take my chances." Actually he was afraid that the dog could do exactly what he said, but he refused to let that fear show, knowing that it could be disastrous. He had to appear confident. Perhaps he could throw the dog on his back and nullify the other head with a foot.

The dog evidently wasn't certain either. "You have courage, man," he said. "And you do seem to know how to fight my kind. But I also know how to fight your kind, so we do not know who will be the victor."

"We do not know," Van agreed. He charged the dog.

Again the creature avoided him. Van barely kept his footing as he slowed and turned, whipping his padded arm around to counter the expected attack from the rear.

"I do not understand you," the dog said. "Why do you risk your life to save the most obnoxious brat in the colony?"

"Because he is a child, and does not know better. With proper adult supervision, he can learn to be a decent human being. I must see that he has that chance." But as he spoke, he wondered. Tara called the boy "Nothing," and in reality that was what he was: nothing. There were aspects of this encounter that made description by the term "unbelievable" inadequate. Yet he had to play the game through, whatever its rules. In the game, there was a boy.

The dog circled, looking for an opening, and Van circled

with him, never letting down his guard. It seemed to be a standoff.

"Would *you* try to raise such a child?" the dog demanded.

That was a challenge of another nature! "I'd hate to try," Van admitted.

"We aren't getting anywhere here," the dog said. "I'll make you a deal: I'll spare the boy and leave you alone, if you adopt him."

Van glanced at the boy in the cage. The boy stuck out his tongue. What an albatross such a brat would be! Yet the offer did have to be considered, because it was a peaceful way out of a violent situation.

"I don't think my wife would agree," Van said. And there was another surprise: He now thought of himself as married to Violet, in the fantasy realm. That was another rule of the game.

"She would agree," the dog said.

"How can you know that? You just want to make trouble in my family."

"She would," Tara called.

The girl had shown him her reality. He could not doubt her word. He sighed. "Then I will make your deal," he said heavily.

"Done." The dog turned and ran away through the forest.

Tara approached. "That was brave and wonderful, Van."

"It was desperation," he replied. "I couldn't get rid of that dog any other way.' He went to pick up his sword.

Tara opened the cage and helped Nothing out. "I guess you think you're pretty noble stuff," the boy called at Van. "I guess you think I'm grateful."

"I doubt it," Van said.

"Well, I'm not! I don't even like your stinking house, and I'm not going to do anything you say."

Van unwrapped his robe and put it on. He slid the sword back into its scabbard. Then he came to the boy. "Do you want to walk home with me, or be carried over my shoulder?"

he asked evenly. "I'll give you a hint: You will find walking more comfortable."

"Listen, dung-head—" Nothing started. But he had to stop as he dodged out of the way of Van's grasp. "I'll walk."

"Henceforth you will not use language like that," Van informed him as the three of them started back down the path.

"Like what, pee-brain?"

Van lifted a hand. "Like that."

"Yeah? And what're you going to do about it?"

Van set the hand firmly on the boy's head. "I will ground you until you reconsider."

Nothing laughed. "And what will you do when I ignore your grounding?"

"You will not ignore it."

"Or what, slop-face?"

"Or you will cease to exist," Van said. He started to change his name, mentally. *Duff.*

The boy began to fade. "I got it!" he cried.

"I thought you would," Van said, returning to his real name.

"You have a way with kids," Tara observed.

"It's the military way," Van said. He had simply pictured the boy as a loudmouthed recruit. There were ways to tame such folk in a hurry, without violence.

Violet made a place for the boy that night. She was thrilled to have a child so quickly, but confessed privately that she had hoped for a girl. "And you have not yet seen the dragon," she said worriedly.

Van doubted that the dragon would be worse than the dog. But the boy was bad enough. Suppose the dragon rejected Van, and Violet was stuck with the boy?

"Let me love you tonight," Violet said. "For I fear for tomorrow."

Nothing jumped out of his bunk across the room and came over. "I'll watch!"

"You'll do nothing of the kind," Violet said severely. "You need your sleep."

"Awww." Nothing looked rebellious.

"Return to bed," V called from the hearth. Van relaxed, relieved. He trusted V.

Nothing began to walk away. "What about when you do it in daytime?"

"Then you may watch," Violet agreed.

Oops. Van waited until the boy went back to bed and the light was out. Then he inquired. "Children watch?"

"Of course. Oh, I see your problem. In the world you came from, where everything is so physical, children don't watch. But here sex is just for fun and commitment and family unity. When we want children, we adopt them from the forest. We teach them what they need to know, and part of that is love. How could they understand it, if they did not see it?"

Van thought about it, as she kissed him and hugged him, and after a while it began to make sense. He cast off another aspect of his former life-style. This was not the world he had known. It was a better world.

In the morning they went to see the dragon. The other villagers merely nodded as the three of them passed, and Tara emerged to wish him well. Then they took the path up the mountain.

Van remembered how the Colonel had said that the dragon had killed Victor. The dragon was a mock-up, but it had done the job. Now Van believed that he would encounter a real dragon, and it could indeed kill him. If it didn't like him. Because it would know his heart.

And would his heart be good enough? How could he know? But he could doubt! Because he was a spy for the science world. He had told V, and V had not been surprised, but V knew only his mind, not his heart. Where was his heart?

He glanced at Violet, beside him, so lovely. She turned her face to him and smiled.

"Oh, Violet," he said. "I am afraid."

"But why should you be, Van?" she asked. "The dragon is our lord; he knows the truth. There will be no pretense before him."

"That's why I am afraid." He kissed her, holding her as close as he could without hurting her.

"Hey!" Nothing said. "Do it now, so I can watch."

Van wished he hadn't had to adopt the boy. He could see that any life he had with Violet was going to be seriously compromised. Even if it was acceptable for a child to watch, he didn't care to have an obnoxious child kibitzing.

"Why do you think the dragon will not like you?" Violet asked.

"Because I am a spy for the outsiders. They sent me in to find out what is going on here, because their instruments aren't picking it up."

"But we know that, Van! We were all brought here from outside. The outsiders don't believe any of this."

"But I have to report to them."

She shook her head. "They won't believe you, Van."

He considered it, and was relieved. All he had to do was tell the truth: that there really was magic here, and that it governed the lives of all the colonists. They would think him to be lying or crazy. Except—

"Suppose they shut down the project?"

"The dragon wouldn't let them do that," she said reassuringly.

He hoped she was correct.

At the top of the hill he saw the dragon. It was a monstrous serpentine winged figure whose head was large enough to gulp down the body of a man.

"We must wait," Violet said. "You must meet the dragon alone." She shivered. "Now I am afraid!"

Van kissed her again. It was very sweet. Then he nerved himself and went forward to meet the dragon.

The huge head swung around to orient on him. "Be at ease, Van," the dragon said. "I am satisfied with you."

Just like that?

"Do not speak aloud of this," the Dragon said. "There is one other test for you, but it is not mine. It is that of those who sent you. I can not prevent this, for they are not of my domain. But I will finish my business with you before they come."

Business? Van still hadn't adjusted to the notion of the dragon's instant acceptance. How could the dragon know his heart, without even looking?

The dragon smiled. "I knew it yesterday, Van. The dog is my creature. So is Nothing. If there was abuse in your heart, it could have shown then." He glanced past Van. "Nothing! Come to me."

The boy left Violet and walked forward.

"Now wait!" Van protested. "I adopted that boy."

"You don't want him," the dragon said. "He is an obnoxious pest. I will exchange him for a better child."

"You can't just switch our children!"

Smoke puffed from the hot nostrils. "I can."

Van drew his sword. "You can't!"

"Oh, I like you!" the dragon said. "You have the heart of a hero. But your way does not govern here."

Van stepped forward, lifting the sword. But the dragon exhaled flame. It surrounded Van, setting him afire without pain. He was unable to move. The creature's power was overwhelming.

Nothing came to stand before the dragon. The enormous eyes focused on the tiny boy.

Please! Van thought. It was the only way he could express himself now. *I made a deal with the dog. I know the boy is obnoxious, but I can handle him. I don't want him to die by your agency any more than I did by the dog's agency. He deserves his life. You gave me my chance; give him his chance.*

"The boy does not exist," the dragon said. "He was never more than a manifestation, there only to test for the ugliness of hearts. He can not remain with you."

But—

"But you may keep the child—in her true aspect," the dragon continued. He breathed on Nothing, and Nothing changed. Where he had stood was the most adorable little girl Van could imagine. Niceness emanated from her. "I give you Veeda. She will be the joy of your life, as she has been of mine. She is the best of all my children."

The little girl turned and smiled at Van. "I love you, Daddy," she said. "You stood up for me when I was mean."

The fire faded, and Van was free. He put away his sword and squatted to hug the darling creature. He remembered that Violet had wanted a girl, but had accepted the boy. Violet, too, had passed her test.

Van stood as Veeda went to embrace Violet. He addressed the dragon. "You know my heart," he agreed. "I never suspected."

"You should have," the dragon said. "How could an N child join a V hearth?"

Van clapped his palm to his head. Of course! V had accepted the child, and that was possible for only the right letter. Even Violet had not thought to rename Nothing.

"Now grasp this," the dragon said. "At dawn tomorrow the colony will rejoin its parent world. All of you will come here to me for the transfer. Do not be late, for once the portal closes you can not pass. The colony will become a settlement in our world, and will manifest the things of science as persuasive illusions, so that we of magic can better understand the creatures of science. In time perhaps our two cultures can adjust to each other. In time, perhaps, we can teach the ways of peace and the living world to the other. With your help. This is why we extended our presence to the world of science, though here our power is slight, limited largely to illusion. In our own world it is the other way around, and we have difficulty even perceiving the manifestations of science. The concept of war remains opaque to us. I regret that we had so little time to let you adjust, Van, and I realize that this has been hard on you, but the science folk are preparing to move against us and we have little choice. We have to get out of their way."

Van knew that it was so. The two worlds differed not only

in magic and science, but in fundamental philosophy. The science people had seen the magic world only as a place to be conquered and exploited. They had sent in things of science, whose effect there had been limited and diminishing, just as magic things were in the science world. So the invasion forces had been nullified. In future it might be possible to prevent the invasions from ever getting started. He would be glad to help with that effort.

"We hold the members of those invasion forces in benign captivity," the dragon said, following his thoughts. "We are providing women and employment for them, and gradually they are learning. The members of this colony are different; all of you loved magic at the outset, and were ready to fathom our way. But those others remain hostile. So we depend on you to be our liaison—"

Suddenly there came a noise from beyond the dragon. Violet screamed. Van looked up—and there was a military helicopter bearing down on them. The science folk were attacking!

Van drew his sword. "Get away from here, Violet!" he cried. "Take Veeda!" Then he moved to block the way, so that no one could pursue them down the path.

The machine landed and helmeted warriors debouched. They charged Van—and suddenly all he held was a stick, while they had guns. So much for heroics. In a moment they had him; he was the one they wanted.

"I don't understand," the Colonel said. "You are in that village barely two days, and suddenly your mind is all cluttered with junk about the supernatural. They feed you hallucinogens?"

Van shrugged in the fatigues they had put him in. He hated this foreign clothing. It chafed both his body and his soul. "No. They showed me the truth."

"That they do things by magic? Come off it, Sergeant!"

"Your devices can't pick up on it, because science doesn't fathom magic, any more than magic fathoms science. It's an enchanted world over there, sir. You'll never be able to exploit it, because you can't send in military equipment. The farther a tank gets from the aperture, the less valid will be the principles on which it operates, mechanical and philosophical, until it grinds to a halt. That's what happened to your invasion forces. You'd be better off trying to understand—"

"I understand that you had repeated sex with that fat pig just as if you liked it, and then you went and felt up a damned ten-year-old girl! Then you went out with the girl and messed with a mongrel cur. Then you came back for more disgusting sex. Where the hell was your mission, Sergeant?"

Van looked at the red-faced man with new appraisal. What filthy attitudes the oafs of this world had! Unable to see beauty, they saw obscenity. Yet his duty required that he try. "Sir—"

"Enough of this nonsense!" the Colonel snapped. "We're going to deprogram you, Sergeant. We'll cure you of your delusions. Then maybe we'll get at the truth."

"Lotsa luck, sir."

Then the orderlies took him away. They left him in a padded cell.

Van didn't care what the Colonel believed. He had to get out of here! The colony was going home at dawn, and it was dusk now. But how could he escape a padded cell? Nothing he said would impress the orderlies, who thought him crazy. And he might as well be, because there was no magic here.

Or was there? He knew how science faded the farther into the magic world a person went, and magic faded similarly here. But this complex was not far from the village. Could there be a little magic here?

It was mostly illusion, anyway. Illusion wouldn't help; he needed the reality of a key to his cell. He didn't even know how to craft an illusion.

But he did know how to make a fire, maybe.

He inspected the walls and floor of his cell. It was as he had thought: This was not a professional job, but an amateur one. This was a military base, not a prison or mental hospital.

They had had to make do. They had tied mattresses in place, and the mattresses were stuffed with material which was surely flammable, because these were old "surplus" mattresses, the sort that no longer passed flammability standards. The military never threw away anything; it stored it for eventual use, no matter what it was.

He worked at a seam until he was able to pull out some threads and open it. The job was tedious and time-consuming, because the mattress was tough and his fingernails were short. Eventually he got the stuffing, and made a little pile of it. Then he sat between his pile and the front bars, concealing it, and concentrated.

Fire, fire, light my hearth.

Nothing happened. Well, he hadn't expected it to. But he had just begun. He needed to focus his hope and belief.

Hours later, without success, he began to get depressed. If he didn't get to the dragon by dawn, he would be stuck in this dreary world for the rest of his life!

Oh spirit of my hearth, he prayed. *Oh V, I beg you, give me strength for this magic!*

Then he tried again. This time a tiny curl of smoke rose from the stuffing. He was doing it!

Buoyed by that, he intensified his concentration. The smoke thickened, then billowed, and then a tongue of flame showed. Victory!

Thank you, V! he thought. *You are truly watching out for me.*

He fed the flame with more stuffing, and then with the corner of a mattress itself. The stuff did not burn readily, but it smoldered well. The thick smoke was spreading out into the building. The fire was established; it no longer depended on magic. It would interfere with the science world just fine.

In due course an alarm sounded. The soldier in charge of the wing dashed in. "Get a damn extinguisher, you idiot!" Van shouted. "Want me to burn to death?"

Rattled, the soldier dashed out, to return a moment later with a hand extinguisher. He started to spray through the bars, but couldn't get to the farther reaches of the cell. The smoke ballooned as the struck mattresses hissed.

The man came up to the bars and poked the nozzle through, trying to score more perfectly. He was of course a fool, as Van had hoped. Van grabbed his arm and then his body, holding him through the bars. Sure enough, the cell key was on him. Van took it and let the man go.

The soldier opened his mouth to shout. Van tossed a smoldering divot of mattress at him. While the man tried to get it off him, Van unlocked the gate and stepped out.

Just in time! Several other men were arriving at the scene. Van hunched low and caught the first in the chest with his shoulder. The man grunted and went down. This unit certainly wasn't combat-ready!

He charged through the building, pausing only to duck out of sight as the commotion of the fire brought more men. He made it to the Alien Plot door and rammed into it. But the thing was locked, and he didn't have the key for that. He couldn't get out!

Could he go out the front, circle the building, and climb the fence that enclosed the Plot? No, that was barbed and electrified; he'd never make it. He could get out front and lose himself in the woods, but that would do him no good; it was the plot he had to get into.

Oh, V, what can I do? he thought.

Forget V; his fire is down, another thought came. It was the dragon! *How do doors open in the science world?*

They have keys to unlock them. But I don't have the key to this door.

Then get the key from the desk.

In the desk? Could it be?

He lunged to the desk across the room. Sure enough, the security-oblivious dopes had left it in the drawer! He grabbed it and ran back to the door. In a moment he had it open. Then, as an afterthought, he held the door open and bent the key sharply to the side until it broke off. He slammed the door shut. No one else would follow him for a while. Not with the broken key jammed in the lock.

He ran out from the wall toward the village. *Not that way,* the dragon thought. *Come to me.*

Van realized that much of the night had passed in his slow effort to build a fire. He had to get to the top of the hill before dawn.

Lights flashed in the sky. Oh, no—the helicopter was coming after him! He had blocked the door, but the troops weren't limited by that.

Van plunged into the dark forest. Branches tore at his clothing and flesh, but the concealment was good. The copter would not be able to find him here.

The copter did not try. It swung across toward the hill. Oh, no! It knew where he was headed, and would wait for him there. What was he to do now? He couldn't just hide and wait; dawn would finish him.

"Here."

Van knew that voice: It was the two-headed dog! "I'm not here to fight you!" he said, looking desperately for some weapon. The Project personnel had thrown away his stick, and if it had reverted to its sword form, it was still up on the hill.

"No fight," the dog said. "I'm going too. The dragon sent me. Follow me."

Of course! The dog would be better off in the magic world. But it wasn't enough. "That machine will stop me. It'll stop us all. We have to get it away from the hill."

"How can we do that?"

"Another fire!" Van exclaimed. "Can we light one here?"

"We can try," the dog said dubiously. "It's not my skill."

"I might do it, but it could take hours." Then he thought of another ploy. "The village—can you get a coal from a hearth?"

"In my mouth?"

Obviously not. "Then lead me there, quickly. I'll start a fire there."

"You may not have time to reach the dragon, if you do."

"But at least the others will escape!"

I'll do it, the dragon thought. *I can pass people through only at the key site, but I can start a fire anywhere. That village is no longer needed.*

"But the hearths!" Van protested. "The magic letters! We can't burn them up!"

"The people took down the letters," the dog said. "They wouldn't go home without them. The village is a husk."

"Then let's go!" Van cried, relieved. He ran after the voice of the dog.

Soon there was a light from the direction of the village. The dragon had started the fire. It expanded rapidly, illuminating the night sky.

Sure enough, the helicopter left its perch on the hill and moved to cover the fire. The diversion was succeeding.

Come to me, all of you! the dragon thought. *We must complete this before the science thing returns.*

This distance wasn't far, but it took Van another half hour, struggling cross-country in the dark. His body felt like a mass of welts. But he made it to the top of the hill, and saw the magnificent dragon standing there, glowing faintly.

"Come on, Daddy!" a sweet little voice cried. It was Veeda.

Van swept her up and stumbled on. He saw Violet waiting beside the dragon, lighted by the glow; she had not gone without him. No one else was there; it seemed they had already made it through.

Then the helicopter returned.

Van put forth his remaining energy and sprinted for the dragon. "Through! Through!" he cried at Violet.

She turned—and the dragon swallowed her.

Van almost stopped running. Then he realized that this was the way of it. The dragon *was* the portal. He plowed on. "Through!" he gasped at the dog.

The dog ran ahead and leaped into the dragon's open mouth. But now the light of the helicopter was spearing down.

It illuminated the dragon—and lo, it was merely the mockup, lifeless and pointless.

Then the light moved on. *Now!* the dragon thought.

Van held Veeda out before him, and dived up and into the place where the mouth should be.

He entered a gullet-tunnel, sliding on his belly, the child still held before him. His body seemed to turn inside out and do a cartwheel without changing its orientation.

Then it stopped. He found himself standing in a pleasantly warm place. But where was it?

"We're here," Veeda said. He had forgotten he was holding her! "Now I'm all-the-way real."

"Ah, there you are." It was Violet's voice, as she approached. She came to kiss him and take Veeda. "What was illusion there is reality here. I hope you like it, Van."

Now light was coming. They were standing at the top of the hill, watching the first gleam of dawn. All of the beautiful people were there. The tops of the great exotic trees were beginning to show, and the smells of strange spices wafted down. A breeze stirred, caressing them.

Van knew that this was only the beginning of their job. They would have to teach the people of this world all that they knew of science and economics and politics, before this knowledge was lost, so that a more perfect defense against the brutal other world could be forged. So that no one would have to be hurt, and there would be no ravaging of nature here. Some of them might even have to go back, on spy missions, so that there would be no ugly surprises. It would not all be easy or fun; some might die on such missions.

But meanwhile they would be part of this magic society, living in harmony with their world instead of exploiting and destroying it. For these people were not only physically perfect, they were emotionally perfect. Science, in the other world, gave man power, which he too frequently abused. Magic, in this world, gave him understanding.

"I like it, Violet," he agreed.

The world became gorgeous around them.

Nonent

When I started my career as a hopeful writer, I wrote my pieces, sent them off to the least unlikely publishers, and entered them on my list at the time of first response. I wrote "Nonent" in 1967 and it was #63 on my story submission list. In that year my story numbers would pass the year: that is, I had tried sixty-nine different pieces by the end of '67. Most of them were rejects. Show me a writer who has never been rejected, and he'll be assassinated by the first real writer who learns of it. Rejection is the nature of being a writer.

However, the rejections were getting less impersonal. PLAYBOY said the story was little more than an in-joke. F&SF said it would be an almost impossible task to render this incredible notion into some sort of plausible form. GALAXY said it was good to see someone writing short stories, but this wasn't their cup of tea. So what was this incredible notion, this in-joke that was the wrong kind of tea? Well, it's a story about rejection, and shows exactly how much attention your manuscript will get from the average editor. Editors don't like to have this truth bandied about, of course. But it's the heart of the alien plot.

So when Brad Linaweaver asked for a story for his *Off the Wall* anthology, I sent him two: "E van S" and "Nonent." He

accepted both, which shows that he'll never become an editor
in real life, because though it is obvious that he didn't read
them, he doesn't know that it is an editor's job to reject, not
accept. Naturally with this story in it, his anthology was
doomed, and it found no publisher. This shows, of course,
that this volume, which he co-edited with Elinor Mavor, was
a success on its own terms. The idea was that a number of big
name writers would contribute stories so controversial that
even they had encountered difficulties placing them. An equal
number of iconoclastic stories by unknowns would have a
chance at being published in the same volume. At least that
was the idea. Too bad he ruined it by including "Nonent."

Nonent

Call him Nonent, for he is a distinct nonentity. Call him
also male, for the female of the species would naturally be
identified by the four terminal letters of the description. As a
matter of minor fact, he is about as nonentitious as it is worthwhile to imagine; should he ever appear in a narrative again,
you may be certain it is an insignificant effort. Fill in Description A, for undernourished, inimical alien, and derive a moment of pleasure from the frustration of his ill-advised plotlet
to abolish Earthly values.

For Nonent did indeed plot, and was indeed frustra-
tioned, for a reason that would have been obvious to any
knowledgeable native. Or, if you happen to belong to that
vanishing and slightly suspect minority who prefers the illusion of surprise, you may suspend your disbelief in Earth's
pregnability and toy with the notion that this superfluous
preamble is merely an artifice to prolong the story and to
divert your attention from the approaching demise of civilization as we like to think we know it.

Now Nonent, by a line of reasoning the alert reader
should find alien, deduced that the essence of Earth's intellectual establishment, and therefore its nucleus of stability, lay in

the dissemination of imaginative graphics: i.e., printed fiction. He concluded that the abolition of this form would inevitably lead to the dominance of the mass vocal and visual media, and the wholesale dissolution of the dangerously literate element. Earth would become degenerate, and in due course destroy itself—which, of course, was the object. Fill in Motivation C, for galactic disinfectant objectives.

But the project had its awkwardities, for there turned out to be an unconscionable number of nucleii in the anarchistic publications system. A more sedate civilization would have centralized its output, so that the defunctioning of a single complex would have the desired effect; but on this world the essential medium was allowed to run rampant. It would take Nonent, he calculated, 9ine years to supersede each output singly—and he had only 3hree months before his report was due. Most of that period was already allocated to the other inhabited worlds in this sector. He was in a pitiable predicament. Failure to discommode this planet on schedule could lead to a frownsome reprimand.

But Nonent was fashioned of greener goo than some. He could almost smell the District Supervisor curving his beak into a toothsome slurp. "Nonent, 2wice you have underachieved . . ." No, he would never subject himself to such abuse, not while Earth existed! He would ingenuitize, he would overconquer, he would superprevail even over the ridiculous Earthly multiplicocity!

He calmed himself. Surely an experienced C Motivator like himself could distangle the confusion óf graphemes of an isolated planet, once he put his thought upon it. So there were ubiquitous nexii—so he should evolve some routinely brilliant technique to ungruntle them simultaneously. A common impulse of demise. A—

He had it! All of the publishers of consequence depended upon "free-lance" material—that is, contributions by unsolicitors. Most of them even boasted of this liability. All he had to do was forward each a missive—

Nonent applied his vasty intellect to destructive writing.

In an impressively constricted interval he produced an essay of marvelous perfection and symmetry: mere perusal by humanoid eyeball of the opening 100undred words—7eventy-8ight, computed editorially—should clamp an irresistible compulsion upon the average brain, forcing addictive reading until the terminus. Hi-Q persons could be hooked in less, idiots in more—but only an illiterissimo could go beyond the initial page without succumbing, in which case he was below the legal limit anyway.

And on the final page, where secretaries, censors and other functionaries wouldn't happen across it, was the formula-X mindwarp configuration. Nonent meticulously averted his own orbs while committing this section to print, lest he be hoisted, petardwise, by his own device.

It stood complete—but first he had to test it. How underfortunate if some trifling lapse or inversion allowed any of the recipients to escape! Nonent prepared 3hree copies on 10enminute evanesce, shoved each under the respective doors of his adjoining left, right, and opposite neighbors, and retired for 12welve eventless minutes.

He raised his snooperscope. He looked through the walls. Left sat in his living-room easy-chair, one hand lifted as though holding a sheet of paper, though of course there was nothing there anymore. Right stood in her kitchen, one hand holding the vanished essay, the other stirring a pot of vegetables. There was no trace of animation in her expression; she was as sodden as what she aimlessly stirred. Opposite happened to be an 8ight-year-old child, part of a family unit. It would never become adult.

Complete success! Nonent gleefully printed a full order—then, expostulated by a maudlin something, prepared 3hree renditions of the antiwarp configuration. He was not, after all, a bad alien; he merely had a job to do. Consider it serendipitous that in due course Left lowered his hand while assuming a baffled expression, Right glanced at the clock in surprise and turned off her range, and Opposite picked up another comic book. It would not after all be courteous to remark upon a presumed weakness of character in Nonent; none of these neighbors were of the literary establishment. Certainly such mercy was more to be pitified than censurated.

But there would be no such foolishness in connection with the divers publicatory offices, however, for the antiwarp had to be viewed within an hour of exposure to be effective. Nonent knew that Earth's technology would not normally master this configuration for 70eventy years. Since only another editor, or person investigating the effect, would look at the essay (alas, he could not print these copies on evanesce, because of the unreliable time factor), the elimination would be highly selective. The point was to leave the nonimaginative minds intact, so that they could proceed unhamperated to their natural end. Earth would end *un*naturally long before the antiwarp was conceived.

Nonent had worked it out precisely. The essay was set up in exact submission format, titled "Devastating Configuration," and addressed to each editor concerned. To make absolutely certain the piece was mistaken for a free-lance entry, he accompanied each copy with a note requesting a prompt reading, and a stamped, self-addressed return envelope. He had no interest in such returns, but this did lend the final note of verisimilitude, and it occurred to him that some might actually come back marked "Publication has been suspended due to editorial mindwarp." Yes, indeed.

Nonent issued the mailing, left a polite cancellation note in the milk bottle, turned off the air-conditioner, and took off for the next planet. In the dreary fluxations of space travel he prepared renditions of the essay in all the remaining dialects of Earth, since the nullification could not be considered complete until every thinkable center of imaginative notions had been uncentered. He would have no more than a week at the end in which to conclude things on Earth, but he was sure this would be sufficient to verify the success of the first mailing and to execute the other shipments.

Alas for Nonent! As the discerning reader has long since anticipated, this plot was a fated failure. Upon his return he discovered Earthly civilization undemised; not even a headline rippled the placidity of Parnassus. Periodicals appeared on schedule; novels released themselves; prices rose.

Anticredulously, Nonent checked his box number. It was strenuously overcapacitated with return envelopes. Virtually his entire edition was back on his tactiles. He contemplated the pile with horrification. How had he failed?

He tore open the soonest manuscript. His effort fell out and a neat white slip of paper fell to the floor. Ah! They had provided him the reason. He picked it up, eagerly assimilating the answer to all things—"The editors have given your material careful attention; unfortunately it does not quite fit our present needs. We regret that the large number of manuscripts received prevents individual comment, though this does not imply any criticism of merit. Thank you for thinking of us."

And a handsome signature.

20 Years

This story became a mystery. As I set up to write this introduction, I checked for the story's history: When did I write it, where was it published or rejected, what have I had to say about it before? But I couldn't find it in my records. I remember writing it, and I remember it getting rejected, but my records didn't. What was going on, here?

The answer seems to be that I wrote this story when my literary agent was handling my marketing, and he didn't give me reports on it, so it never got entered in my records. Had it sold, there would have been a monetary record. But it didn't. So it was lost. Perhaps for up to twenty years. Until this moment.

20 Years

The Dragon reared up on its hind four legs, beat at its armor-plated belly with steel claws, snarled horrendously and snorted fire. The Nymph screamed and yanked pitifully at the silver chain that fastened her nude body to the boulder.

Once Wife had looked almost like that in her splendid nubility. But she had grown obese after marriage despite regular hunger-satiety shots, and finally applied for early euthanasia for relief. The autopsy showed diabetes, undiagnosed in life and actually aggravated by the shots. She had skipped her health appointments for a decade, because of an unreasonable fear of hospitals.

Hero drew his shining sword and challenged the Dragon as it made ready to gulp the luscious Nymph. "It annoys me to see any animal grow rambunctious," he said.

The Dragon paused, assimilating the implications. It decided the insult would do. It turned at bay. Its eyes were small for its size, and protected by sturdy nylon eyelashes, but its tempered teeth were large. Fire was its main weapon; it would burn him down before he could strike its impervious iron hide with the sword.

A business competitor had reacted like that once. The man had founded a rival company to market a product whose attributes infringed the Clofiver patent, and Hero had sued. But the competitor made a private payoff to a developing-world politician and obtained a non-Earth product sanction that was technically immune to interworld prosecution. Hero had not slain that Dragon; he had in fact taken a beating. He had lost a third of his preferred customers and suffered a stockholder revolt that almost unseated him. He still felt fury at the memory.

The Dragon's flame shot out in two thin streams: pseudonapalm, that activated the pain receptors without actually harming the skin. Hero hurdled one, came down in the yard-wide space between them, and charged. The Dragon could not swipe at him without singeing its own claws. Dragons, contrary to folklore, were not immune to their own heat.

He swung the sword with all his might at the great nose. But at the height of his stroke he paused, realizing the futility. That nose was soft copper—but the skull and skeletal structure of the creature were high-grade steel. His sword's diamond edge would shatter against that. He could only infuriate the Dragon this way, not slay it.

He had learned caution the hard way. The Dragons of

galactic industry were ruthless exploiters, consuming the small independent operators without qualm. They had monetary and legal resources that no little outfit could match. But they tended to be bureaucratic, their reactions slowed by red tape, and alert policy combined with luck could wrest small concessions from them. So his Clofiver—clover-flavored fiber—business had survived, but never truly prospered. He would have saved himself much financial grief if he had enlisted as an officer in one of the giants at the outset.

No, the nose-swipe was useless. Instead he rammed the sword point-first up the Dragon's left nostril as the jet of fire abated. The inner membrane was ceramic, and the diamond point and edge sliced through it. At the end of the thrust the weapon intercepted the printed circuits of the complexly wired brain, shorting out key synapses. The Dragon collapsed, twitching.

"Sir, you have saved me!" the lovely Nymph exclaimed, rearranging her copper tresses to course more aesthetically around her golden breasts. "It might interest you to know that the last six Heroes have failed. In fact, only two of the past thirty-one—" She stopped, perceiving his lack of interest. "Well, of course I shall grant you one wish, the thing you desire most in all life."

Hero laughed, somewhat bitterly. "Be at peace, damsel! I saved you only because of the challenge. Obviously the Dragon never eats you, delectable as you surely are, or you could not talk so glibly of all those past failures."

She was not disconcerted. "Naturally there is a certain amount of showmanship involved," she admitted. "The Dragon does eat me, but after that the repair crew releases me through an emergency exit in its posterior. But when you play the game and win, as you just did, we do pay off. You have just won my kiss, which will make you up to twenty years younger than you are now."

"So the ticket says. But my rejuvenations have served me well several times before, so that now I am eighty—with the body of a man twenty-five. With euthanasia close at hand I do not need another rejuvenation."

"Sir, you don't understand," she protested. "This is not rejuvenation; it is a chance actually to live over up to twenty years of your life—with your present abilities."

Hero considered, leaning on his solder-stained sword. "May I ask a technical question, in that case?"

"Certainly! We have no desire to deceive a Hero!"

"You are, of course, a human girl about twenty years of age, employed here on planet Heroic Fantasy for decorative purpose."

"I am. And you are a retired Citizen of Earth, exercising your privilege to spend a month at this galactically popular resort before reporting for mandatory euthanasia. So?"

"So how can you rejuvenate my legal status? No exceptions to the eighty-year life-limit are permitted. This is why I took your advertising as carnival froth. A paradoxical promise."

"There is really no problem, sir. There is no paradox. Our reduction is achieved by excising an actual segment of your prior life—a simple matter of focusing a selective time-fix, cutting out that span of your existence, and suturing the extreme ends together. The computer handles that; the kiss is merely for fantasy verisimilitude, you understand."

"That was a bit more technical than I required," Hero said, grimacing. "But still, legally—"

"Legally, you never lived that span. Your lifeline has literally been shortened. So your deadline for euthanasia is extended accordingly. In effect, you have only lived sixty of the past eighty years, with twenty skipped in the middle—"

"I understand all that, now!" he said, obviously not understanding it. "But the expense—it must cost a billion dollars to operate on past time like that. The ramifications, the effects on other lives—how could you possibly afford to—"

She shrugged with a practiced but impressive motion of shoulders and breasts. "It *is* expensive—but this is a money-making challenge. You can't beat the oddsmakers!"

"But all it costs is a dollar to enter! And you said two of your last thirty-one clients won! I'm a businessman; you can't tell me that a billion-dollar payoff for an average fifteen-dollar investment is—"

"Actually, the average is one success in twelve tries," she said. "That's governed by law. If we had too few winners, we would have to slow down the Dragon. And I assure you we do pay off to the customer's satisfaction. Every game on Fantasy Planet is honest. It all works out."

Hero shook his head. "Must be a loss leader! Well, I'll take your kiss! I can certainly use twenty more years!"

"Excellent!" she said. "Remember, you are limited to one span; you can't break it up into several excisions. The suturing is too complicated to permit—"

"Yes, certainly! So I can lose a span of one day—or of twenty years—or any length in between."

"That's right! Normally there is much good along with the bad, so unless you had an extremely bad twenty-year run—"

"My whole life has been a bad run!" Hero said. "Let me consider a moment . . ."

"Would the timescan help?" she inquired after more than a moment. "Once we excise, that segment of your life is gone forever, so—"

"Yes, I'd appreciate that."

She took hold of the stem of a tall magic sunflower and tilted the big disk toward him. On its myriad seeds were printed numbers: one through one hundred, plus fractional intervals dividing each year into days and hours and minutes. He touched a combination more or less randomly.

The buttons faded and the sunflower face became lens-like. He saw through it into a picture of—dirt.

It was as though the camera were scanning the ground from a height of six inches. Hands came down and patted the dirt, shaping it into ridges.

Perplexed, Hero watched. "You pushed four years, five months," the Nymph said. "Of course you do not appear in the scan yourself, unless you happen to see your reflection. It is *your* view of the universe . . ."

"Age four . . ." he said, marveling. "I was playing in dirt! That was before magnetic plastisand came on the market, before the sanitary laws forbade . . ." He continued to stare, morbidly fascinated. "It's been sixty years since children played in genuine dirty dirt! I had forgotten . . ."

"The timescan is more accurate than memory," the Nymph reminded him. "This is no mockup. You really did play—"

"No, no, I understand, forget it!" he said irritably. "The unique experience of dirt! Germs, refuse, bugs and all!"

The picture faded and the sunflower buttons manifested again. "Of course," she agreed, humoring him.

He punched another combination, more carefully this time. Now he saw through the eyes of his twenty-first birthday. He remembered being disappointed in his achievement of majority. It had ushered in the responsibilities of adulthood in a phenomenally complex universe; the searching for suitable employment in a chronically depressed economy; the awareness of the crushing inevitability of taxes and inflation, the threat of enforced space service; possibly even subjection to the colony lottery. Surely he could well spare those migraine years!

He saw a glass door—they still had *those* then, before the threat of planetary vibro-bombing outlawed glass construction—and a flash of display window with quaint bottles lined within. A liquor store—a seeming anachronism, for beam hallucinogens soon crowded out most of the cruder brain distortants.

The gaze picture continued down a street, with wheeled vehicles moving along, gusting pollutant gases from their pipes. Even the police cars! What a lawless age!

Now he remembered the specific scene. On his birthday he had gone to buy liquor, for there had been an age limit on the purchase of the brands above 200 proof. Armed with his certificate-of-majority, ready to trot it out triumphantly, he had taken a bottle of Saturn 500, capable of providing complete intoxication two-and-a-half times as rapidly as could pure alcohol, and with no hangover—and the stupid clerk had never challenged him! What a disappointment! He knew what had happened: the store had checked his age-record the moment he entered, so needed no other proof. It seemed that birthday splurges were common then. And the Saturn 500 had tasted awful—but he didn't even have the satisfaction of feeling miserable afterward.

He looked up, shaking his head. What a rich tapestry of experience, even in his minor frustrations! There was tremendous detail in the least of life's endeavors.

He skimmed through the later years—conventional, rather dull ones, incorporating his unhappy marriage, mediocre family, and mundane business projects. He had bought the patent on a technical process for refining clover-essence fibers for aromatic bindings on quality books—at a time when reading was going out of fashion. But Clofiver had caught on, thanks to his dreary perseverance. It had been used in the bindings of the ledgers of the first Neptune tourister ship—fortuitous publicity there!—and later for the prestige edition of the Encyclopedia Galactica. That had given it reputation among the developing worlds, and many small orders had come in—until that competitor interfered. Regardless, Clofiver had prospered moderately, and now his hard-nosed grandson had eased out the founder and put him on early pension—another damned indignity, considering his rejuvenation!—and the company was still expanding.

Success did not equate to satisfaction. How many hurts he would have avoided, had he anticipated them. How many things would he have done more effectively. Only through his ignorance and misfortune had he been relegated to his hell of mediocrity. He had progressed from dirt to indifference, and nobody cared.

"Have you decided which period to excise?" the Nymph inquired, delicately hinting that he was wasting her time. She thought no more of him than the rest did; she was merely playing her polite part.

"Yes, I have."

"Excellent!" she exclaimed with false enthusiasm. "Which part of your life—?"

"None of it," he said with a surge of victory. "I refuse to kiss off any of my experience, not even one minute, good, bad or indifferent. I just wouldn't be *me* without that body of hopes and hurts and frustrations."

"But sir," she protested. "We can't let you go to euthanasia unrewarded! You slew the Dragon and won—"

"You have rewarded me sufficiently already," he said. "You have made me realize how very precious my own unaltered life is! Experience is far more meaningful than bliss!"

She sighed, her eyes wandering to a new customer just purchasing a Slay-the-Dragon ticket. Her hand went automatically to her hair, which had strayed from her bosom. "If that's your decision—"

"You've never had this happen before, have you!" he said, watching the repair robots clamber over the Dragon. Other robots were checking the Nymph's chain. "Your prior winners—"

She smiled brilliantly. "You're wrong, Hero! That's why this is a profit-making game. Not one of my winners has accepted the prize!"

I remember one of the rejections of this story: Harry Harrison, saying that *he* would have accepted the kiss and loss of twenty years. Well, perhaps. But maybe he hadn't thought it through sufficiently.

I finally found my original story folder—I keep a folder for every piece I do—with the first and second drafts. I wrote it in Mayhem 1972. So it *was* lost for nigh twenty years.

December Dates

In 1985 I received a request from a local newspaper: They were having a story issue and would like something from me. So I pondered, and worked up a notion. I believe that my daughters felt that it was entirely predictable, I being an old man who for some reason unfathomable to them still likes to look at young women. I set the date of the action somewhat ahead, as is customary in science-fiction stories, and it has now become dated, as is also customary. But I leave it as it was; let the reader suspend his disbelief just enough to accommodate it.

December Dates

It was the evening of the May/December Ball, a week before Christmas 1990. It ran from nine to midnight, and was totally punctual.

Ned met his date at the entrance foyer, as agreed. They picked each other out of the throng by reading each other's name tags. Only when he spotted the one that said Margaret Morrow did he raise his gaze to face-level; he had not wanted to form any prejudicial impressions.

She was lovely, in a formal gown whose light brown hue exactly matched that of her hair and eyes. He was relieved; he had been afraid she would be plain, and this one night that was not what he sought.

"Mrs. Morrow, I am Ned Brown," he said.

"Of course." She took his arm and they moved on to the main chamber, where the music was starting.

They paused at the huge mirror set in the wall opposite the dance floor. "Don't we make a fetching couple!" she exclaimed.

Ned nodded agreement. The mirror showed a man of about 25, tall and well constructed, with a full head of pale brown hair and even teeth. The woman, at this slight distance and changed perspective, was even more attractive than he had judged before, being poised and slender. She smiled, and it was like a flash of sunlight in the chamber.

"Shall we sit for a bit, Mrs. Morrow?" he inquired, glancing at the tables at the edge of the dance floor.

"Meg," she said. "I'm really not married."

He had known that, of course; she was a widow. They sat and talked while couples moved and whirled to the music.

"After a year's correspondence, it's good to meet you," Ned said. "I must say, I really looked forward to this—and would have been more impatient had I realized how lovely you would be."

"Well, you did have my picture," she reminded him.

He laughed. "And you had mine. But it was meaningless."

"But I look like this all the time," she said.

He nodded. "And I look like this all the time, from the inside. But the mirror tells me I am really 60. My doctor tells me I can live another 30 years, if I don't overdo the Mays, but who would want to dance with December?"

"I would," she said.

He took the hint and brought her to the dance floor. The music at the moment was slow, and he liked that, for she was a delight to hold—slow, moving with the limber grace of youth. He was savoring every moment.

In due course they sat again. "I wish this could last forever," Ned said. "But the May only lasts six hours at most, and sometimes only four. There'll be a real scramble at midnight."

"Would it really be so bad if they changed?" Meg inquired.

"I gather you are satisfied with your age and health," Ned said. "That's fine, for you. But in my natural state, I am somewhat stooped, and bald, and I have a paunch, and liver spots on the back of my hands. I did not take care of myself, and I paid the price. I think most of these present are in worse condition than I. For us, these few hours of May—of temporarily restored youth—are the high spots of our declining lives. Without them, life would be a graying morass."

"But your letters suggested that you were wealthy," she said. "You can afford to go Maying any time you want."

"I am wealthy," he agreed. "But we pay another price for May. It takes days to recover completely from the depletion of the body's resources, and if it is done too often, a person's anticipated lifespan is significantly shortened. Youth is not cheap, as you have surely discovered."

"No, I've never done this before," she said.

He glanced at her, surprised. "Never Mayed before?"

She shrugged. "I didn't mean to get into this. I don't have a membership, just a one-shot pass. This is it, for me."

"I'm sorry," he said, embarrassed. "I didn't realize. You never wrote of finances. Had you told me, I would gladly have—"

She shook her head. "No, please, Ned. I never took money from a man, and I'm not about to start. I don't need to be any age but what I am."

"Yes, of course," he agreed, but he was shaken. It had never occurred to him that his correspondent was in a different financial situation. How boorish it must have been of him to even mention the matter.

"Let's dance again," she said, to cut off the silence that had developed. This time it was a fast dance, and she was good at that, too, a pleasure to see as she was moved. *Ah, Youth!* he thought. However much Meg denied it, she was taking full advantage of these few hours.

But the awkwardness persisted after the dance. Ned tried to evoke a different mood. "Where were you when Kennedy was shot?" he asked.

At first she seemed perplexed, then startled. "Me? Where? Why I wasn't—" She broke into embarrassed laughter. "What a question! Let's dance."

Ned was glad to do that, not because he enjoyed dancing—though with his youthful body, he did enjoy it now—but because Meg was such a joy to hold.

So it was they spent the evening and the three hours were over in what seemed more like thirty minutes. Abruptly the ball was over, and the anticipated scramble was on. One man's treatment gave out early, and he suffered the embarrassment of visibly aging in public, his skin passing from robust youthful health to wrinkled pallor, his clothing hanging on his flabby arms while it stretched tightly across his developing paunch. December was reclaiming its own. The others averted their gazes, but the man was plainly mortified, as was his date.

Somehow this reminder of mortality and age made this contact with Meg more precious. Ned found that he couldn't just let it go. "Meg, we must do this again," he said urgently as they reached the foyer. "How about next week—Christmas Eve?"

"Oh, I couldn't!" she protested, dismayed.

Because she had no additional pass for May. He had forgotten. "I mean December," he said quickly, covering his error. "You and I, as we are. Please, I must see you again!"

She tried to demur, surely ashamed of her appearance as a woman in her sixties, but he insisted, and she had to agree.

"Christmas Eve—December," she said. "I—not in public!"

"I'll come to your house," he said. "A private date, just the two of us, as we are. December."

She nodded wanly as they parted.

Ned made it safely to his hotel room. He had time for a quick shower before his change began; then he lay down and let it proceed while he watched television. The change was hardest on the oldest folk, or those in poor health; Ned remained fairly robust for his age, so could handle it with reasonable dispatch. Nonetheless it was always depressing to return to his real form. It was said that every May/December Membership holder had memorized the legend of Cinderella, and all detested the stroke of midnight, when things reverted to grim normalcy. Certainly this was true for him!

In the morning, bald, stooped, paunchy and with liver spots, plus a few minor complaints he hadn't bothered to mention to lovely Meg, Ned Brown took his flight back to his home city. *He* knew his depression was part of the body's process of recovery from the strain of temporary youth, but this time it was worse than usual. He asked himself why, and realized that it was because of Meg. As a correspondent of his own generation—actually she was a few years older than he— she had come across as a lovely personality, nicely in tune with his times and his foibles. As a person, artificially youthened, she had been a beautiful woman. Now the two merged in his mental picture of her, the understanding and experience of the old grandmother, with the bounce and spontaneity of the debutante. In short, the ideal woman.

Wouldn't it be wonderful to enjoy perpetual youth with such a woman! But even for three hours it had been a ball, literally. That was of course the appeal of the May/December Society; it gave old people the chance to be young again with those who understood. Truly young people did not understand the preciousness of youth; they squandered it in damaging habits, heedless of the penalty they were bringing on themselves. Exactly as Ned himself had, and Meg. Oh, yes, they understood each other, almost too late! Now they could taste briefly the delights they had frittered away in the past, in retrospect.

But something nagged him. Some subtly wrong response, something she had said, or hadn't said. He couldn't quite pin it down. Plagued by that doubt, Ned did something of which he was not proud. He investigated Margaret Morrow. He had connections that made a private personal inquiry simple; he had to do this routinely in business connections. But he felt that he was in some way betraying her.

In three days he had the report. It was filled with information about her life and family and economic situation, but he skimmed over that. One thing leaped out at him, causing him to sit down hard. That was the word "deceased."

He stared at the report, appalled. Margaret Morrow was dead! She had died December 10, hardly a week before the ball. She had a progressive illness that she thought was under control; evidently she had been too optimistic.

Then with whom had he danced at the May/December Ball? It had to be an impostor!

He verified that there had been no foul play; Mrs. Morrow had died of natural causes, attended by her family. Too bad he had not been notified! Now someone else had used her precious May-pass to take her place. That infuriated him.

No, he realized as he pondered further. Mrs. Morrow had had no further use for that pass, obviously. Perhaps she had given it to a friend, and the friend had garnered what joy of it she could. That was a human failing he could not condemn. It was his own gullibility that angered him; he had never suspected.

Now he had a return date with her. No wonder the impostor had tried to avoid it! Well, he would keep the date, and face her with her deception! That would show her!

But as the time approached, he realized that his righteous ire was fading. What he remembered was the way Meg looked and felt in his arms, her youth and beauty, the way she gazed into his face as he spoke, as if rapt. She had deceived him, true—but she also had given him one excellent evening. If she had borrowed a few hours of youth from a dead friend, at least she had given back a few hours of delight to one who would otherwise have been caught without a date. She had not tried to prolong the relationship or to take anything from him; she had simply completed the date her friend could not.

From that realization his mood swung the other way. That anonymous woman had actually done him a favor! She had brought light into his life, making his date precious. What did it matter who she was? He liked her as she was.

No, he was more foolish than that. He liked her as she had appeared at the ball. As the Mayfly. Liked her very well. "There's no fool like an old fool," he muttered.

A relationship was of course impossible. Ned had no hankering for old women, only for that fleeting aspect that this particular woman had shown him. He could turn young as often as his body could tolerate it—every week or so, perhaps—but she could not, because she could not afford the expense. There could be no other dates like the first.

Then he snapped his fingers, making his decision. He could make it partway right! This was Christmas, wasn't it?

He boarded the plane the afternoon of December 24, ready to make the date. But weather intruded, requiring a landing at another city, and a long taxi ride to his destination. Ned fumed, but could do nothing. He arrived at Margaret Morrow's house disheveled and three hours late.

She was there, and she was indeed old, late sixties at least. She had tried unsuccessfully to make herself presentable with thick makeup. She had fixed a Christmas dinner, but his lateness had made it somewhat cold and stale. "Oh, this is so awful!" she exclaimed, near tears.

"My fault entirely," he said. "The weather—"

"Yes, of course. I was afraid—I'm sorry you had to go to all this trouble—for this." She spread her arms as if revealing the disaster that was herself.

But Ned insisted on having the meal, and it really wasn't bad when allowance was made. Meg obviously meant well, but had a problem coping with the situation. She grew increasingly nervous as an hour passed. "You'll be late getting back—you'll miss your flight," she said.

"I have a hotel reservation for the night," he reassured her, but she did not seem relieved.

Ned decided it was time to spring his surprise. "I have a Christmas gift for you," he said, handing her an envelope.

"Oh, I couldn't—there was no need . . ." she protested.

"Open it."

Nervously she opened it, then gasped. "A May/December Membership!" she exclaimed.

"I want you to have it, so you can be young whenever you want. Don't worry, I can afford it."

She was flustered. "But I couldn't possibly accept—I never asked for . . ."

"Why not?"

"Because I'm not—not what you think. I . . ."

"I know that Mrs. Morrow died, and that you took her place. The name of the membership has not been filled in. You may enter what is appropriate; they will honor it."

She gazed at him, her eyes tearing. "But why?"

"Because I would like to have more of your company—as you were at the ball. I know this is foolish of me, and certainly you do not have to spend your precious hours of youth with me. I want you to have them anyway."

Her body seemed to be losing its cohesion. "I—that's most generous of you, Ned. But I just can't accept. You see—"

Then she lost her balance, and began to fall. Ned leaped to catch her. "You're fainting; I'll help you to the chair!"

"No, no," she said. "It's just . . ."

The heavy makeup crumpled and flaked off her face, and her dress became distorted on her body.

"What's *happening* to you?" Ned cried, alarmed.

"It's—it's the change," she gasped. "I'm reverting. I had the treatment. I meant you to be gone before . . ."

"A May-December metamorphosis?" he asked. "To *what?*"

She brushed off her face, and now the features of the

young woman he had dated before manifested, smudged by the refuse of her makeup. "To my natural state," she explained. "I am Meg Morrow, your friend's granddaughter, named after her. Margaret was so anxious not to disappoint you at the ball, and when she knew she couldn't make it, I promised her to . . ."

"Her granddaughter!" Ned exclaimed. "Then you're . . ."

"Really twenty-two years old," she finished. "I used the pass to get myself made older, so you wouldn't know."

It hit him with unpleasant force. Naturally a beautiful girl her age would not want to spend time with a man his age! She had filled in for her grandmother for one date, but that was it. He, in his idiocy, had thought there could be more. "I apologize for my misunderstanding," Ned said. "I never meant to impose myself . . ." He shut his mouth and turned away, realizing that he could only make it worse. What a Christmas this was!

"Oh, no, you never imposed," Meg said. "It was so nobody could accuse me of throwing myself at a rich man."

Ned paused. "What? You never—?"

"I read your letters, and they were so warm, and you made my grandmother so happy in her declining days, and young men never did turn me on, they're so immature—but who would believe I liked you for yourself? I mean I'm just a jobless girl who wasn't even born when Kennedy was shot, and—and I just had to get rid of you somehow." She was definitely crying now.

Ned turned back, realizing that though his attempt to give a gift had been misdirected, the reality was much better than the illusion. "Meg, I think we should talk about the New Year." Then he opened his arms to her.

Ship of Mustard

I wrote this one in 1963, and it had such a history that I wrote a five-page introduction to it for my first collection of stories. That was *Anthonology,* not the volume published under that name, but the 1969 original, which was a compilation of all my unsold stories. Naturally, that, too, bounced. Once an editor learns that a story has been rejected elsewhere, his limited mind locks into the reject mode, and the game is over. "Ship of Mustard" suffered, in the course of five versions, some nineteen rejections. Now, after a couple more decades, I'm finally getting this spicy story into print. I'm ornery; I just don't give up easily on my stories or novels.

I got the notion for the story when I pondered what it would be like if women had the sex drives of men, and vice versa. Actually, the foolproof verification of paternity mentioned in the story has been developed in the intervening years, but it doesn't seem to have changed male or female nature. Ah, well.

Ship of Mustard

"What's a four-letter word for a mustard plant used for feeding cattle?" Phai asked, attractive brown eyes intent upon her crossword.

"Flax?" Isys offered helpfully.

Phai shook her head. "It ends in E," she said. "Blank A blank E. And I don't think flax is a mustard, anyway."

The others gathered slimly around. "I didn't know they fed mustard to cattle," Annye said.

"It's an Earth crossword," Phai explained. "They do strange things on the home planet. Maybe the hot stuff gives their bulls more vigor."

"We'd better grow a few tons soon, in that case," Annye said. There was a general titter of agreement.

Glorie turned away. "It's bad enough being cooped up in an orbiting space station with the does outnumbering the bucks five to one, but when the bucks are kids—"

"Orbiting henhouse, you mean," Bethe said. "And the roosters are chicken."

Their added off-color speculations were interrupted by a hesitant knock on the door. "It's a public office, you barren mare!" Isys called nastily. "Don't knock—barge in like the rest of us."

The door eased open tentatively. "I was assigned to the, er, 'shack,' " a nervously masculine voice said. "I'm not sure I'm in the right—"

Five pairs of eyes met across the outer desk. "A man!" Isys whispered, stricken. "And I went and called him a—" She bounced off the desk and tripped forward, smoothing out a shapely derriere and flinging back long tresses. "Battle stations, girls—I'll snare him."

"I was looking for the—" the man repeated uncertainly. He was fair, young, and naive. Isys took him gently but very firmly by the arm, not missing the opportunity to clasp his hand in hers.

"This is the Radio Monitor Section of station Athena," she said brightly. "Otherwise known as the shack. Which reminds me—what *can* we do for you, you handsome hunk?"

The man made an ineffective effort to recover his arm. "My—my name is Billiam Kandric," he stammered. "I was retrained as an office h-handyman. This is my first day off hydroponics. They told me to report to the sha—the Monitor Section."

"Why, how nice!" Isys exclaimed, kneading his arm suggestively, "we see so few members of the handsome sex here at the shack. Fresh off the farm, too. I'm sure you'll be very . . . handy, once we get you broken in. There are five of us, you know." She squeezed his biceps and pulled him to the center of the room. "Girls," she called cheerily. "Girls, you can stop soldiering now. This is Mister Billiam, our brand-new man."

Billiam found himself the cynosure of an inquisitively feminine circle. "So tall," Phai purred, rubbing against him. "I'm sure he's . . . capable," Annye put in, capturing his other hand. "I think I'll give him a welcoming kiss," Glorie said eagerly.

Billiam backed off in alarm. "Th-thank you," he said, twisting away from the approaching lips. "But I mustn't keep you from your w-work."

Bethe hooked his head from behind and nibbled on his right ear. "Don't you worry about a thing, honey man," she breathed comfortingly. "We hardly ever get a call. There's plenty of time . . ."

"Cut it out, you in-heats," Isys said, her voice much sharper than it had been when she addressed the man. "I saw him first."

"Oh no you don't!" Phai retorted. "Share and share alike, in this office."

"But we can't share him all at once," Glorie said, clutching the subject so determinedly that her nubile bosom almost smothered him.

Billiam wrenched free heroically, sacrificing a lower button, and fell against the wall. "Please, please," he said, eyes searching for some escape.

"We could draw lots for him," Annye suggested.

"Somebody lock the door while we thrash this out," Isys said.

"I'm only here for odd jobs. If you don't n—need me—"

"We *need* you," Phai assured him. "We haven't had a man in the sack, uh, shack for three months."

"I have it!" Bethe cried. "The gal who fills in that missing crossword word gets first crack at the meat!"

Billiam blushed furiously and sidled toward the exit. Glorie dived in front of him, slammed the door and turned the key. "You can't get out without this," she said, dropping the key ostentatiously into her cleavage. "Just like the late show. All you have to do is come and get it."

"I've got it!" Phai trilled. "Kale. That's the word!"

"That's not mustard," Bethe said. "That's a vegetable. If you don't know a vegetable by this time—"

"Mustard is a vegetable," Phai said. "I think. Let me check the dictionary."

"Uh-uh. Only a disinterested party gets to look at the book."

"What disinterested party?" Glorie demanded. "There's a whole man-day at stake."

"If only you'll let me—" Billiam said, vainly trying the door.

Eyes met again. "Can't get any more disinterested than that," Bethe murmured. "At least we're getting some use out of that archaic lock-and-key system. If only there were some *men* in this orbit."

"Oh, Mister Bill-yum," Annye called. "We have a nice little job for you."

"You do?" Billiam stumbled forward, pathetically eager.

Annye handed him the dictionary. "Look up 'kale' and tell us whether it's a mustard."

"But why—"

"You'll find out soon enough."

Billiam thumbed through the volume. "It says—it says kale is a mustard."

Phai smiled beatifically. "You'll never regret this, sir," she said, approaching him with gleam in eye.

"But I thought you had something for me to do."

"That's right, man-baby. If you will just loosen your collar a bit and come over here to the corner . . ."

"Let me see that crossword," Isys said with bad grace.

Static sounded over the loudspeaker. "That's mine!" Bethe said. "There must be a ship coming in for groceries." She rushed to her stool and began twiddling dials.

Two were left at the center desk. "Things are back to normal," Annye said.

"Dull," Glorie agreed.

"They just don't put the old fire into the handsome sex anymore."

"Oh, I don't know," Glorie demurred. "It's there, if you manage to arouse it. I heard that only last week someone slipped a little Iberian beetle into a chap's glass of milk, down at the dock restaurant."

"Was he a good specimen?"

"Certainly—for Athena. Think they're going to waste a culture like that on an anemic stamen? He wasn't muscular, but he had the waviest thatch of red hair. The waitresses were fawning over him disgustingly, but he was a true-blue virgin. Wouldn't even look at them."

Annye sailed slowly. "So one of them—"

"She sure did. They managed to clear out the other customers before it took effect . . . then, sister! They all stripped down, casual as you please, and just waited for nature. He got sort of uncomfortable—didn't know what it was, you see— but when he saw those young musclebusted nudes parading by he tore loose and planted three of them before getting control over himself. I never heard of anything like it."

"Right there in the restaurant?"

"Would you quibble if you had a chance like that? He wasn't chaperoned . . ."

Annye smiled dreamily, "Is there any of that beetle around the shack?"

"The stuff's illegal. Too bad; I had a powerful one on the line last month, but he lost his nerve. I told him he was absolutely safe; I'd keep his secret and he could use any protection he liked. But maybe he suspected that everything in the apartment was placebo. Couldn't get a rise out of him."

"It's getting so a girl can't get planted once in six months," Annye complained. "No wonder so many of us are stuck with menial positions. Twenty years ago there might have been a reason for it. If a man sowed too much garden, he could be in debt for the rest of his life because he was economically liable for his offspring. But now the average gal covers the expense, just to get the proper mileage. Still that old conservatism makes him insist on a wedding band before he puts out."

"Except for the hybrids . . ."

"Who'd touch one of them? There's no challenge when you know he's sterile. I'd as soon make love to a carrot. A girl's got to believe that it can sprout."

"I know what you mean," Glorie said. "A man just isn't male without live seed. That's his whole attraction—the potential to fertilize. Oh, for the privileges of matronhood! Take away that promise, and the act isn't worth the trouble."

"Sometimes I regret living in a matriarchy," Annye said. "It has its advantages, and I know the men aren't fit for technical responsibilities. But when reproduction is the chief and only route to success—"

"Well, the station will collapse entirely if the birthrate drops any more. And what will happen to all those long-distance ships needing hydroponic renovation then? We have to keep up our personnel."

"If only Earth would allow some replacements. We need renovation, too, and not hydroponic."

"Uh-uh. Take an act of the World Congress, and you know how long *that* takes. They set this up two generations ago as a self-sustaining vegetable stand on the theory that lifetime tenure would increase efficiency, or something. So we have to grow our own replacements. Now it's a matter of individual initiative."

"But what good is initiative without a *man?*" Annye glanced into the corner. "Say, look at Phai work him over!"

Phai had her blouse unbuttoned. "Men are visually stimulated—I hear," she said in a conversational tone. "Come on now, Bill-yum, manchild—admit it. Wouldn't you like to lay your handsome head on that?"

Glorie watched with clinical interest. "She certainly keeps herself in fighting trim."

"Pretty good technique, too. I think he's yielding."

"I've heard that back on Earth the men actually chase the women," Glorie said.

"Well, back on Earth the situation is different. There are almost as many men as women, so landing one isn't so much of a status symbol. And they call Paternityping a violation of privacy."

"Violation of privates, you mean. So the man isn't responsible for his seed?"

"He's responsible, all right—if they catch him. But their crude blood typing only proves that he could be the father, not that he *is*. So the mother is stuck with the progeny. *She* has to raise the kids. Most women can't afford the cost of incubation in Earth gravity, so they can't preserve their figures by aborting three months after conception. Can you imagine carrying a fetus to full term, and then giving natural birth?"

"Ugh," Glorie said, making a face.

"But here in Athena, with the foolproof Paternic analysis, the man is nailed proper. He knows what he's in for."

"It's a funny system, you know. If there were too many men, or overpopulation . . . but Paternityping just makes things worse. We need bold men, not frightened boys."

"They miscalculated. No Earthman would hesitate half an iota if he saw Phai spread out like that. But here a man really has to watch his step."

"Watch his what?"

Annye looked into the corner again. "Speaking of which—sister! She's darn near grounded him already."

Glorie's mouth dropped open, but she wasn't looking at the corner. "Annye—what you said—"

"It's the plain truth. He's really standing tall."

"No—I mean about Earth-women not having incubation, and all. We do—but only one-fifth as many manbabies come out of those machines as girls."

"That's the whole problem. Did it take you this long to notice, dearie?"

"But there has to be a reason. Those first-generation matrons have control over the incubation ward. Do you think they're cheating?"

"You mean, killing off the males before birth, so there'd be no possible threat to the matriarchy?" Annye frowned. "I wouldn't put it past them—but this particular wrinkle has been checked out. My friend in Nursery says there's absolutely no funny business there. The birthrate is just plain low, and skewed to the distaff. The few males born are anemically sexed, too."

Glorie still wasn't satisfied. "But there should be just as many boys as—"

"On *Earth,* yes. Athena, no. My guess is that some kind of space radiation screws the he-sperms and invigorates the she-sperms, so—"

"That's almost as disgusting as natural birth!"

Annye shrugged. "Earth doctors claim it's all in our minds, so nothing is done."

"Our *minds!* Rampant transvestism among the X-Y chromosomes, and all they say is—"

Isys came over, waving the crossword. "Look—I've filled in another vertical. R A blank E. Kale doesn't fit."

The other two pored over it. "You're right, dearie. It's no go."

The three faced the corner. "We'd better break that off before she finds something that does fit," Isys said, alarmed. "Field's open again."

"Barely in time, too. Phai! Get your hand off his—"

Bethe had to put on her earphones to blank out the ensuing scuffle in the corner. A man's voice came through the intermittent static with startling clarity, ". . . calling station

Athena . . . Earthship *Spaceward Ho! calling station Athena . . ."*

Bethe's dark eyes lighted. "This is Athena Radio Monitor. Are you docking here?"

In a moment the others were jostling behind her. Billiam was free to reassemble himself, relief and disappointment smeared across his face.

"A genuine purebred Earth ship?" Annye asked. "With *men* in it? Not an outspace shuttle?"

"Shut up," Bethe snapped, not entirely pleased with the audience.

Isys turned up the gain on the loudspeaker.

". . . regulations require me to inform you before docking that Spaceward Ho! is a prison ship . . . 351 young men sentenced for sexual aggression . . ."

"Excuse me," Glorie said, leaving the huddle.

"You mean they're *oversexed!*" Bethe said.

"Three-time losers," the ship captain's voice said grimly. "Uncontrollable around women of any age. We're bound for—"

"How about granting them indefinite parole right here? They can't get away from Athena!"

"Madame," the captain said, "such humor is in dubious taste. I'll list our supply requirements now so that there is no dangerous delay. As follows: three tons potatoes, five hundred pounds fresh lettuce, two—"

"Captain, that was no joke. We can arrange—"

"I'm afraid I haven't made clear that these men are extremely—" The captain faltered, exhibiting the quaint Earthly disinclination to speak bluntly in mixed company, even by radio. "Of course, they've all been sterilized, but—"

The excitement collapsed. "Wouldn't you know it," Isys groaned, "hybridized. Dead seed . . ."

"Captain, what are *you* doing tonight?" Bethe began, as the others drifted disconsolately away.

"Well, we still have Billiam," Annye said philosophically. "Phai had him about ready to break ground—where is he?"

"The door's open. He's gone!"

"But Glorie had the key—"

Isys picked up the crossword and studied it. "Forget it, girls," she said, looking tired. "She's got him." She held up the paper without further comment.

There, neatly printed in the four spaces, with the open dictionary lying nearby for verification, was the name of the mustard plant: RAPE.

Soft Like a Woman

In 1986 I received a solicitation from David Drake and Bill Fawcett: Would I contribute a story to their forthcoming collaborative adventure series THE FLEET? I didn't want to agree unless I was sure I could come through, so I tried to work out a story. When I had the notion ready, it was as easy to go ahead and write it immediately as to wait. So in three days I had the 11,000 word piece complete. That was very fast writing; it just happened to come together well. I believe it was the first story they accepted, and I think it helped them place the series with a publisher. However, the internal chronology of the series required that my story be placed in the second volume, *Counter Attack,* published in 1988. As far as I know, the series did okay, and I'm glad to have helped.

I have been called a sexist by feminists. It's a smear, because I have strong attitudes about sexism, which I detest. I have a wife who went to work in 1962 so that I could stay home and try to be a writer, and who earned less than she would have in the same position had she been a man. That made it that much harder to survive the lean years of my writing career. I have two daughters I want treated fairly. If there's a job requiring heavy muscular effort, men are likely to do better. But most jobs today are intellectual or not heavily

physical; women are as qualified for these as men and should
be given the same chance and pay as men.

It became apparent that to some militant feminists, sexual interest is by definition sexist. I am a man, and I love the
look and feel of women, but that is not sexism. Sexism is when
a woman doing the same job as a man earns only two thirds
as much, simply because of her gender. Sexism is when there
are male and female workers on a job, but only the females get
razzed. Sexism is when the teacher calls on boys rather than
girls in class, because boys are supposedly superior. I think if
the feminists got their definitions straight, they'd have a better
chance of doing something about the problem.

While I do not consider sexual interest *per se* to be sexist,
it can slide into it when men do not treat women with the same
courtesy or respect with which they treat men. So I elected to
make my point in a story. "Soft Like a Woman" is a savage
indictment of sexism. I wonder what the feminists have to say
about this one?

Soft Like a Woman

"Now it gets tight," George said. "We're shielded, but
they can spot us if they know where to look." He glanced up.
"I need a break. Whose turn to pilot?"

"Mine," Quiti said.

"Never mind, cutie," George said. "It's a man's job."

"Listen, I'm qualified!" she snapped. "I've had the same
training you had! I'll take my turn."

But Ivan came up behind, his big gloved hand sliding
across her posterior as if coincidentally. "Soft like a woman,"
he murmured. Then: "I've got it, George." Just as if he was
talking only about the piloting.

Quiti masked her outrage. Even here on the mission, they
were treating her with the contempt they deemed due a
woman! She had smoldered under it throughout training and
her tour of duty at Port Tau Ceti, clinging to the hope that it

would be different on an actual mission. Now she was on it, and nothing had changed. She might as well have been a housemaid.

"Hey, make me up a sandwich, will you, honey?" Ivan said without looking at her. "I forgot to eat."

The worst of it was, he wasn't even conscious of the insult. None of them were. They all took it for granted that she was along for tokenism, if not pure decoration. They did not abuse her, or force their attentions on her openly; they simply did not take her seriously.

There was no point in aggravating anyone right now; their mission was dangerous enough without that. She opened the supply chest and made a sandwich: actually two slabs of hardtack, as it was called, of complementary flavors. Any one slab contained all the nutrients a human being needed, but was too bland for interest.

She handed Ivan the sandwich. "Thanks, cutie," he said, absentmindedly, his eyes on the planet ahead. The shield made its outline vague, but made the outline of the scout ship even less clear to any observer on the planet.

"The name is Quiti," she reminded him. "Kwee-tee."

"Sure thing, cutie."

She gave up. He wasn't even listening to her. It was no worse than being called "monkey," as some of her training-mates had, because of her planet of origin. The truth was that the human species was beginning a new radiation, with subspecies forming in a necessary adaptation to the extremes of their host planets. In the three thousand years since coloni-zation had begun, some changes had been engineered geneti-cally, and some had been by mutation and drastic natural selection, so that evolution had leaped. Somehow all that other people noticed about her particular subspecies was its supposed simian characteristic, rather than its mental one. But her kind could still interbreed with the others, which meant it was definitely human, and no one could tell by looking at Quiti now that she was not identical to the "standard" variant of Earth. That, perhaps, was part of the problem: The men here saw her as a sex object, just because she was young and full-fleshed.

Morosely, she watched the growing planet of Formut. It was the most Earthlike of the bodies in this primitive system. Its only distinction was that it was the closest habitable planet to the neighboring system that contained the human colony of Bethesda, which the Fleet hoped to recover soon. It had two Khalian batteries that could inflict devastating losses on any passing convoy. It was the Fleet's intent to make a diversionary thrust, a decoy gesture, through this system, to distract the Khalians from the main thrust elsewhere. That would be useless if the batteries wiped out the token force at the outset.

Therefore those batteries had to be taken out. This could not be done from space without doing irreparable harm to the planet, and since the natives were not the enemy, that was out. But they could be tackled from behind, as it were: by a surprise attack from the ground. That was the present mission: Two five-man ships were to infiltrate the planet and take out those batteries. Then the ships would report and wait for the Fleet to pick them up in a week, as they lacked the power to escape the planet's gravity well.

It seemed simple enough—and it was, if all went well. Each ship had small arms and one plasma weapon. Because this was technically a hostile planet, there were no reloading cartridges; it was essential that the enemy not be able to take over the weapon and use it against the infiltrating party. The three shots of its initial loading should suffice; if not, it would probably be too late.

The loaded weapon weighed twenty-five kilograms. That was why there were two crews of two men each: to haul the hefty one-point-three-meter pipe expeditiously to an appropriate line of sight with the battery, and to haul it away again without delay. Whether there would be pursuit was uncertain; it was not known whether the Khalians had full complements here or merely minimal site crews. If the former, things could quickly become, as George put it, tight.

Their chances of survival and safe return were rated at

seventy-five percent. Those were considered good odds for this type of work. The men acted as if there were no danger at all, calling it a milk run (with significant glances at Quiti's bosom), but they knew the risk. They used only first names, not even knowing each other's full names, to protect their identities in case any one of them fell into enemy hands and was interrogated. They were, for all their insensitivity, good men.

Two crews of two. Why, then, was she along at all? To guard the ship. If enemy forces threatened to take it, it was her duty to push the destruct button. That would strand the men and, incidentally, blow her to bits—but the ship would not fall into enemy hands. Would she push that button? Yes; that was part of her training. However lightly the men might take her, they knew she would do that much of her job.

Still, they wouldn't let her participate in the real action, despite her ability to do so. She was by their notion merely a woman, existing principally for the entertainment of a man. The men of the two ships on this mission had a pot on for the one who first managed to, as they put it, ground her. They didn't even bother to conceal this game from her. Each day they each put another credit in the "honey pot." The longer it took, the more the victor would have. There were of course certain rules: Force could not be used, and no false promises were allowed. Nine men and one woman: They figured the end was certain, with only the timing and the identity of the victor in doubt. That was her value to them: the challenge. It was all perfectly good-natured on their part. They all admired her body, and said so rather too often. They took it for granted that she admired theirs. They were, after all, men.

This was why so few women volunteered for front-line service. Even when they got it, they didn't get it. She had thought she could fight through, demonstrating her competence, and make a place for herself. So far, she had not been given the chance. Soft like a woman, indeed!

They made it to the planetary surface, and skimmed in toward the objective. The land below seemed to be solid mountain and forest, with no sign of civilization. The two

Khalian batteries were a hundred and fifty kilometers apart; their companion ship would orient on the other, so that the twin strikes could be accomplished almost simultaneously. That was the ideal.

They glided to within fifteen kilometers. That was as close as they dared take the scout; they did not want to trigger any alarms. The indications were that Khalian forcefield alerts were limited to ten kilometers. That might change, after this mission! From here they should be able to climb a hill and establish a direct line of sight to the battery. That was all that was required.

Jack opened the port, letting the planetary atmosphere in. They had all been given shots to adapt them to the local air, and the ship's receptors had tested for verification of compatibility. This was an Earthlike planet, slightly smaller than Earth but with a denser core, so that gravity at the surface was almost the same. There was enough oxygen to sustain them; it was the trace elements that the shot protected them from, so that there would not be cumulative damage to the lungs and blood. The plants and animal life were similar too, not in detail but in fundamental metabolism.

George and Ivan were the first team. They girt themselves with water and rations, and each picked up an end of the pipe. "Be back soon, cutie," George said. "Catch yourself a little beauty nap."

Ha ha, she thought. Catch yourself some other beauty, chauvinist!

Henry drew his laser pistol. He checked it, then pointed it at the fourth man, Jack. "Disarm yourself, slowly," he said. Jack looked at him, startled. "What?"

"I am a Khalian operative," Henry said. "I am taking the three of you prisoner. Your mission is over."

Jack smiled. "Some joke! The Khalia don't take prisoners. Come on, we have to go, so we can get the tube back fast when these weaklings wear out."

"Second notice," Henry said grimly. "I prefer not to have

to kill you. I'm not a Khalian, I only work for them. Disarm yourself."

"I don't think he's joking," George said. He started to lower his end of the plasma pipe.

Henry's laser swung around to cover him. "Hold your position!"

Jack's hand dived for *his* own laser. Henry snapped his weapon back and fired. The beam seared across Jack's throat, opening it as if a knife were slicing. Blood spewed out as the man fell, his eyes wide with amazement rather than pain. The other two men dropped the plasma pipe and reached for their weapons. Henry swept his beam across both of their throats. Both fell, unconscious and dying; the blood pressure at their brains was gone.

Now Henry turned to Quiti. She, like a complete idiot, had stood aghast, unmoving, stunned by the speed and horror of the event. "Disarm," he said.

He had her covered. Slowly she removed her laser and dropped it.

"Out of the ship."

She stepped carefully across the bodies and out the open port. Why hadn't she drawn her weapon and fired while he was lasering the others?

The surface of the planet was lushly green. This was a jungle region, the kind the Khalia liked. They had landed in a long glade fronting the steep base of a mountain ridge; this provided both cover from observation by the battery personnel and a place to land comfortably.

She braced herself to run, but Henry was right behind her. "Make no sudden move, cutie. I especially don't want to have to kill you."

After what had just occurred, she had no doubt of his ability to kill her. Her training had been rigorous, but obviously he had had some that was not in the manual. She stood outside the ship, facing away from him, making no move.

She knew she had only a moment before he emerged.

Anything she was going to do to protect herself she had to do now.

She put her face in her hands and sobbed. Her fingers pushed up through her pinned-back brown hair.

He emerged, his pistol keeping her covered. "Soft like a woman," he muttered disdainfully, echoing Ivan's remark. He stepped away from the ship, coming to stand before her. "You know the routine, honey."

Slowly she lifted her face, her fingers sliding down across her forehead and her tear-wet cheeks. She gazed at him, her fingers actually poking into her mouth.

"Don't try your pitiful look on me, cutie," he snapped. "Just get your clothes off. Be thankful you're to be a slave instead of a casualty. I won't see you again after I turn you in, so it has to be now."

It did make sense, she knew, in his terms. The Khalia did not take prisoners, they took slaves, and not many of them. They would interrogate her, not caring what damage they did to her body or mind in the process, and use her as a slave thereafter if she remained sufficiently functional. Her self-hypnotic ability could dull ordinary pain but would not help her against the savagery of that. She had known from the outset what to expect from the Khalia; not for nothing had humans named them after the ancient Hindu goddess Kali, dark creature of destruction and bloody sacrifice. Now she knew what to expect from their human agent, whose lust was of a slightly different nature. It was pointless to make open resistance; he would only laser her just enough to incapacitate her, perhaps severing the nerves of her arms and legs and blinding her, then have his will of her body as she suffered. Some men were like that, preferring the writhings of a woman's agony to those of her joy.

She removed her uniform, carefully folding the sections of it and setting them on the ground beside her. She did not take undue time, knowing that stalling would gain her nothing. He watched, evidently enjoying the striptease show as her breasts and buttocks came into view. She had counted on that, and even moved a little more than she had to, to make those portions flex and quiver. She wanted him watching her body, not her face. Her teeth were clenched, her lips very slightly parted. Soon she stood naked except for her heavy military socks.

Henry nodded. "Cutie, I always thought your body was the best," he said. "Now I'm sure of it. You sure don't look like a monkey to me."

She did not answer. She merely stood, teeth still clenched, waiting for his next directive.

"Very docile, aren't we," he remarked. "But I'm not fool enough to take chances. Go fetch the emergency cord."

She walked in her socks to the ship. The odor of fresh blood was strong inside; the bodies of the men lay in pools of it. She used her self-hypnotism to keep her mind clear, treating the bodies as if they were merely meat, and stepped carefully to the storage compartment. Henry kept her covered from the port. She made no false move; she had seen how accurately he aimed his laser, and how quick his reflexes were.

She got out the rope and brought it back. Now there was some blood on her socks; she had been unable to avoid it. But this was no time to be squeamish about details; her own blood, and the success of the mission, were on the line. She said nothing.

Back outside, Henry made her go to a nearby copse of young trees. There he made her form nooses and put them over her own ankles and wrists; then he had her lie down while he looped the ends of the cords around trees and drew them tight. Only then did he put away the laser and strip off his own clothing.

Quiti was spread-eagled on the turf, her arms and legs anchored by the cords so that she could not bring them in. Still she kept her teeth clenched and spoke no word. Her fit of grief as she first stepped out of the ship was the only expression of emotion she had allowed herself.

"It doesn't make any difference, you know," Henry said as he kneeled beside her and ran his hands along her body. "I never expected your desire, or even your approval; I just want your body, one time. You can sweet-talk me or curse me or just play zombie; my pleasure comes from having a lovely woman who would never submit voluntarily." He squeezed her right breast, then her left. "Soft like a woman," he said again, trying to provoke a reaction. She made none.

He built himself up to a pitch of erotic excitement, his strokes and pokes having the opposite effect on her, then straddled her. He let his weight come on her, moving his chest against her breasts, squeezing the last bit of sensation from the contact before getting into the primary act. He did not try to kiss her, evidently cautious about possible biting. The right side of his head was near her face, the outline of a vein showing as his excitement mounted.

Suddenly her head jerked up. The pin she had clenched between her teeth jabbed into the vein. His head turned, stung—and her second thrust with the pin caught his right eye, puncturing it.

Now he screamed with pain and rolled off her, clutching at his face. The pain was in his eye, but the venom was in his vein, moving toward his heart. The pin was poisoned; she had held it dry between her lips the whole time, awaiting her chance to use it. Only a tiny weapon, a barb that projected beyond her lips only when those lips flattened against the target, but a deadly coating.

Within thirty seconds Henry's heart stopped. His body convulsed as its other functions tried to continue; then he was dead.

Quiti turned her head to the side, and carefully spat out the pin. It was deadly yet; she wanted none of its coating on her. The riskiest part of her operation had been the setting of it between her teeth; had it scratched her as she slid it down from her hair to her mouth, or had her forced tears wet it so that the venom dripped into her mouth . . .

She had survived, and even gotten through uninjured, though her body felt unclean where he had handled and kneaded and pressed on it. She would have accepted the rape if she had to, to get the proper opportunity to score on him with the pin; fortunately she hadn't had to. She wasn't prudish, but she preferred to indulge on a voluntary basis, not involuntary. Some year, when she found a man who truly respected her, she would show him what kind of pleasure a healthy woman could give.

But she still had a problem. She was securely bound, and could neither slip the nooses nor bring a hand in to untie them. She had tied them herself, but had done it right, because Henry would have known if she had not. She had done nothing to provoke him, because one slap across the mouth would have killed her, had he but known it. She had protected herself and her pin by making no other moves.

But there was one other thing Henry had not thought about. Quiti was of a variant humanoid species that had redeveloped prehensile feet. The terrain was extremely rugged on her home planet, with rugged vegetation to match; man had largely returned to the trees. Genetic manipulation had restored what other humanoids had lost: the ability to use the feet almost as cleverly as the hands. Hence the contemptuous nickname "monkey." Her kind tended to run lithe rather than fat, because excess weight was a liability when swinging in the trees. She really could climb like a monkey, and hang by one hand or one foot.

Quiti, already the butt of sexist attention because of her gender, had not cared to add to it by showing off her feet. Therefore she had worn special shoes, braced to accommodate her feet so that she could walk in comfort, that made them appear normal. She had left her socks on when she stripped for Henry, maintaining that concealment, also aware that that slight bit of coverage made the rest of her body seem more naked. So the man hadn't challenged it; he already had access to the portions of her that interested him.

The feet, unlike the hands, were set at right angles to the supporting limbs. Thus they were able to do what the hands could not: twist back to set their fingerlike toes against their own ankles. First she flexed the toes to slide off the socks; then they set to work on the nooses, loosening them. What a main-stream human could not have done at all, she did readily: She untied her feet with her feet. She could have done it before, but again had wanted no indication of her potential. The man had had to believe that she was entirely helpless. Indeed, she had been helpless enough, while he held that laser pistol!

Once the feet were free, she hiked her body up to give slack to the wrist ropes, then raised her feet to untie the remaining knots. This limberness was part of it; those who depended on trees for support had to be able to take and hold a grip with any extremity, and to exchange grips readily.

She dressed quickly, not bothering with the blood-tainted socks or the shoes; her feet were tough, and it was good to have them fully functional again.

Now she had a job to do. She returned to the ship and lifted the twenty-five-kilo plasma tube. She wiped off the blood that was caking on it, then had an idea. This thing was intended to be carried and operated by two men, but there was a harness so that one man could do both in an emergency. She made her way to the supply chest and brought out that harness. It would add to the total weight of the package, but she needed it.

She put it on the tube, then hefted the assembly to her back. It was an awkward process, but she was in fit condition and could handle it.

The plasma pipe had to be fired line of sight. She was close enough; all she needed was elevation. So she headed up the mountain before her, using hands and feet to draw herself up efficiently. The men had never given her a chance to prove herself; she regretted that they could not see her now.

That reminded her, in a moment when her guard had dropped, of their brutal deaths. A choke formed in her throat. They had been, for all their unconscious snobbery, decent men; they had not deserved to be so casually slain. She had not been close to any of them, and not just because of the sexism; she simply preferred not to mix duty with pleasure. After she proved herself in combat, and had credits of her own, she could consider romance. She could have accepted a secretarial or maintenance position, as many women did, but had insisted on front-line duty, partly because of her need to prove herself and her planet. Now at last she had her chance to do that duty as it should be done. But how terrible that this chance had come only because of the brutal murder of the rest of the complement!

She was soon panting and sweating. The air was pleasant, but the loaded climb was more than enough to compensate. That tube weighed half as much as she did!

She persevered, and soon reached an outcropping of rock that overlooked the relatively level expanse beyond. And there was the battery! There was no mistaking the huge laser cannon, that could score on anything that passed within a light hour and farther if the target was stationary in space. The Fleet dared not pass within range of that monster!

She eased the tube to the ground. She removed it from its harness and set it up against a split rock, wedging it into place. She put her eye to the scope set along its top, and nudged the tube until the distant cannon came across the cross hairs. That was all that was necessary; there was no recoil as such, only a blast of light—swift plasma blasting through the air.

She fired and there was a crack of thunder, not from any detonation of the weapon, but from the heat of the bolt's passage through the air.

The cannon disintegrated, and a fireball formed.

Quiti smiled. She had taken it out!

She started to put the harness back on the tube, but then hesitated; it was still too hot. Maybe she didn't need to carry it back to the ship anyway; it was for one purpose only, and that purpose had been fulfilled. She had better get herself back to the ship as fast as possible, for the hornets could soon be buzzing. It depended on how solid an establishment this battery was; if it was a full complement, there would be auxiliary forces patrolling the region, and these would be searching for the source of the attack. Let them find the plasma tube, much good it would do them now! Even if they figured out how to fire it, where was their target?

She hurried away as the sound of the explosion reached her. What a satisfying noise! It made up in part for the losses her mission had taken; these were now echoed by worse losses for the Khalia.

The return was much faster than the trip out had been. Now she was able to use feet and hands to full effect without the enormous burden of the weapon. She could clamber along branches that were too weak to support her loaded weight, and leap from tree to tree instead of trudging along the ground.

She hesitated as she approached the ship. Henry's naked body, its mouth open in the rictus of the agony of death, reminded her of the slaughter within. But she had to enter, because she had to make contact with the other ship. They were supposed to coordinate after their missions were accomplished, and compare notes on the outlook for avoiding capture by the enemy during the coming week. It could get pretty tight. The broadcasts were coded; if the enemy ever broke the code, there would be real trouble. But of course if the enemy had cracked the code, this mission would never have made it to the surface of the planet. The ship's special radio would be a real prize for the Khalia!

She nerved herself for the blood and entered the ship. She stepped over the bodies again and went to the radio chamber. She activated it and gave her message: "MISSION ACCOMPLISHED. FOUR LOST. STATUS? QUITI." Then she touched the Send key, and the radio fired out a compacted blip of coded information that only an alert and properly tuned receiver could catch, and that only a Fleet receiver could interpret. On a primitive planet like this, with its nearest base a smoking ruin, the chances were excellent that the enemy would never even realize that a message had gone out.

In a moment the radio gave the response, in its machine monotone: "MISSION DITTO. NO LOSSES. STAND BY FOR UNION. GOOD JOB, QUITI. LUTHER."

She slumped with relief. She had feared that something similar could have happened to the other crew. Soon they'd be here to clean up the mess and make the necessary reports, and she could go back to being innocent, ignored "cutie." Then she could relax the hypnotic block that kept her sane and functional during this crisis.

Cutie. Something bothered her about that. Of course she resented that demeaning nickname, but that wasn't it. There was something else.

She wanted to get out of the ship, away from the horror it contained. But she delayed. What was nagging her? Her intuition, supposedly a foolish female trait, was operating, and she had learned never to ignore it.

Something about the message. She reactivated the radio. "Replay message," she told it.

It repeated the message, exactly as before, concluding with "Good job, Quiti." And of course the sign-off of the mission leader, Luther. It was the first time he had complimented her on her work; he was just as bad as the others about her status as a participant. But of course she had done a good job; she had completed the mission when the men could not. The compliment was in order.

So what was bothering her?

She played the message back another time. Then, abruptly, she had it.

Luther had given her name correctly. Luther wouldn't have done that. None of them would. To them she was "cutie" and nothing else. Except "honey," or possibly "monkey." That alone was irrevocable, because it was unconscious.

Luther had not sent that message.

That galvanized her. She almost leaped into the "tack" chamber and grabbed several slabs of hardtack. She gulped down water. Then she took a survival pack, stuffed the hardtack into it, and another package of water, and slung it over her shoulder.

She almost danced over the bodies, heedless of the tacky blood her toefingers encountered. She plunged out of the port and ran across the glade, adjusting her pack. She flung herself into the foliage at the edge of the slope.

She continued on up the mountain, her ears alert for the approaching scoutship. It should take it a while to arrive, since it had to orient on her ship, and its crew might not have been ready for an instant takeoff. But she had to cut the risk as much as possible.

She made it to the ledge where the plasma tube lay, in half the time she had taken before. The weapon was undisturbed. There was no sign of activity at the defunct battery; evidently it was after all only a minimal complement, with no reserves for the unexpected. That was a break for her.

She hefted the tube in its harness; it was now cool. She carried it back toward the ship, but not along the precise route she had taken. She located an outcropping that overlooked the site of the ship. The ship itself was not visible; they had of course parked it under the cover of overhanging trees at the far edge of the glade. The lengthening shadows covered any other evidence of the landing. But she had a fair notion where it was.

She set up the tube, aiming it down toward the ship. Then she waited.

After about fifteen minutes she saw it coming, flying low and somewhat clumsily. It came in for a landing some distance from her own ship.

As its motion ceased, she reoriented the tube and touched the firing stud. The arriving ship went up in a fireball, and the sound smote her. The range was almost too close for such a weapon!

Now, belatedly, she experienced doubt. Suppose she had misread the situation, and Luther really had used her proper name? Had she just murdered the rest of her mission? Feverishly she descended, leaving the tube behind again, and her pack of supplies with it. She was tired, but the route was now familiar; it seemed only a moment before she was there.

The first thing she saw was part of the body of what

looked like a monstrous weasel, evidently blown from the other ship.

She had not been mistaken. *That was a Khalium!*

Obviously there had been an enemy agent on the other ship too. Not only had he stopped the mission, he had contacted the Khalia and turned the ship over to them, together with its invaluable radio. That was why they had been able to answer her coded message. Had she not been tipped by that single failure of sexism, she would by now be captive again, or dead. Instead, she had reversed the ploy, and taken them out.

She was, then, the only survivor of the mission. She would have to pilot the ship herself, and try to do the job the other ship had not done: take out the second enemy battery. Well, she was a qualified pilot, and she knew the approximate location of the battery. She could do it.

Or could she? That battery would not be caught off guard; the destruction of the first one would have alerted it. Any alien vessel approaching it would be vaporized in short order.

She considered a moment. Then she got into her ship, went to the pilot's cubby, and activated the system. She started it moving, and taxied it out into takeoff position. She set the autopilot for the destination, with a two-minute delay before implementation. Then she got out, and ran for the mountain again.

The ship took off without her. In moments it was airborne. It rose to low cruising height and oriented; then it flew directly toward the battery.

Quiti climbed the mountain. She had hardly made progress before she heard the boom of the exploding ship. The battery was alert, without doubt.

With luck, the Khalia would assume that that was the end of her. It would seem that she had lured them into a trap, destroyed the other ship, then set out to finish the job on her own—exactly as she had considered doing. They might send a crew to clean up the mess in the glade, but they would not set out in pursuit of her, because they thought she was dead. She hoped.

Now she was alone, without a ship, stranded on a foreign planet. What was she to do?

She knew the answer. She had a mission to complete. She had to take out that other battery, before the Fleet passed this region. She had one charge left in the plasma tube.

But the battery was a hundred and fifty kilometers away. She sighed. She would simply have to walk.

First she slept, for night was closing and she knew better than to waste her strength traveling blind. Then she walked. She hauled the plasma tube down the mountain and through the jungle at its base. Away from the glade the vegetation closed in solidly with brambles, spiked yuccas and thorny vines. She had to don her shoes to protect her feet, but then it got worse and she realized that she could not make progress of the kind she had to, through this mess. She had no more than a week to reach that battery and take it out with her final plasma charge; that meant she had to cover at least twenty kilometers a day. On a flat plain, carrying only her travel supplies, that would be a significant hike. On that plain, carrying half her weight in the mass of the awkward plasma weapon in addition to her supplies, it would be a savage workout. Across this tangled, ragged morass of jungle, it was practically impossible. She was healthy, not superhuman.

An enemy aircraft flew over. She ducked under cover. That was another problem: The closer she got to the battery, the more enemy surveillance there would be, hindering her progress.

She rested, panting. There had to be a better way! She would have to eat ravenously just to maintain her strength, and her supplies were far too limited. She should have brought out all the hardtack, before sending the ship on its doom flight. She was making mistakes, and she couldn't afford them! She would have to forage—and she had not been briefed for that for this planet, as no such trek had been contemplated by the brass.

The brass spent too much time on their fat posteriors, and not enough in the field! Foul-ups and emergencies were always possible; she should have been briefed for every contingency. If she had been in charge—

She shrugged. Such speculation was pointless. They would never let a woman be in charge of anything. She was here, and she had a job to do. How was she to do it?

If she couldn't trek to the battery in time, was there another way to take it out? Yes; all she needed was to establish a line of sight. From the ground, that meant getting close, but if she fired from an elevation, she could do it from here. All she needed was a suitable mountain.

The trouble was, there were too many mountains here! She would have to climb the tallest, so as to see over the lower peaks. She had taken out the first battery from the lower ledge of a mountain close to it, but the farther one was much more of a challenge. She dreaded hauling that heavy tube up the steep slopes! The added weight of her supplies made it that much worse.

But if the vertical distance was small, she could make separate trips for supplies. And if there was a spring or river in the vicinity, she could go frequently to it for drinking water. And if there were edible fruits, or animals she could laser and cook, she could forage. There was an advantage in operating in a set location; foraging would be much easier.

She could even make temporary trails, or at least she could memorize the local characteristics of the terrain, so that she would not blunder into anything bad.

There would still be a lot of work, but at least it was feasible. She felt better. Now she could afford to eat and look about.

That afternoon she found her mountain. It was not the tallest in the vicinity, but it was taller than most, and had a fairly nice ridge along the side away from the direction of the battery. That meant there would be few brambles or tangled masses of foliage to drive through. At the base was a spring; she had found it because of a faint animal trail leading to it.

That meant that the water was potable, and that no civilized creature used it. (She was assuming for this purpose that the Khalia and their minions were civilized.) Near it was a tree bearing unfamiliar fruit; the presence of scattered rinds and seeds near it suggested that animals ate the fruit, which meant it was unlikely to be poisonous. Nothing was certain, of course, on an alien planet, but the odds were in her favor. At any rate, it was a gamble she had to take. The fruit was fleshy and juicy; she would eat it here, and save the dry and solid hardtack for the upper reaches, as it was structured for traveling.

Next day she hauled the plasma tube to the base of the mountain, not too close to the spring. There was after all no sense in making her presence obvious. Then she returned to the region the ship had been, because she needed the cord that Henry had used to tie her with. It should come in handy in the difficult upper region of the mountain. Also, it occurred to her that the less evidence of what Henry had tried to do to her, and how she had escaped, the better. She doubted she would ever have occasion to use such a pin again, but others of her sex might.

She knew by the smell when she got close. The rope was there, as was Henry's body and that of the Khalian. Flies were feeding, very like the ones on her home planet, and indeed, like those of any planet; the little winged predators seemed universal, with only their insignificant detail differing. She got the rope first, untangling it and coiling it about her arm and shoulder, then went to inspect the enemy more closely. She had seen mockups of the Khalia in training, but this was the first actual body she had encountered. She was surprised to discover that it did not look like a monster, but more like a slaughtered pet. Only the hind section was here; the head and forelimbs had been torn off in the explosion. It was furry, with short legs, like a magnified weasel, and about one small ankle was a metallic bracelet.

Military identification? Or jewelry? Could this have been a female, like herself? Soft like a woman? That bothered her, and she turned away. She felt no grief for the traitor Henry, who had mercilessly killed her companions and tried to rape her, but the concept of the alien female got to her.

She knew better than to bury the bodies, of either species, or even to disturb them. That would only make evidence of her survival, and the lack of such evidence was her greatest protection. So she left them, breathing easier as she got away, and not merely because of the clearing air.

Then she heard something. She ducked under cover and waited.

It was a party of creatures, not wild ones. The enemy was coming to this site!

She drew her laser pistol. If they discovered her, she would have to fight.

They passed close enough to alarm her, but evidently were not aware of her. One Khalium, walking somewhat awkwardly on its short hind legs, and two of what were evidently the natives: man-sized humanoid bipeds with feathery scales. The Khalium was clothed only in its fur, but the natives wore uniforms of some sort. But the only one to carry a weapon was the Khalium; that made the relationship clear enough.

For a moment she was tempted to laser the Khalium. She could so readily kill it from this ambush! But she refrained, partly because she didn't like one-sided slaughter—she had seen too much of that recently!—but mostly because she intended to do nothing that would give away her existence. She would kill if she had to, but not unprovoked.

The party went on into the glade. There was a burst of alien chatter. Evidently they had found what they sought: the remnant of the violence here. They were simply an investigatory party.

Quiti used the opportunity of their distraction to remove herself from the vicinity. The encounter was reassuring, actually; it seemed to confirm that the enemy had no awareness of any human survivors. Her ploy with the scout ship must have been successful.

She brought the rope to her mountain base camp, then

ate some more fruit and settled into a tree for the night. That was one thing about this perilous mission: The nights made her feel right at home!

Next day she started the hard work. She hiked up the ridge, carrying her supplies and rope. She used hands and feet to grasp the projections of rock, and to get her safely across a fissure that had a solid fallen trunk as a natural bridge. She was not merely climbing, she was scouting out the best route for her next trip. When she was uncertain of a particular path, she climbed back down and tried another. What she could do when lightly loaded did not necessarily establish what she could do with the heavy load. How glad she was for the bug repellant in the survival kit; a cloud of flies followed her constantly, now.

When she found a suitable landing that she deemed to be at the reasonable limit of her hauling capacity, she fixed its location in her mind. Then she left her supply pack, and started back down, carrying only her laser pistol. She did not intend to be caught defenseless again.

Back at the bottom, she ate more fruit, drank deeply, and curled up in her tree for the night. She had to conserve her strength for the next day's effort. She had used three days getting properly set up; she hoped to complete her mission in three more, with a leeway of one. It was always best to have a margin for the unexpected.

In the morning she hefted up the plasma tube in its harness and set out. She had planned well, and made good progress at first. Then the heat of the day and her own exertions caught up with her, draining her strength. She sweated profusely, but had no water; that was in the spring below, and at the camp above. All she could do was rest briefly, cooling a little, then go on.

The tube had been heavy at the start. It grew heavier as she went. It overbalanced her, making her steeper ascents dangerous; she was afraid she would reel and fall and injure herself, ruining everything. Sweat made her hands and feet slide, and her grip weak. She felt like an ant carrying a spaceship up a vertical cliff.

Then a storm came up. At first this was a relief, for it brought down gusts of cool air. Then the wind intensified, as if trying to pluck her from the slope and hurl her down. Then the rain splashed across, making the entire mountain slippery. But she plowed on, knowing she had no alternative.

She reached her camp behind schedule; it was almost dark, and her fatigue had drained her of hunger. She forced herself to eat a little, and to drink a little, and slept. Perhaps an hour later she woke, and ate and drank a little more. She had to restore her body for the next day's effort.

Somewhere in the night she decided to take a gamble. She needed to find the final site on the next day. That meant she could leave the pack here, because she wouldn't need to worry about eating after she fired the plasma tube. Food was just to sustain her for the great hauling effort. She could travel faster without the pack, and would save more strength.

At dawn she woke, ate quickly, and moved her sore body on up the slope, making the next path and carrying her supplies up. Her stiffness eased as she got into it, but another thing developed: itching eyes, blurring sight and frequent sneezing. She was allergic to something growing here!

No, it was probably worse. All this hard exercise and complete exposure to the planetary atmosphere was causing her shot to wear off sooner than otherwise. She was losing her adaptation to this environment. It struck first in the breathing system and the eyes, most exposed to it, but it would progress inevitably into her system and do more damage there. If she rested, that might slow its progress—but she couldn't rest, because she had to complete her mission.

So she gritted her teeth, this time for real, and plowed on. The implacable slope continued, never ending, always draining her diminishing energy—and she hadn't even started carrying the plasma tube yet on this stretch. The very thought of it increased her fatigue; why couldn't they have made it weigh five kilos instead of twenty-five!

She spared her eyes by looking ahead, noting the situation, and climbing through it with her eyes closed. But she couldn't do the same with her breathing. She had less trouble when she breathed exclusively through her mouth but what was she doing to her lungs? She didn't know, but decided to operate the best way she could for now, and damn the consequence. If she got—*when* she got the tube in place and completed her mission, then she could relax into terminal asthma. Not now.

Tomorrow was her last scheduled day, to haul up the tube. Today she had to find a suitable site. If she couldn't get the tube there tomorrow, then she would use her reserve day. If that wasn't enough . . .

The afternoon was progressing, and there was no sign of the top. She was climbing pretty slowly now, conserving her strength, trying to take the very best route. But the mountain loomed monstrously before her; she could not possibly reach the top today!

But maybe she didn't have to. If she circled to the other side, and looked, she could ascertain that minimum elevation required to sight the battery over the mountains between them. That would prevent her from wearing herself out trying to climb higher than she needed. She should have realized that before; evidently her thinking was suffering too.

Yet her thinking had not been all that great before. Why had she stood idiotically frozen while Henry lasered down her companions? If she had only acted properly then!

But further thought absolved her somewhat. She had reacted as any person would have: stunned by the suddenness and the awfulness of it. The men thought Henry was joking; had they realized the truth, all three could have gone for their weapons together, and one of them surely would have gotten him. She had been no worse than they. The difference was that they had been immediate targets, because they were competent males, while she had not, because she was an incompetent female. Had Henry respected her ability, he would have whipped his laser around and sliced her throat too. So it was contempt that had saved her—and perhaps her sex appeal. Soft like a woman. A justified epithet, it seemed.

She found an almost level ledge and followed it around. What a relief to stop climbing!

She had made progress. The mountain was smaller here, so that she circled it much faster than she would have at the base. Soon she was looking from the other side.

The way to the battery was blocked by an adjacent mountain. Its peak rose high enough to cost her another two days of climbing. That was hopeless.

But this mountain was not only taller, but broader than that one. Maybe she could see around it, if she continued to the side. She went on—and realized that a third mountain was overlapping the second, its slope rising as the slope of the second descended, blocking off the necessary line of sight. Damn! The two might be many kilometers apart, but the effect was solid.

But she kept on. When her compass indicated that the bottom of the effective cleft between the two other mountains was in line with the battery, she resumed her climb. Every few feet she blinked the allergic tears out of her eyes and made another sighting. How much farther did she have to go?

On the third such sighting, she spied a glint. With wild hope she climbed just a few more meters, squinted desperately, and verified it. She had sighted the barrel of the huge laser cannon! How nice of the Khalia to keep it polished! The slanting sunlight highlighted it; otherwise she could have missed it.

Her tiredness receded. She set down her laser pistol to mark the exact spot, and started back down. She wanted no extra weight at all, on the morrow! She would barely make it to the tube before dark, but now she could do it. She could take out that battery!

When she slipped and started to fall, and barely caught herself, she realized that she was pushing too hard. Her vision was blurry, and her nose was running so persistently that she had simply stopped wiping it and was letting it drip on the ground. But she had to pay attention to where she was going, and not assume that what she didn't see couldn't hurt her. She had to make sure of every grip, for this was no cakewalk.

She slowed, and darkness did indeed catch her before she reached the tube, but it hardly mattered because her vision was so bad. She pounced on the pack and gulped water and gobbled hardtack and dropped almost instantly into sleep.

All too soon dawn intruded. Quiti consumed most of the rest of her supplies, and slapped on more repellant. This preparation would have to do; she would not be back here unless she completed her mission.

The last day's tube haul had started with a mass half her weight that had seemed to grow to double her weight. This time it started at double. She staggered, and doubt assailed her like the forming swarm of gnats. It was as though each tiny fly was a formulation of doubt: Could she make it? "Yes I can! I will!" she exclaimed, making a small snort of determination—and mucus dribbled from her nose. She would have laughed, had she had the energy, had it been funny.

The harness settled into the accustomed sores on her back and sides, and she plodded on. She was proceeding on hands and feet, like a pack animal; the angle of the slope facilitated this, and so did the weight and balance of the burden. So did her dripping eyes and nose; the drops fell cleanly to the ground now, instead of down her chin. She was making progress; that was all that mattered.

But her strength was fading. She knew that she wasn't going to make it to the necessary site; the seeming heaviness of the tube was crushing her steadily down.

She would have to do what she had hoped not to do: draw on her last remaining reserves by hypnotizing herself. In her weakened state it wasn't safe; her body might function, but her mind could start going, perhaps hallucinating. But it was that or failure.

She did it, and in a minute slipped into a semitrance. Now the weight of the tube diminished to its proper amount, and she picked up speed. She felt better, but she knew it was illusory. She dared not squander any of this energy; when it was gone, she would be done for.

She reached the ledge and started the horizontal trek. This should have been easier, but it wasn't; her muscles were reaching the point of absolute fatigue that even the trance could not overcome.

Then she heard voices, and knew that her mind was starting to go. It was as if the protein required for her physical system were being drawn from her brain, depleting its sanity. She listened; there was no way not to.

"So you fell for our little charade, eh, cutie? Too bad for you!" It was the voice of her superior officer, the one who had assigned her to this outfit and this mission. "I never did have much faith in you, sweet thing, but the regs say I had to give you a chance, so I did. I sent you out on what we call a sheep-and-goat mission, wherein we ascertain which is which, if you see what I mean."

The trouble was, the voices would seem increasingly real as her strength diminished, until finally she believed them. Then she would do what they told her to do, and that might be anything. For the sake of her mission, she had to hang on to the single shred of reality that guided her to the completion of her mission.

"So here's this soft li'l thing, all dulcet and rounded, and they made book on how and when she'd catch on. They were all in on it, of course; only one can be proven at a time, for obvious reasons."

She didn't believe the voice yet. That was a good sign.

"So when they land, they go into the act. The designated spy draws his mock laser pistol and makes his move. Will she react in competent military fashion, or will she go to pieces, woman fashion? Alas, she does neither; she merely stares. So he shoots them, and they twitch their chins and open up the catsup vents. Does she act now? She does not. She just stares."

She was rounding the mountain. She still knew reality from illusion, but her certainty was diminishing. The mission—a mere test?

"So he gives her one more chance," the voice continued. "He goes into the Rape Sequence. This is so phony she *has* to catch on. A real spy would immediately radio his cohorts, of course . . ."

Quiti grimaced. She was starting to believe. What was she doing here, hauling the tube up the mountain, when she had failed her examination at the outset?

No! That blood had been real! That attempted rape had been real! She had to believe that; otherwise . . .

"The radio, cutie," the voice said. "How do you explain that? Why didn't he call?"

She didn't answer. Once she started answering, she would be locked into the phantom reality, unable to extricate herself. That was another trap of a deteriorating mind.

Then she reached the apparent cleft between the other peaks. It was late afternoon; the day had passed in a seeming instant, but she was close, very close. The voice had tried to distract her from reality; it had succeeded to the extent of distracting her from the horrendous struggle of the climb.

Now came the hard part: climbing the last short distance. Her arms and legs were leaden, and the voices were yammering at her. Was it worth it to continue? Why *hadn't* he radioed? Obviously the other agent in the other ship had; at least one Khalian had joined him. He should have radioed; that way he would have had the other ship there before he raped her, and—

There it was! He had said he would not see her again, after he turned her in. So he had waited to make his report, so as to give himself time to have his business with her. The Khalia would not have cared one whit for his illicit passion; he had to take it first. And that had cost him his life. Then, when she had blithely radioed, they had realized what had happened, and tried to catch her anyway. The Khalia would have used a translator to speak, not knowing her nickname. So he, too, had lost the gambit.

And now she was there; she saw her laser pistol marking the spot. She eased herself down, so tired despite the hypnosis that she had to do it slowly lest she collapse and not be able to recover. She removed the harness and propped up the tube. The last glinting of the sunlight reflected from the laser cannon in the distance; she knew her target.

"Of course you realize you are stranded," the voice said. "We aren't going to waste a good ship trying to pick you up. Everyone thinks you're dead, anyway."

Maybe she would be, soon. Certainly she lacked the strength to climb back to her pack, halfway down the mountain slope. She had no supplies, no water, and sweat had dehydrated her. She had taken a calculated risk, and she had won: She would complete her mission. She would also lose her life, but she had known that. Better to sacrifice it this way, than by having to blow up her ship and herself with it! She oriented the tube, blinked her eyes madly to clear them for just this moment, and caught the cannon in the cross hairs. "Let them explain *this*, spook!" she exclaimed. And pressed the firing stud.

She remained conscious long enough to see the fireball form. It was a direct hit! Then she faded out.

"Suck on this, cutie," the officer said, putting a free-fall drink-tube to her mouth. "Slowly; don't choke on it." Then, after a moment. "Uh-oh, I shouldn't call you that, should I! My apology, Quiti."

"Call me what you want, spook," she muttered. "I'm dying, but I completed my mission. You can't hurt me or it, now."

"She's delirious, sir," another voice said. "But we got her in time; her vitals are good. She's one tough lady."

The restorative fluid was acting on her. She opened her eyes. She was in a ship, on a bunk, and her superior officer was holding the squeeze bottle for her. Therefore she knew it was a terminal fantasy. But she liked it; phantoms weren't all bad.

"I don't expect you to assimilate this right now, Quiti," he said. "But I feel obliged to tell you myself, before I go, because I have some culpability in the matter."

She sucked on the bottle, content to listen to the spook as the strength of the phantom elixir flowed through her. Her dream would have it that she had slept a day or so and recovered somewhat, and that now she was recovering faster. Anything was possible, in illusion.

"It was a setup, but not the way you may have supposed," he continued. "You see, the Khalia were able to convert some of our personnel to work for them. We don't know what inducement they used; that's part of what we wanted to discover. We didn't even know who the agents were. But we had narrowed it down to a few units, and this was one of them. So we put all our suspects on this mission, and—"

Even for a vision, this was getting outrageous. "I was a suspect?" she demanded.

He nodded. "Not too many from your planet in the Fleet; we weren't absolutely sure of your fundamental loyalty, or of the pressures or temptations you might have. Also, the matter of being an attractive young woman in an all-male complement—there are those who might get resentful." He had scored there! She shut up.

"Every one of you was bugged. Even Ivan, the only one on your ship who was in on this. When the spy revealed himself—or herself—Ivan was to activate the stun box in his pocket and render all of you unconscious until he disarmed and confined the spy. But as it happened—"

"He never had the chance," she finished. "Henry fired too soon. Ivan was holding the plasma pipe when—" She stopped. Now she was believing the vision!

"None of you had a chance," the officer agreed. "On either ship. Except that one of them did wound the spy, there, so that he had to be put away by the Khalia when they arrived; they have no use for spies whose work is finished and who are likely to be a burden."

"Bugged?" she asked, catching up to an earlier reference. "You heard it all?"

"We heard it all—up to your broadcast," he agreed. "The bugs fed into the radio unit, and it was programmed to emit a coded ball at the same time as it was used for any other purpose. So we got your whole story up until that time." He smiled. "Once the second battery blew, we extrapolated the rest, and came for you in a hurry. It was safe after that, you see; they had no battery to hit us with. Had we tried before—" He shook his head.

"You mean—this is real?" she asked, amazed.

"And I'll tell you something else, Quiti," he said. "Off the record, until it's official. You did a man's job, no affront, and restored the viability of the whole plan. You'll be getting a double promotion, and next time there's a mission like this, you'll be in command. They already have a code name for it: 'Soft Like a Woman.' Others won't know exactly what that means, which is part of the point. There's a new respect for your planet spreading through the higher echelons, and for the capacities of women in the service. No one will call you cutie anymore."

She lay back dazedly. "Oh, I think I'll keep it. I don't mind it now."

He stood. "I have other business; got to go. But you know, you are awful cute. I never saw a prettier recovery of a lost mission; it will go down in the textbooks."

"Oh, I thought you meant—"

He winked. "That too. Now get some sleep."

"Soft like a woman," she repeated, liking it. Then she did sleep.

Imp to Nymph

Back when I discovered that it was possible to market novels from summaries instead of writing the entire manuscripts first, my income tripled. Because then I no longer wrote novels which didn't sell, I wrote only novels which had already sold. In that heyday of early success I tried a number of summaries, and some were never sold, so they went into my file, biding their time. I, as a writer, have of course never had a bad notion, only ignorant editors. This is true for all writers; ask any of them. But then what happens to those excellent notions that can't find homes in print? Well, sometimes they mutate to other forms. Usually I have made a story salable by lengthening it into a novel, as I did with "Ghost," "A Piece of Cake" (published as *Triple Detente*), "Omnivore" and "Balook." (When it's in "quotes" it's a story; when it's in *italics* it's a book; when it's CAPITALIZED it's a series or magazine.) One early story, "Tappuah," waited a quarter century before becoming the lead-in to a collaborative novel with Philip José Farmer, *The Caterpillar's Question*. But in this case I went in the opposite direction.

Back in the late 50's, when I was in the US Army in

Oklahoma, I diverted myself one day by looking up words in my big dictionary. I started with the word "Imp," then looked up the synonyms, and their synonyms. I made a kind of crazy chart, and in time it filled the pages. I got hundreds of words, covering most of the fantasy spectrum, from that one little opening wedge. I realized that this could be a fun contest game: Let folk each pick a word, and whoever's word goes farthest wins. Or maybe try to document a chain of words leading from a set beginning to a set ending, using a dictionary and limited to it. It may have been in the course of that first exploration I encountered the terms "Incubus" and "Succubus," which have served me in good stead ever since. Those are demons who come to sleeping folk, and get very, uh, intimate with them.

Later I decided to work that notion into a novel, *Imp to Nymph.* I made a summary—but this was back in the humorless-editor stage of my career, and it found no publisher. Lester del Rey of DEL REY BOOKS considered it in 1975, but in the end he went for Xanth, and I can't fault that. Xanth was, as it turned out, an idea with more future than Imp. So the notion languished in my file.

Then in 1982 a German publisher asked me for an original story for an anthology. So I wrote "Imp to Nymph" as a 9,000-word story with a German setting, and it was published in the GOLDMANN FANTASY FOLIANT I in 1983. I got a sale in America, but the magazine folded before publication. So finally I gave it to the World Fantasy Convention, and it was published in the Program Book for the 1987 convention in Nashville, Tennessee, where I was the fantasy guest of honor. Thus this story has been published, but the chances are you haven't read it. It's a good example of the long genesis some of my pieces can have. For those of you who are hopeful writers (which seems to be half my readers) the moral is plain: Never give up on a piece. Writers have longer lifespans than editors, and can sometimes outlast them and get into print despite them.

Imp to Nymph

I glanced down as I rode my carpet across the Rhine. This was one of those relatively unspoiled sections of the great river, decorated with fine old estates and elegant castles, some dating back to the twelfth century. There was no prettier region than this in all the world, to my mind—at least so it seemed from this high vantage. If I were to fly lower, I knew I would begin to perceive the problems man had brought to the grand river: the pollution of its water and shores, the destruction of age-old forests, and the crowding in of modern dwellings. Therefore I kept the carpet high. I was not an environmentalist by profession, after all; I was a police investigator.

But that was a truth I should not even think about now. I had to school my mind and emotion to reflect my cover-identity, so as not to give myself away by any inadvertent signal. This was my first important case, tracking down the fate of one Herr Schlucken who had vanished much in the manner of his namesake, the hiccough. Like several other people, he had been traced to a certain region, where the trail had ended, and his heirs wanted to verify—

No. I was not supposed to be aware of such things. I was now an idle, wealthy, spoiled child of a Cologne industrialist who was abroad more than he was home; all he required of me was that I be discreet. That was very limiting. One bad head-line involving the family name, and my allowance would be drastically cut. I had already been restricted to Germany, after an obscure incident in Paris. This identity of mine was of course verifiable; my department did know its business. Of course if high order black magic were used, the ruse would crumble—but that was part of the point. No legitimate business would employ black magic, and so its use would only advertise illegitimacy.

White magic, naturally, was legal and widely used; this convenient flying carpet was an example. No traffic congestion for me! The carpet would find its way promptly to its destination with no concern on my part, though I could give it directions at any time. Few machines were that good. Black magic, in contrast, was illegal, but also widely used. The authorities did not worry about the small infractions, such as one-mark curses; many of them were of such inferior grade that Satan Himself would be disgusted with them. But some of the infernal celebrations could get ugly, especially those involving human sacrifice, and had to be watched. It was one thing to trick innocent young women into kissing billygoats in the belief that these animals were transformed friends; it was quite another to summon genuine demons to murder business competitors. Demons were not only unethical, they were dangerous, because they were often smarter than their summoners and would try to trick mortals into voiding the spell of control. A demon unbound could cause terrible mischief before sufficient white magic could be brought to bear to bind it again. There had been a case in Berlin that almost triggered a nuclear confrontation. A number of people were still rather nervous about Berlin.

But such crimes were obvious. It was the subtle ones that caused the headaches. When people simply disappeared without apparent motive or explanation or violence, we couldn't be certain whether magic was involved at all. So we had to be prepared for anything, and I wasn't sure I was. I felt inadequate—

I put the thought from my mind. The carpet was descending now and I didn't want any local spirits reading my mind and reporting my real mission to the object of my investigation.

No, that thought, too, had to be stifled. Probably there were no special enchantments here; this was really a routine assignment, for they did not assign inexperienced investigators to really significant cases. There could always be surprises, however. So I was merely a young man of high libido and low ambition, ready to pay handsomely for his pleasures. I was supposed to know nothing about the sinister aspect of magic;

I was an innocent who had answered an intriguing ad in the underground press. The same ad marked on Schlucken's last newspaper.

The address was an imposing, rather massively ugly castle with none of the pretty spires I had half hoped for, set some distance back from the river, within a fenced wooded estate. A private place, of course. I stifled a thrill of nervousness, then decided to let the emotion run its course. An innocent young man would naturally be worried at this point, for anything could happen in a place like this. Perhaps they would cheat me, delivering nothing more than illusion for my money. A middle-aged woman, for example, could be made to seem like Marlene Dietrich in her youthful prime—for a few hours. It was rumored that more than one ambitious man had committed suicide when he discovered what he had actually dallied with.

I landed in the front yard. I noticed that there was no driveway; magic was the only way to enter here. Good; I had really hoped it would be magic, and not some mundane scheme or fraud. I've always liked magic, just as I've always liked money, perhaps because I grew up with so little of either. And, though I blush to confess it, the part I was playing did have some basis in fact. The libido part, I mean. It would be fun to meet a genuine nymph.

I got off the carpet, rolled it up, and carried it under my arm. There were two life-sized decorative stone griffins at the front steps; I hoped they did not come alive until after I was safely inside.

A well-dressed, rather portly middle-aged man met me at the door. "Ah, you are punctual, Herr—"

"Anton," I said quickly, as if embarrassed. "Just Anton. No title, please."

The man smiled with comprehension. Evidently he was used to dealing with secretive clients. Naturally a man would not care to let his associates know he had a captive nymph at his disposal, though there was nothing actually illegal about that. Polite society just didn't quite understand about nymphs. "Of course. And I am Karl. Just Karl. I have no identity at all, beyond this estate. I am here only to implement the policy of my employer. You have the agreed fee?"

We were getting down to business rapidly. "Twenty-five thousand marks, in cash, used bills," I agreed. "This had better be worth it!"

"There is no guarantee," the man said.

"No guarantee!" I exclaimed angrily, playing my part with enthusiasm. "For this kind of money, I expect an absolute guarantee. And I want to see her first. I don't want to get stuck with an ugly—"

Karl shook his head. "There are no old or fat or ugly nymphs. They never spoil. That is not my concern. Come, sit down, Anton." He ushered me into a somber antechamber that reminded me of a mortician's waiting room, though it was in fact richly upholstered with tapestries on the walls and carpet on the floor. "There are things I must clarify for you."

"You said twenty-five thousand on the phone," I snapped, true to my impetuous character. "I won't pay more!"

Karl raised his hand in a gesture of unconcern. "My employer always honors his word. The fee is not at issue. But what you ask for can not be handed to you on a platter."

"All I want is a nymph," I said. "Just as your ad offered. A creature who never eats, never sleeps, never eliminates, has no free will—a luscious female-figure who will do exactly what you say—always, with no argument and no kissing-and-telling, or moods or times-of-the-month or headaches, or whatever."

"Or whatever," he agreed wryly. "A nymph is all you describe, the ideal sex object. You do not desire any personality at all?"

"Of course not," I said, aware of the contempt in which he probably held me. "All she needs is to understand orders, and perform well. And to keep out of the way when I'm busy with something else. I don't want her for conversation, you know."

"I had gathered as much. You do not suppose it might get dull after a while? My employer wants to be sure you understand what you are getting. A nymph, generally speaking, is hardly more than a body. She may have a mind, but it is completely unschooled, childlike."

"A body that never grows old," I said. "Completely sexy, completely obliging. No real woman is like that. Not once she gets her hooks into a man."

"I would not know," he said, resigned. I wondered momentarily about that; did he never indulge in the wares himself? Maybe he had been placed under a spell of abstinence, to keep him honest.

"Now that that's settled, bring her in," I said. "I've got the money right here."

"That is part of what I need to explain," Karl said. "I can not deliver the nymph to you. You have to fetch her yourself."

"Fetch her myself!" I exclaimed. "Why should I pay you the money, then?"

"What my employer offers is merely the key to the door," he said. "The nymph will obey only the man who fetches her out. If I fetched her, she would be mine, not yours. That is the way it works. These soulless creatures are incapable of multiple loyalties; we call it bonding."

"Bonding," I repeated. "You mean like a hatchling duckling seeing its mother the first time?"

"Yes. Once that bond is made, only death will break it."

"Hey! You told me they're immortal!"

"They are. You are not."

"Oh," I said, momentarily disgruntled.

"I am the keeper of the portal, not the deliverer of the goods," Karl continued. "But I am obliged to advise you of certain cautions before I accept your money. The first is that this portal is magic, and that it opens on wild enchantment."

"Wild?" I asked, perplexed.

"Undifferentiated magic," he explained. "You are accustomed to selective effects, the so-called white magic, that is essentially beneficial. As you must know, there are other types of magic, some inimical. It is best to avoid those other types, unless you happen to be conversant in such arts. This is a wild zone, where all types mix, rather like a wilderness. You must be very careful where you step and what you invoke."

This didn't sound like a person who planned to cheat me with illusion! Was this after all a false lead? I wasn't really looking for a nymph, but for a missing man. "I don't want to go into any wilderness!" I protested. "I just want my nymph!"

He nodded patiently, evidently accustomed to dealing with louts like me. These butler-types have remarkable stability. "You will be given a charm to protect you from untoward effects," he said.

"So I won't be in any danger?" I asked nervously. Actually I rather liked the spice of danger, but could not say that now.

"Not if you are careful. I will explain the situation in as much detail as you wish; that is my duty. But once you pass through the portal, you are on your own. My employer does not protect any person from his own folly."

This sounded less and less like a swindle or murder trap. Why should Karl bother with such a warning, if he didn't intend to deliver? "Let's have the protective charm," I said, staying in character. "I didn't come here to sit around and talk."

"First the situation," he said firmly. "This castle consists of many sealed chambers. In each is a supernatural creature, confined there by the physical walls and enchantments of this locale. Thus we have a complete array of specimens—"

"A zoo," I said, catching on. "Or a pet store. With nymphs!"

"I would not express it so crudely," he said. "But that may be a useful analogy. There are indeed nymphs of many kinds; nereids of the sea, oreads of the mountains, dryads of the trees—"

"I want an apartment-nymph," I said. "I don't care about the sea or mountains or trees." Which was not strictly true. I cared strongly about all three, which might be one reason I had taken this job. I wanted to protect the world from the further depredations of man—and from the illicit use of harmful magic. Black magic could be a worse addiction, and do more harm than any potent drug. But it wasn't wise to reflect on that, here. I was supposed to be a superficial idler.

"A generalized nymph," he agreed. "One who can enter any habitat without being committed to it. That is a higher-class creature than some. Therefore you should search for the chamber labeled NYMPH."

"Search for?" I asked.

"The rooms are jumbled," he explained. "Each is labeled—but you must travel a route of affinities to reach your goal."

"Look," I said, affecting impatience. "I didn't come here for any long discourse on affinities! Are you going to let me go in after my nymph or aren't you?"

"Anton, I must warn you against going in unprepared," he said. "There are certain devices of convenience, and formidable pitfalls for the unwary. Some careless clients do not emerge."

So this *was* the place! But I was playing the part of an impetuous, thrill-seeking youth; too much caution would make him suspicious, and as yet I did not have enough evidence to arrest him. "Just give me the charm and let me into the zoo."

He seemed almost to sigh. "I really must advise against this impetuosity. There are special aspects that—"

I shoved the money at him. "Deliver."

He shrugged and accepted the wad of bills. Now I had half a case against him; he had accepted payment. If he failed to deliver, or if what he delivered were illicit, he was mine. But that was incidental; I still needed to locate Schlucken to wrap it up completely.

Karl walked to a wall-cabinet and brought out a cloth bag with a loop-strap. "There are twenty-five magic talismen here," he said. "Each one passes you to the chamber of your choice. You must save the last one to return here, or you will be trapped in the, uh, zoo yourself. My employer will not help you if—"

"Yes, yes!" I said impatiently, pretending I didn't understand the significance of his warning. If I lost the last token, I would be out of luck. "Where do I start?"

"And the charm," he said, taking down a sword.

I contemplated the sword, taken aback. It was a huge, gleaming double-edged blade with a kind of enclosed hilt to protect the hand. "I don't know how to use a thing like that!" I protested quite sincerely. I had had training in assorted firearms and barehand techniques of combat, but not in ancient weapons. "I'd be likely to cut off my own foot!"

"It is enchanted," he said. "Anyone who holds it becomes expert. You must carry it; this is a requirement of the transaction."

"Oh, all right," I said. We put the sword in a sort of harness and fastened the harness about my body. The sheathed sword now lay against my left leg, the hilt projecting slightly forward. I felt like a costumed fool.

He led me to a blank panel. "Take a talisman and touch the surface," he said. "Then step through promptly, before the portal closes. The entry-point is random; the rest you control. Remember, this is the only way you can pass between chambers; do not mislay the talismen."

Small chance of that! I fumbled in the bag and fished out a small disk. It reminded me of a subway token, but it was more than that. It was silver, with arcane images engraved all over it—four-leaf clovers, evil eyes and other obscure symbols of power. I kept a straight face, though my pulse gave a start. I've studied some magic, of course; it's a requirement for this type of employment. I knew a number of fairly simple but potent spells, though I would never be a real sorcerer; the police academy makes sure we have the basics down pat. Thus I was instantly aware that this was no faked-up amulet; this was genuine! I could feel the subtle power associated with it. The police lab would love to have this for analysis; it had surely not been crafted in any conventional shop! My knees felt weak; I was onto something here, and might need all my untried expertise to get safely free.

But first I had to spring the trap, or I would have no case. If this was as big as I now suspected, I would get points toward an early promotion for it, so I was not about to let it slip away. I touched the panel in the center, with the token.

The word IMP flashed before me, printed on the panel.

"Be ready to draw your sword at any time," Karl told me. "Now step through."

Step through a solid panel? I poked my finger at it, discovering that the talismen had vanished. My finger sank into the opaque surface. It had become unsolid despite its appearance. I watched my arm disappear into it as if amputated, but there was no sensation. Dematerialization—a standard magic device, but still impressive in this context. Something else nagged me as I shoved through the panel. If there really was strong magic here, as there seemed to be, then there could indeed be supernatural danger. I paused halfway inside the panel. "What, specifically, do I need this sword for?"

"For the monster," Karl said. "It pursues all who invade this region, and it can pass through walls without use of the talismens; our spells do not confine it. But the monster takes time to orient and close on you; move quickly and you will complete your mission before it arrives."

"The monster!" I exclaimed. Rash youth that I pretended to be, I still should have taken time to learn more about this. A magic monster could be real trouble! But the panel was beginning to thicken around me, and I had to move on through before I got stuck in it. In a moment I stood in an irregular chamber with seven walls slanting this way and that, each bearing a prominently printed word. The ceiling resembled that of a cave, with small stalactites projecting down. The floor was a bed of coal, with patches of fire consuming it. On one side was a sort of jungle gym.

There beside the gym stood the imp. This was a childlike figure with cute little snub horns and a bobbed tail and hooves on his feet.

"Hey, a tourist!" the imp said. "I'll take a piece of that!"

A small pitchfork appeared in his hands. He stepped toward me, his little eyes glittering malevolently.

"I'm just passing through," I said. I'd never met a genuine imp before, and didn't care for this one. "Stay out of my way and we'll get along just fine."

"Sure, sucker," he said, and charged.

I'm a bachelor, but I've had some experience with children. That's one reason I intend to have none of my own. I stepped aside as he came at me, and the pitchfork jammed into the wall and stuck there. "You want a spanking?" I asked.

The imp was mortified by his failure. He backed off, his horns turning red. I kept a covert eye on him while I read the signs on the walls. They were, clockwise from where I stood: SPRITE—ELF—HOBGOBLIN—FLIBBERTIGIBBET—DEMON—DEVIL —SPIRIT.

I realized that these were creatures loosely associated with the imp, perhaps clarifications of his nature. He was small, like an elf, and horned like a devil, and supernatural like a spirit. But neither he nor any of those other creatures were what I wanted.

Evidently I would have to select one of these related beings, traveling the route of affinities, and hope it was closer to my need. To locate Schlucken, I had first to locate NYMPH. I would keep trying; I had plenty of tokens.

I fished in the bag and brought out a second talisman. Which wall should I touch?

"Take your time, tourist!" the imp said. "Till the monster comes!"

"What do you know about the monster?" I demanded.

He grinned nastily. "Nothing, nothing at all, chump!"

Of course the little devil wouldn't help. But he had reminded me about the monster; I could not afford to dally too long. So which creature should I go for?

I certainly didn't want to tangle with a demon or devil, and I didn't trust the hobgoblin, and I didn't know what a flibbertigibbet was, so I took the one most likely to be female: the sprite. I touched my token to that wall and stepped through. Just as well, for the heat of the coals was making my feet uncomfortable.

The new chamber was twice the size and irregularity of the prior one. Walls angled in and out like the surface of an accordion, each bearing its printed word. The scenery was bright and green, with several trees rising; the ceiling was quite high, to accommodate them. There was no fire, and the air was pleasantly cool. This might be a cell in a zoo, but it resembled an enclosure in an open forest.

The sprite drifted close. It was a ghostly, neuter shape, cloaked in white, whose face was obscure. "Yooou coome for meee?" it inquired with a voice like distant wind.

"Uh, sorry, no," I said quickly. "I'm really looking for a nymph." And for vanished Schlucken, so I could nail a seller of black magic, or maybe a murderer. Karl had not given me enough to go on for a clear-cut case. So far, this castle was exactly what he had claimed it was, and that wasn't enough for my purpose.

"Theeere," the sprite said, pointing with a discarnate arm to one of the wall-panels.

"Thaaank—uh, thank you," I replied. This creature was eerie, but helpful. Better than the imp. I walked to the panel, passing APPARITION, SPECTRE, GHOST and SHADE on the way. The one I arrived at was FAIRY.

Well, they were female, weren't they? That was on the way to NYMPH. The sprite's advice seemed good. I dug out another token and touched it to the panel. In a moment I was through—and found myself in fairyland.

It was beautiful. The bushes and trees were luminescent, and sparkles radiated from the clear pools. Pretty little winged fairies flitted about. Each was only a few centimeters long, no larger than birds, but human in form.

I looked for the labeled walls, but they weren't evident. I seemed to have stepped directly into the realm of the fairies. Alarmed, I cast about, ready to step back through the wall I had come by—but it was gone. I stood in an open glade, and whichever way I turned there was only similar scenery.

A fairy flitted up to me. She was a perfect little female, completely nude, like one of the modern adult dolls children like to dress and undress. Her wings moved so rapidly they buzzed and were hazy, like those of an insect. Indeed, she might have been a dragonfly, but for her face and shape, or a hummingbird. "You look lost," she piped.

"I am," I said. "I'm looking for walls with terms on them." Her smile was a miniature flash of white in her face.

"They are here. You have to see through the illusion."

"Oh. You mean this only seems like fairyland?"

She frowned, and a tiny tear fell from her eye. "Alas, we are far from home. Would it were not so! We pretend and prettify our cell, but—"

This made me pause for reflection. My mission was to locate, rescue, or verify the fate of Schlucken, and to arrest the perpetrators of the crime. I had not been at all concerned with the situation of whatever other people or creatures I might encounter. Now I wondered; if Schlucken were captive here, a part of this fantastic zoo—what of the others? Did the fairies have families back home?

It was easy to find out. "Who are you?" I asked the fairy. "How did you come here?"

Another tear fell. "We may not speak of such matters to the tourists," she said. "Please go away."

I realized that she was afraid of being punished if she talked. I was not in a position to do anything for her, and would only get her in trouble—and perhaps myself as well—if I tried. "Show me the route to NYMPH and I'll go immediately," I said with a certain regret.

"I'm not sure of the roster," she said. "It changes. But here are the walls." She waved her arms, and the illusion faded, revealing the stark outlines of the chamber. On the walls were the words SPIRIT—SPRITE—PIGWIDGEON—DEMON—ELF—FAY—NIX—BROWNIE—all the cousins of the fairies, one of which I had already checked out. I'd managed to find a female, but not of the right size or species. I still didn't want a demon, and didn't know what a pigwidgeon was. How about a fay?

I shrugged. This was more of a puzzle than I had anticipated, but I had used only three of my twenty-five tokens. I could take a chance on the fay. It seemed as good a course as any. This was turning out to be an interesting experience.

I drew out another token and touched the wall. The disk vanished and I stepped through—into a tiny stone cell, like a dungeon cubicle. It was really two-sided, the walls bowing out to form a narrow crevice between them.

On a stool sat hunched a small furry figure with pointed ears. This was the fay, of course, in solitary confinement. One wall had the word FAIRY—I must have just come through it—and the other had ELF. I hesitated, looking at the fay, who might stand a meter high if he got off his stool. Should I speak to him? I disliked seeing any creature, natural or supernatural, in such dire straits. But what could I do for him, anyway? I was only a tourist. I took out the next token and phased through the ELF wall.

This turned out to be another of the larger chambers, resembling a cavern hewn from the side of a rocky mountain. Several little men labored over stone lasts, evidently making shoes. Smoke smudged up from a fire smoldering in a pit. The irregular walls said IMP—SPRITE—FAIRY—FAY, which were the ones I'd already pushed through, and PIXY—PUCK—SPIRIT, which I had not. I really was not making a lot of progress, so this time I would seek advice.

I approached the nearest elf. "Pardon me," I said politely. "I'm a tourist—"

The little man looked up from his shoe. He was about the same size as the fay, and his ears were pointed, but a wary intelligence showed in his face. "Obviously," he said.

"I'm looking for a nymph, and—" I broke off, for a sudden pain had occurred deep in my gut.

"Better hurry," the elf told me.

I leaned against the wall, trying to alleviate the discomfort. It wasn't intense, but I disliked any undefined illness, especially when it might interfere with my mission. "Why?"

"It'll cost you," he said, and held out his callused little hand.

"Cost me?" I asked blankly.

"One talisman," he said, "for three questions. That's standard."

The little entrepreneur! He was charging me for information! But maybe this was fair enough. I still had plenty of tokens, and if his advice could save me several, it would be worth it. "Agreed," I said, fishing out a disk. "Clear answers to three questions. No riddles or evasions or useless stuff."

"Right," he agreed, hand still out.

I hesitated, but gave him the token. "Ha!" he exclaimed. "Now I can go home! I've got a pass!"

"Not before you honor our deal," I reminded him.

"I'm an elf," he said stiffly. "Goblins cheat; elves always deliver. I told you it's a standard agreement. Ask."

"What is the fastest route to NYMPH?"

"That way," he said, touching the wall that said FAIRY.

"But I just came from there!" I protested. Actually I had just been through FAY, but it had been FAIRY before that. The elf merely nodded, waiting for the next question. He evidently considered me something of an idiot. And I felt like one, for I found I didn't know what else to ask. His first answer hadn't been very helpful, and I didn't want to waste more time on it.

"Look, tourist, I want to get out of here," the elf said. "I can't wait while you hem and haw and poke at your belly."

I stopped checking my uncomfortable abdomen, somewhat guiltily. "Suppose I just tell you what to ask?"

"Do that," I said, wishing that the pain in my gut would go away. It seemed to be getting worse.

"Ask about the risk involved in crossing your trail."

Crossing my trail? I shrugged. "Very well, give me a full account."

"You must use one talisman to enter each exhibit," he said. "Or to go home. But there are other restrictions. If you return to a chamber you've visited before, that's known as crossing your trail. No harm in that, except it means you've wasted a talisman, and they cost you a thousand marks apiece, which isn't exactly goblin dust. But if you enter a given chamber a third time, your trail ends there, and you must take whatever is in it no matter how many talismen you have left, and if you happen to be out of talismen, whatever is in that chamber takes you. So it's all right to cross your trail when you've gone wrong as you have this time—but don't make the same mistake again."

I realized that Karl would have told me this, if I had waited for him to finish. The penalty of my impatience was becoming evident. Yet I had had to play my part properly, even if it meant trouble. If I ever hoped to locate the man who had sought a nymph, I had to make sure not to arouse suspicion.

"Thank you for a good answer," I said, suffering another wash of discomfort in my abdomen that made me wince.

The elf eyed me appraisingly. "And you had better ask about the monster," he said.

"Yes—" I agreed painfully.

"It is zeroing in on you now," he said. "It doesn't like intruders, and it sniffs them out relentlessly. If they dawdle too long, it catches up. You can tell when it is getting near, because you feel a pain. You can fend it off with that sword, but you're better off staying well away from it."

"Thank you," I said, experiencing yet another surge of discomfort. At least now I knew what caused it!

"And now I'm going home!" the elf said. "Farewell, fellow inmates. I hope you find your own tickets soon!" He went over and touched the token to the floor, and sank through it and out of sight.

So that was the way to leave the zoo! I hadn't thought to inquire. It was a good thing I had seen this. Evidently whoever touched a token to the floor passed through it and directly into his own world.

My gut-pain eased; the monster must have taken a wrong

turn, perhaps sniffing out the elf's progress instead of mine. It was not unreasonable to assume that the creature was sensitive to the use of the magic tokens; that was what distinguished a tourist from an inmate.

I looked at the walls. The elf had told me to return to FAIRY—but that meant crossing my trail. I didn't want to do that, yet. It would only limit my options. So I considered the three new walls; maybe SPIRIT would get me there. I brought out another token and touched the panel.

"You'll be soorryy!" an elfin voice singsonged as I phased through. Well, I might indeed be sorry—but now I was committed.

I came into a somewhat smoky region where fires and shadows seemed to war with each other. Several figures moved about, but I couldn't quite determine whether they were solid or otherwise. Their features were vague, seeming more clear in peripheral vision than directly. Maybe my personal discomfort distorted my concentration. I didn't like this place, so I marched up to the first convenient wall, marked APPARITION, and expended a token on it.

The new chamber was the largest and gloomiest yet. I had to pause to let my eyes adjust to the poor light, and my gut felt worse. That monster was shifting closer—and I still wasn't making progress. I was already sorry I hadn't taken the elf's advice, and backtracked to FAIRY. There had surely been better alternatives from that chamber than from this! I walked around the exhibit, having to peer closely at the labels because of the poor light. SPECTRE—PHANTOM—DOPPELGANGER—SHADE—GHOST. They were all spooky things! But my gut was hurting worse. I was breathing in small pants, trying to ease it, though I now knew that the source was not in my body. I had to get where I was going, quickly!

I reached for a token—and something horrible loomed before me, mostly eyes and teeth. It was an apparition, of course, but it scared me. I wasn't sure my sword would have any effect on something that wasn't exactly solid. So I punched my token at GHOST and crashed through.

The next chamber wasn't much better. It was like the interior of a haunted house, with a rickety wooden floor, peeling-papered walls, and a broken window directly across from me. A ghost floated up, all eyeless moan—and I jammed my next token into the nearest wall, labeled SPECTRE.

Now I was in a dank nocturnal forest, with rain drizzling down on me. It reminded me of the time I camped as a teenager in the mountains of the Black Forest near Switzerland, and got lost in the rain. I liked nature, but that had been too much! And so was this. A grim winged thing swooped at me, and I dived for the nearest tree, token extended. The tree was labeled SHADE, and I disappeared into it and emerged into a barren plain where a huge animalistic shape howled and turned toward me. Almost blindly I lunged at the sign saying PHANTOM and phased through, not caring where I went so long as it was elsewhere.

I was in another dismal chamber, and something translucent rose up before me. I had no wish to dally with a phantom, so I cast about for the next, even though I knew I was wasting precious tokens by my hurry and panic. My inexperience was showing, and I was just getting myself deeper into trouble.

This easy quest had become difficult.

The walls said GHOST—ILLUSION—VISION—SPECTRE—APPARITION—SPIRIT. Hadn't I already been to most of these horrors?

The translucent thing moved to enfold me in its awfulness. I threw myself at VISION. I landed in an ordinary living room that seemed somehow familiar. An older but elegant woman sat in a rocking-chair before a television set, halfsmiling.

Well, this was different. This place was so cozy it reminded me of home.

Home? It *was* home—as I had known it a decade ago! The layout, the curtains—

Then the woman's identity penetrated. "Mother!" I exclaimed, amazed. "What are you doing here?"

She looked up at me, her gaze bland. And I remembered

that my dear mother had died two years ago. This was a—vision.

I wrenched my attention back to business. Most of the labels were repeats; I realized that I was being driven inevitably to cross my trail, which would put me in jeopardy of finishing in the wrong chamber or using up my diminishing store of tokens pointlessly. I took the first new one I saw, CHIMERA, not willing to remain any longer in the presence of a person I knew was dead. It had been a jolt to see my mother! I still loved her; that was the problem. The years of my childhood and the happy unity of my family were gone forever, and it was best not to dwell on them now.

I passed through the wall, and suddenly I was in an ancient Roman arena, with a huge audience seated above the pit, and from an open cage was striding the most horrendous monster I could have imagined. It was like a lion in front, and like a serpent behind, and had an otherwise caprine body. Smoke issued from its nostrils as it breathed, and I knew that where there was smoke, there was fire.

Simultaneously my gut-pain intensified. The pain suffused my body as if something were being stretched to the bursting point; my arms felt weak and my hands were sweating, yet I felt cold and I was shivering, with goose-pimples appearing on my skin. I staggered, feeling somewhat faint. Was it terror, or—

Oh, no! *This was the monster!* Instead of avoiding it, I had unwittingly phased right into its arena! My abruptly worse pain was the proof of that, for I am not normally a coward. Foolish, perhaps; stupid, at times; but cowardly, seldom. When I am afraid I feel it more in the chest than in the bowel. Confusion and pain had led me into folly.

I heard the cheering of the spectators. They were ready for the slaughter. I had suddenly come to the end of the line. It seemed everyone had known about this appointment except me.

No, the crowd was probably illusion, and this was really

a much smaller chamber than it appeared. Still, the threat from the chimera was real enough.

But my mission had not been accomplished! I might be a fool, but I didn't want to die here and I didn't want to fail in my assignment. My father was a good man, and he would be most upset. He hadn't really liked my decision to go into this line of work. So both my survival instinct and my pride stiffened my resolve. If I had to go, I'd go fighting.

The monster moved toward me, and I almost doubled over with the pain. I certainly wasn't cut out to be any barbarian hero! But I did have a weapon.

I gritted my teeth, forced my body erect, and reached across my torso and put my right hand on the hilt of my sword. Abruptly the pain abated. My fingers closed firmly on the handle and the blade slid from its sheath mostly of its own volition, feather-light yet solid. The sword assumed a ready position, and it gleamed as if with eagerness. What an instrument!

The chimera paused. A column of fire shot from its mouth—but the sword moved to intercept it, and the flame ricocheted off the surface harmlessly, though I felt the flash of heat. In the back of my mind had been the hint of a notion that I might have been given a flawed weapon, one that would betray me in the crisis, but this was a splendid sword! And yet that bothered me, professionally. If Karl was sending people in to their deaths, why should he provide this valuable weapon? This suggested that I had misjudged the man; maybe he was dealing honestly with his clients.

But now the monster roared and leaped at me, banishing idle speculations. My sword whipped up, slicing at the open jaws. The chimera drew back its head in midair, so the blade only clipped the tip of its nose. That tip flew off, and the monster dropped to the ground, blood flowing. My sword swung back, going for the neck, thirsting for more blood, but the monster flinched aside.

In the magic violence of my swing, I forgot the bag I

clutched in my left hand. Several tokens spilled out and bounced and rolled across the ground.

I couldn't afford to lose those! Automatically, foolishly, I squatted to recover them, forgetting the monster. Oh, what folly! I have done stupid things before, but this set a new standard of idiocy.

The chimera batted at my right hand. One claw struck the guard around the hilt, harmlessly; but another struck my wrist. The shock was terrible. I wrenched my arm away, letting go of the sword. I had been disarmed!

I scooped up a couple of tokens and launched myself at the nearest sign set in the wall of the arena. It said PHANTOM—a repeat. I didn't care; I had my life to save!

I landed in the dismal chamber with the translucent thing looming before me. My gut-pain returned; I had lost that aspect of protection from the monster when I lost the magic sword. I saw a panel ahead; GHOST; I thrust the second token I had recovered at it and plunged through. I had to get away from the chimera!

Now I was back in the haunted house. I had crossed my trail again! I forced myself to pause, despite my concern about the monster so close behind. I had to get organized before I got wiped out!

I checked my tokens. I had six left, I had lost two or three in the arena, but I still had some leeway. I was lucky; I could have done far worse, considering my carelessness.

My gut knotted. I heard the roar of the monster. Feverishly I scanned the walls: APPARITION—SPECTRE—SPRITE—say, that was one of the earliest ones!

The chimera came through the wall, breathing fire. I made a flying leap for SPRITE, token extended.

I made it. Now I knew where I was going. I ignored the floating sprite and went directly for FAIRY.

I was back in fairyland, or the illusion of it. I had four tokens left. Now I would go to FAY and—

Wait! FAY, I remembered, led only to two others, FAIRY and ELF. No alternate route there, for I had visited FAIRY twice already, counting now. The elf had not told me to retrace my former path, he had told me FAIRY was the fastest route.

The little hummingbird fairy flew up. "Oh, you are hurt!" she piped, hovering near my right arm, where blood spread from my clawed wrist.

"So is the monster," I said, remembering how the sword had sliced off the tip of its snout. My gut knotted again. Wounded or not, that chimera was hot on my trail! I didn't have time for thought! One of the alternate routes had to be the one.

A blood-smeared snout came through the wall. The fairy screamed and buzzed away. I went for the first untried panel I spied: NIX.

I landed in a pool. I sank into the water, held my breath, and splashed for the surface. Several naked young men were here, with gills in their necks. These were the nix. They did not look friendly. I stroked for the rim of the pool, hampered somewhat by the bag in my left hand and the stinging in my right wrist, ready to clamber out before the nix decided to use me for waterpolo.

My gut knotted. I doubled over involuntarily, inhaling some water before getting my mouth clamped shut. Through bleary eyes I saw the chimera standing at the rim, waiting for me to come to it. The monster was literally burning with anticipation. It seemed that the heat of its own breath had cauterized the amputated portion of the snout, so the bleeding had slowed.

Torn between my gut, my lungs and my fear, I somehow managed to wrench another token from the bag and splash water in the monster's face. Many cats don't like water, and this cat-head was no exception. The chimera drew back in a cloud of smoke, and I banged my token into the section of the pool wall marked NAIAD and twisted through.

I sprawled on a small beach on the other side, gasping. There was a feminine scream as I glanced blearily up to see a young woman swimming swiftly away from me. She moved so rapidly that I knew she was no normal girl; maybe she had a fishtail or webbed extremities or gills. This was of course the naiad, or water spirit.

I sat up as I got the water clear of my throat. This chamber had a circular fountain in the center, behind which the naiad now hid. It was a good place, for a water creature. I felt in the bag—and found only two tokens remaining. One I would need to escape the zoo; that meant I could visit only one more chamber.

My gut tightened again. The monster was coming through! It seemed to take the chimera a moment to locate me again, each time I phased to another chamber, but that grace period was hardly enough. I gazed wildly about and saw the word NYMPH on the wall across the chamber, behind the fountain. I rolled into the water and swam, bag clutched in left hand, token in right hand. The water of the fountain sprinkled on my head and shoulders like rain. Behind me I heard the familiar roar, I clamped my teeth, held my breath and fought my gut, struggling to keep moving. Fortunately the pool was small, and in a moment I touched the wall.

I fell into a parklike region, with green turf for a floor and sunshine beaming down from a skylight. The most lovely young woman I had ever seen stood before me, clothed only by her waist-long golden hair. Here at last was my nymph!

"Have you seen a man named—?" I began, remembering my real mission. Of course, Schlucken might never have made it to this chamber; I almost hadn't!

Another roar interrupted me. I had no time to look for the missing man; I had to save myself. But the nymph could be a valuable witness if I took her along.

I scrambled to my feet, staggered forward, and grasped her by a slender bare arm. What a figure she had! "Come with me!" I gasped, and jammed the last token into the ground as the monster leaped through the wall.

We landed in the antechamber, the nymph in my arms. She was a remarkable armful! I tried to disengage, getting my bearings.

Karl was awaiting me, impeccably dressed. My pain was

gone, except for the scratch on my wrist, and I was abruptly conscious of my bedraggled state. I was soaking wet, and was embracing a nude nymph. I really wasn't sure how we had gotten so close together; maybe she had jumped close as we sank through the floor of her chamber. I tried again to pry her away from me, somewhat awkwardly, but she was like glue.

"Stand clear!" I muttered—and instantly she obeyed, standing contritely beside me.

I looked at Karl. "I lost the sword," I said, embarrassed. "But I found the nymph."

"So I see," Karl said gravely. "The sword fell back into this room when it was separated from you; it is spelled to do that, lest the monster get hold of it. It is the sword it really wants, for then its power would be magnified beyond all reason." He indicated the cabinet, where the sword had been returned.

"You mean—if I hadn't carried the sword—the chimera never would have chased me?" I demanded.

"Perhaps," he agreed. "But you would have had no protection, had you encountered the monster randomly. It seeks the sword in order to abolish the one thing that can destroy it."

I decided to drop that matter; I had indeed blundered into the monster on my own.

"I was concerned that you would not return," Karl continued. "This quest does have its hazards, as I tried to explain to you. But it also has its rewards. I trust you are satisfied?"

I didn't want to tell him my real mission, which was as yet incomplete. But I realized that this castle certainly could account for Schlucken's disappearance, as it had almost accounted for mine, and there was sufficient evidence against Karl for an arrest. Too bad, for he had played fair by his rules. It had been my own folly that nearly wiped me out. But I had a job to do.

"I regret this," I said sincerely. "I must advise you that I am an officer of the law, and you—"

Karl smiled tiredly. "I am aware of your identity, Anton.

How I wish you could arrest me and take me away from here. But that is impossible."

"I'm afraid I must insist," I said. "I shall testify to extenuating circumstances, and perhaps you will get off lightly, especially if you free any people who are prisoners in this castle—"

"My employer will not permit—"

"I must take you in." I stepped toward him, ready for some evasive maneuver on his part, ready to catch him in a standard police come-along spell. With him in custody, and the nymph as a witness, and the evidence that our police experts would find in the castle itself, we should have a tight case.

He did not move. "You see, I also am bound here," Karl said. "I am no more free than the other exhibits. I am bound forever to serve my office—or be tormented below." He glanced significantly downward, and I knew what region he meant. It was a tacit admission that the very blackest magic was involved.

I refused to be bluffed. "Come with me," I said, and grasped his arm.

He shriveled in my grasp as if trying to resist my magic. His face seemed to fall in, and his extremities collapsed. But I did not let go; my grip is spelled to be tight despite the most extreme changes of shape by the arrestee.

"Oh!" the nymph cried, the first word I had heard her utter. At least she was intelligent enough to speak; she would be a useful witness.

I looked at Karl—and saw in my hand the twisted mass of a large mandrake root. This was Karl's true identity. He was correct. I could not arrest him. He wasn't even a man. He had been animated by black magic and had no other existence than that permitted him by his infernal employer. All I would have to prefer charges against would be a vegetable. Karl really was bound here, another zoo exhibit.

I set the root down gently. "You are already more of a prisoner than I knew," I said. "But our experts will take apart this castle, if necessary, to gather evidence against your employer."

But I spoke too soon. The walls of the room were becoming hazy, and soon the castle itself became smoke and drifted away, leaving me standing in a deserted glade. I should have known that the infernal one would not permit any tangible evidence to fall into the hands of the police. I walked disconsolately toward my rolled carpet, the only artifact that remained.

The nymph came with me, jiggling as she walked, her hair washing back to reveal her full body. Now I remembered: She had become bonded to me when I had brought her from the chamber. She was my slave for life. I had no case and no evidence, but I did have her. My fee had paid for her.

What was I going to do with a nymph?

The nymph smiled and took my arm possessively. *She* had a notion . . .

E van S

For years I tried to market humor, but editors told me that humor required a special touch, which unfortunately I lacked. I think editing requires a special touch, which unfortunately most editors lack. Only when I got Xanth into print did I begin to prove that the editors really didn't know much about humor either. Critics, being humorless, still hate Xanth, of course. But what, then, was I to do with those earlier rejected efforts? Two I sneaked into *Anthonology*. I'm sneaking some more into this volume.

Way back in 1963 I was asked to enter a story in a fan contest sponsored by the National Fantasy Fan Federation, or N3F. This was a problem, because I had sold my first story in 1962 so was technically professional. But they wanted me to enter regardless. So I compromised by submitting a serious story I had written in 1958 well before becoming pro, "Deva," and by writing a joke entry that couldn't possibly win, "E van S." Wouldn't you know it, they turned out to be two of the top entries. But I had given "Deva" to a fan editor long before, who had then disappeared—only to reappear after I had given up and sent the story to the contest. This is the nature of fan editors. So it was disqualified because of the fanzine publication. However, the following year the first and second places in the contest were taken by two of my correspondents and later collaborators, and their stories were duly published in IF MAGAZINE in 1964: "A As in Android" by Frances T. Hall, and "Monster Tracks" by Robert E. Margroff. So the contest did do somebody some good.

I was left with the joke story. I never tried to market it, until decades later another writer, Brad Linaweaver, asked me to contribute to his anthology *Off the Wall,* for which odd stuff was appropriate. So now, as my brain slowly softens with age, I'm ready to let readers see it. Beware: This one is wacky. I should explain one of the puns, though: I have a play on the pronunciation of Don Quixote, who was a rather special fictional adventurer in Spain. It is pronounced Don Kee Hotay, but from it comes the word "quixotic," pronounced Quick Sotic. Later a TV cartoon series had a similar play on the word, but I believe I was the first. There are other literary allusions, for those with the inclination and education to fathom them.

Note, incidentally, how little commercial television has changed since 1963. Evidently the same demons are in charge.

E van S

"Curse this TV!" Mary Tate exclaimed euphemistically. It was midmorning. Her brown hair was in uncomfortable curlers, she'd had nothing more than coffee for breakfast, and her bathrobe refused to stay tied. She sat before the television set, hating it but unable to pull herself away. The programs were dull, the commercials repetitive and prolix; watching the thing was a waste of time. Somehow she had been caught up long ago in the interminable run of soap operas and quiz shows. Now, at a uselessly well-preserved thirty-three, she was a TV addict. Her husband usually managed to sleep through his Saturday sports programs, warm beer in hand; but she found no such relief.

Mary wasn't certain exactly when she became aware of the visitor. No one had rung the doorbell, yet there he was, standing beside her TV, a fat-cheeked, curly-haired youngster bearing an impish grin. "You really should watch your language, miss," he said nonchalantly.

"I'm *Mrs.* Nicholas Tate, and I'll say what I please in my own house," she said, surprise making her tone fierce. "Who are you and how did you get in?"

"My name is van S. *E* van S. I'm the little fiend for this sector."

Mary strained her credulity. "A fiend? What do the initials stand for?"

"Evil Spirit, you dope. Say—your husband is Nick Tate? Nick T. Tate? Does he—"

"Get out!" Mary exclaimed. "I was sick of that joke before I ever met the man. The same goes for you. Go home and ask your mother for a spanking."

Van S grinned impudently. "What a handsome temper. But you summoned me here, you know. 'Curse this TV' you said. And since I'm basically a malignant spook, I had to answer. Did you have any particular curse in mind?"

"That was just an expression. A figure of speech. Leave my TV alone."

"Lady, I don't give two sarcastic hoots in heaven what you *thought* it was. You asked for a curse, and a curse you will get. Unless you prefer to work it out," he added, eying her bathrobe lasciviously. "I know an old satyr who'd—"

"Why you unspeakably smut-minded brat!" she exclaimed, whipping her robe tight and making a triple knot in the sash.

Van S blushed with pleasure. "Thanky for them kind words, ma'am. But I guess we'll have to stick to the TV. Technically, that's all you cursed. Oh, there's more iniquity in technicality than your world dreams of, Horatio."

There was something about his emphasis on the final word that caused Mary to distrust its spelling. She grabbed the broom. Speechless with an indignation she hadn't enjoyed in years, she rushed van S.

But he was gone. Not through the door. He had simply

disappeared. She was left brandishing the broom, stupidly, at nothing.

It hadn't occurred to Mary Tate to be frightened. The whole episode, on reconsideration, had been more exciting than any event in years. She had had to be insulted by the imp's remarks, of course—but those earthy insults had possessed complimentary overtones. She wondered whether he actually *was* a fiend.

Preoccupied, she cleaned the house thoroughly, then washed the bleary dishes. It was an hour before she remembered the TV, that had been chattering to itself all along. Silly notion! How could you curse a—?

She sat on the couch and paid attention to the set for the first time since the interruption. It was functioning normally. For a moment she had feared that the picture would be flawed, or the sound gone. But there was nothing wrong.

So the obvious explanation was true. A fresh kid had barged in, overheard her frustrated swearing and taken the opportunity to poke fun at her. He must have slipped out the door when she turned to grab the broom. Somehow she felt let down.

"We take you now to the great Southwest," the announcer was saying, with just the right shade of artificial enthusiasm. "This is Dos Passos, U.S.A., a thriving slum due south of the 42nd parallel, famed for its 'Big Dollar' casino district. Across the rusty tracks is Precinct 1919, the toughest beat in seven states. Here juvenile delinquency is a way of life. The brats start training early . . ."

The picture centered on a filthy street. Garbage lay strewn on the cracked sidewalk, and loose bricks and larger rubble littered the pocked road. A mottled eye of spittle glistened in the foreground. A small child meandered into view, dirty and ragged, eyes on the ground. Pouncing gleefully, he trapped a bright coin peeking out from under a brick and held it up to the light. It was a slug.

Eagerly now, his button-eyes searched out the corner slot machine. It was gloriously vacant. He ran to it, a broken-toothed smile cracking the freckles. He strained on tiptoes, reaching up to the slot—

And doubled over as a sudden fist struck from behind. A battle-scarred bully stood over him, grinning sadistically. Without further ado he kicked the child in the stomach and caught the spinning slug.

But force and determination had no reward. Before the bully could enjoy his spoils, another punk appeared. "Hand it over, slobhead," the newcomer said.

"This ain't your territory, Ben," the bully protested, while the original child squirmed from underfoot and fled. "Get outta here."

Ben pulled a lumpy sock from his pocket and twirled it ominously. The bully put up his fists, but Ben kneed him in the groin and connected with the business end of his blivet. "Now beat it," he said tiredly, "or I'll rough you up. Thanks for the tin."

Ben was a well-built youth of twelve or thirteen, with brown curly hair and direct eyes. "Are you Ben Anderson, the toughest bully in Dos Passos?" the announcer inquired respectfully.

"What's it to you, blabbermouth?"

"Are you going to jimmy that slot machine?" the announcer persisted.

"Hell, no, stupe," Ben said indignantly, turning to the camera. "Think I'm a cube? Nothing *in* that machine. We cleaned it out yesterday. I'm putting this slug where it counts: in the cigvender down the street."

"Aren't you a little young to be smoking?"

Ben scowled craftily. *"Now* I get it," he said, marching down the street and forcing the pickup to bounce over the strewn debris to keep up. "Hell, I don't smoke *real* butts. If I was to stunt my growth I'd lose my 'Top Tough' status. But I'm safe with my brand: Dromedary Ciggs, the *fake* cigarette."

"You mean Dromedaries *don't* stunt your growth, like ordinary butts do?" the announcer inquired with excitement.

"They *can't,"* Ben exclaimed, a trifle too enthusiastically.

"Drommy don't use real tobacco. It's synthetic: tastes like tobac, drags like it—"

"Full-bodied flavor with no unhealthy nicotine or tars—"

Ben smiled expansively, the yellow showing on his teeth. "You said it, shill. So get that sleazy tar out of your system and switch to Dromedary, like *real* thugs do!" He deposited his slug and extracted a pack, holding it up to fill the screen. "You're safe with Drommy, the fake smoke!"

Mary flopped back limply. It had been too long since she'd actually watched a commercial; she didn't recollect that particular one. And somehow she'd always thought of Dos Passos as a person, rather than a place. She wondered vaguely whether Dromedaries were cancer-resistant too.

"And now we bring you the adventures of Donkey Hotee and his mistress 'Quick' Sote," the announcer said soporifically. "Our story opens as Donkey Hotee carries Miss Sote through caverns measureless to man, but quite susceptible to mensuration by equine intellect . . ."

The picture closed on a motley burro picking its way through a maze of obvious stage props and bearing on its sagging back an impossibly luscious redhead. Her hair and makeup were just so, and her sarong artfully exposed one miraculously generous breast.

Miss Sote: Where are you taking me, Hotee?
Donkey: Where the sun never shines and you'll shiver in the—
Miss Sote: But I'm not dressed.
Donkey: (with a lascivious wiggle of one ear) Precisely.
Miss Sote: (with threatening mein) I'll throw a tantrum!
Donkey: The sponsor wouldn't like it—

Mary got up and went to the set, motivated by sudden suspicion. She changed the channel.

Donkey: . . . on now, doll. I hate to have a babe cry all over my horsehair.

It was on all the channels. The TV *was* cursed!

Morbidly fascinated, Mary watched it for the rest of the day. Donkey Hotee's adventures continued interminably: implausible, ridiculous, and often obnoxious. The frequent commercials were worse; she resolved never to use the product.

—A sergeant, chewing out a private for an unnamed offense: "But Sarge—the latrine was off limits for three days—" "That's no excuse, soldier. If you smoked Dromedaries you wouldn't *need* no latrine!"

—A medical report: "So your blood has sickle-shaped cells, and your spouse has hammer cells? Consumer, you *know* what that makes your offspring! But they can redeem their patriotism by smoking Drommies from age three on."

—Again: "Are you listless, run-down, tired of living? Sign with Lucifelzebub, Inc.; they have a warm spot for you. Their waiting room stocks free Dromedary Ciggs."

Mary's husband was late coming home, as usual, and Mary finally ate alone. She turned on the set automatically for the evening programs, but quit immediately when Donkey Hotee reappeared. "Damn that little evil," she muttered, careful not to say it too loudly. No sense getting in deeper.

It continued the following day. Several times she found herself restlessly switching on the set, but giving up when the same odious material showed. It looked as though the curse were permanent. But she refused to give in easily. She set her alarm for three A.M. and rushed sleepily to the set, trying to catch it off guard and perhaps break the curse. A normal test pattern came on. Had she outsmarted it?

E van S materialized a few minutes later, white-eyed and grouchy. "What are you trying to pull, woman?" he demanded.

"I'm breaking your curse," Mary explained, pleased to have caught the demon in an off moment. "See—it's the straight pattern."

"Sure it is," he retorted irritably. "I can't keep the curse on *all* the time. Can't you let an indecent, law-breaking spirit have some sleep?"

"Oh, that's too bad," she moaned with mock solicitude. "Diddums want a nice rest? If you're a real imp, why do you sleep at all?"

Van S scratched his head. "Never thought about it," he admitted. "When in Rome, and all that, I suppose. I'm on topside duty now."

"Well, you won't get much sleep as long as you keep this curse on. I'll wake you up every hour of the night," Mary said gleefully. "Unless you want to work it off, of course. You'd look good in dishpan hands—"

The fiend blushed with fury. "I'll put an aphrodisiac in your husband's beer!"

"Would you really?" Mary asked with interest.

"Oh, come on now. I've got to keep this curse on. If I reneged, they'd assign me to one of the Nether tours."

"That shouldn't be so bad, for a devil."

Van S stamped his foot with frustration. "You keep using the wrong terms. I'm not a demon or a devil or an imp. I'm a little fiend. I don't belong down Below. As long as I put little curses on the clientele and walk the crooked path, I'm okay. But once I mess up—"

Mary eyed him with calculation and decided to drop the subject. She'd have to find some other way to break the curse. Van S vanished gratefully, and she went back to bed.

Saturday afternoon her husband turned on the set and settled back with his momentarily frigid beverage. Mary watched furtively, but baseball came on, instead of the donkey. Did the curse apply only to herself?

"And now the lead-off batter in the first inning is coming to the saucer," the announcer said. Mary listened from the kitchen, out of sight of Nick. If the curse *did* apply, there could be repercussions. "And here comes the first pitch of the game, a banana peeler—and it's a triple-play ball, and the side is retired!" the voice exclaimed. "What a play! And now a word from the Everdull Razorstrop Company. If your child is willful and undisciplined—"

Mary had to cover her mouth to keep from laughing. The curse *was* on. How was Hubby taking it? She dared not look.

"Strike! The pins fall, and the score is ten to nothing. The batter is pouring around third base—fourth base—and he's hauled down on the five-yard line. Coming in for the free-throw is 'Skinny' Meatflab, seven foot-five inches, famous for his jawbreaking toehold—eight, nine, ten—he's out! The pitcher is leading by half a length going into the back-stretch—"

Mary peeked cautiously around the corner. Her husband was sound asleep, warm beer in hand.

The days went by. Mary no longer bothered to sample the programs. She involved herself in fancy knitting, good books and letters to forgotten friends. She wrote up a discussion of one of the better books and sent it to the local newspaper, which naturally printed it; later, several people called to express their interest. She made new friends by mail and phone, and used her knitware for family gifts. Life became interesting, even exciting.

Dusting off the TV one day, she suddenly remembered what had started her new life. She had been addicted to that set—and now she was free, having a grand time with her newly directed energies. "Why," she said, seeing the truth at last, "that was no curse. It was a blessing."

There was a crack of thunder and a biting smell of hot sulfur. A forbidding gentleman in judge's robes appeared in Nick's easy chair. Before him was E van S, a heavy silver collar clamped around his neck, and a chain dangling from it. Van S looked miserable.

"Now you've done it," he accused her tearfully. "It's Hades for me now, for sure."

Mary was baffled. "What on Earth—?"

"Hell, madam, Hell," the seated individual corrected sternly. "I am the Archfiend Inquisitor. You have made a serious complaint, for which I am about to sentence this slackard to an eon of incredible torment. Shall we get on with it?"

"But all I said was—" Mary halted. "Oops—blessings are

against the rules, aren't they!" The Inquisitor looked at her sourly.

"This infernal court will come to order," the Archfiend intoned. "How does the offendant plead?"

"But neither of you looks like a demon!" Mary said, perplexed.

The Archfiend fixed her with a dour stare. "Madam, your nomenclature is careless. We are fiends. Naturally we assume our human shape when on the surface. When in Rome . . . HOW DOES THE OFFENDANT PLEAD?"

Van S hid behind the TV. "Guilty, your excrescence, sir."

"But he *tried* to curse—" Mary put in hopefully, feeling sorry for him.

"Madam," the Inquisitor said, pink horns appearing for just a moment in the chill of temper, "one more outburst and I shall hold you in respect for this court. Do you know what that means?"

Mary was afraid to inquire. It was a reasonable assumption that respect for an infernal court could only be a step toward damnation.

"The offendant will now take the witless stand." Van S cowered forward. "Do you swear to prevaricate, perjure yourself and tell nothing but lies except when the truth would wreak the greatest havoc, so hinder you Satan?"

"Never," van S said.

"The witless is unduly sworn." Suddenly Mary caught on. An infernal trial was the direct opposite to a normal one. If E van S were found innocent, he would be shipped to the lower regions for a fate better than death—or should it be worse than life? And yet he was innocent, er, guilty. He *had* put a curse on the TV. If they sent him down, some other fiend might be assigned to the case, and she might not be so well off. Van S had to be exonerated.

"Just a minute," Mary said firmly. The Archfiend opened his mouth to speak, but she cut him off. *"I'm* the one who made the complaint. Without my testimony you have no case. I withdraw the charge."

The Archfiend glowered. "That would be fair," he said. "Of course, we can't allow it."

This was a setback. She still hadn't geared herself to the niceties (or perhaps nasties) of the situation. "All right. I'm pre-empting the witness, er, witless stand. I hereby declare that everything I say during this mistrial is false. Accordingly, I swear to tell the truth, the whole truth, and nothing but the truth, so help me. Are you satisfied, your honor?"

The Inquisitor grimaced at the appellation. "This is highly irregular," he said. "Normal people aren't allowed to participate in—"

"Precisely. I'm breaking the rules, aren't I?"

Hoist by his own petard, he capitulated. "Proceed, madam."

Mary rubbed her hands together in her best Machiavellian style. "I now call to the stand the offendant, E van S-quire." That unworthy came forward again. "Did you put a curse on my TV set?" she demanded.

"No ma'am," he said piously.

"And did you do this in answer to my statement 'Curse this TV!'?"

"No ma'am."

"And isn't it true that the only thing you were supposed to curse was the TV, and that any incidental benefit incurred is none of your concern?"

Realization lighted the fiend's features. "That's a lie!" he said happily.

Mary returned to the Inquisitor. "So you see, your honor"—she used the term deliberately now, since he obviously disliked it—"the fact that I was blessed has nothing to do with the offendant. He was supposed to curse the TV, and he did indeed curse it. He acted in a perfectly fiendish manner."

The Archfiend was sorely troubled. Then he brightened. "It remains to be ascertained," he pronounced, "whether the set *was* cursed."

This time Mary was prepared. "Exhibit A for the offense," she said. "Turn on my set and see for yourself—your honor."

It came on, stifling his dolorous reply. ". . . treatment, the psychiatrist gradually became identified with the patient's father. The profession fostered this 'Father Image,' holding to the convention that it was beneficial therapy. However, certain masculine juveniles expressed violent parental rejection, that rendered this identity ineffective. It became necessary to develop superior association patterns. The most promising innovation was the 'Sweetheart' image, in which an attractive female doctor—"

"This would appear to be normally dull programming," the Archfiend said impatiently. "Certainly not much of a curse."

"Give it a chance," Mary said. "It sneaks up on you."

". . . creating something of a problem for the Planned Parenthood association," the TV continued. "However, some elementary advice to the more enterprising practitioners ameliorated this complication, and a number of patients showed sufficient improvement to enable them to patronize normal establishments.

"Another advance is Marriage Insurance, that covers all expenses incurred in defending oneself against paternity suits. This eliminates the financial liability of licentiousness. Alimony protection or ready cash for blackmail payoffs are extra. But if you're not getting divorced at the moment, and can't afford romantic releases through enlightened psychotherapy, or if your doctor is simply unattractive, sublimate your cravings with a rich, delicious Dromedary Cigg. Who needs an image at all, when Drommy's fine flavor—"

"Surely this is conventional television?" the Inquisitor said irritably. "I don't recall the brand, but I've seen similar ads."

"But people never watch the commercials anyway," Mary put in quickly. But she was beginning to wonder herself. She remembered thousands of commercials whose taste was just as dubious: the mucous specials coming just at suppertime, the raw sex purporting to advertise new cars . . . *Had* commercials ever operated without benefit of a curse? "The programs are what count. I'm sure there's a terrible one coming up." She shot a warning look at E van S. "Donkey Hotee, for example."

"Don Quixote?" the Archfiend repeated, troubled. "I thought this was the twentieth century—"

"It *was*," Mary replied succinctly, "before the curse."

". . . and now we return to the further adventures of Donkey Hotee: ass him no questions, he'll tell you no tails," the announcer enthused. "As our scene opens, Hotee and his mistress 'Quick' Sote are entering the city of Curio, in the nation of Conster, on the continent of Inn."

Donkey: Ah, just dip your muzzle in that fresh sea breeze from Discrepan.

Miss Sote: Do you mean to say we are on the shore of Discrepan Sea?

Donkey: Be thankful it isn't the Lepro Sea. Terrible cities on its shores. Atro's the worst, but Pugna and Fero aren't far behind. One of them pirated the good ship Citizen when I booked passage at—Tena, I think it was. I thought I'd never get away from there. Old King Mar had a real decalco mania. Wanted to put his brand on my hide. With glue. Know how they make glue?

Miss Sote: What's that smoky building ahead?

Donkey: That one? That's the satis factory. Business is really booming these days, as you can see by the opti mist coming from the chimney.

Miss Sote: But what's a 'satis'?

Donkey: If you don't know a good thing when you see it—speaking of seeing, you'd look better if you got some support for that exposed udder. It makes you look too inti mate. You'd really light up one of the Candella company's garments.

Miss Sote: A Candella bra? I don't know . . .

"I don't know," the Inquisitor said. "Are you *sure* you cursed this set, van S?"

"May the Evil One Himself be redeemed and sent to his salvation if what I have told you is not the rankest falsehood," van S swore fervently. "I do the worst I can, but I never had literary aspirations."

Miss Sote's dulcet tones interjected a comment. "Eating all this fruit has tired me. I think I'll go lie down on an apri cot."

"I know blessed well you were a writer when you lived," the Archfiend stormed at van S. "That's why you were damned in the first place. I'm not interested in your biogra fee. For two cents I'd—"

"Make it one magnifi cent," Mary put in helpfully.

"Keep your abomina bull remarks out of the china shoppe!" the Archfiend ranted. "Bless it to Heaven, now you've got *me* doing it!"

"Steal any more food," Donkey Hotee warned, "and you'll end up in Obee City."

"I will *not!*" the Inquisitor screamed. "I'll steal all the food I want—TURN THAT ACCURSED THING OFF!"

"There!" Mary pounced on the word. "You admitted it. You called it cursed."

The Inquisitor gaped. "Madam, that was a mere figure of—"

"Makes no difference. That's how this whole thing got started. Remember? Just because a person speaks imp etuously—"

"What thoughtful good did I ever do to deserve this?" the Archfiend gritted. "What unsuspected virtue is buried in my conscience? What an angelic picklement! Have your way, madam; he is guilty. E van S is guilty, guilty, guilty! Now—"

"Put it in writing," Mary cackled. "I have a sig nature—"

The Inquisitor puffed hot smoke from his ears. ". . . not with a Wimp, but a Banger . . ." He vanished.

Mary deftly caught the scroll that fluttered to the floor in the fiend's stead and rolled it carefully. "I don't trust that bird. I'd better hold this document in S crow—van S crow."

"I don't know how to curse you enough," he said thankfully.

"A malediction upon you, you little creep," Mary said warmly. "And don't you forget it. Is that true—er, false about your writing?"

"It was a big fib," he said proudly. "Do you think that once in a while you might turn on the set and—"

"I'll invite all my husband's friends over on Saturday afternoon," she promised. "It will make them furious!"

"Damn you to Hell," van S whispered joyfully as he faded out of sight.

"Damn *you,*" Mary replied, stars in her eyes.

Vignettes

In 1982 the quality fanzine NIEKAS put out a volume of short stories. Very short stories. Each was limited to fifty words. Shorter than this introduction. I started out as a natural story writer, and shifted to novels because the fickleness of story editors prevented me from earning a living in stories. But they wanted me to contribute, so I tried. Actually I wrote three, and they duly appeared in *50 Extremely SF Stories* along with the forty-seven entries by other writers. It's really not easy to do a story that short; characterization and description suffer, for one thing. But it can be done.

To the Death

The martial artist had laser-zapped Crogs, wrestled Snogs, and sworded Blogs. Now the ultimate challenge: Swami Noname of Dread.

"Champion, I challenge thee! Rapier, cannon, solar flares?"

The wizened little ascetic looked up from his lotus position. "Ten paces."

"Agreed! Ten paces. But what weapons?"

"Hunger."

Transmogrification

Brownie elves invaded the house, intent on mischief. He garbaged the floor. She greased the dishes. Baby pooped carpets. All caked the oven with soot.

The oven closed, clicked on: disaster.

After school, the children opened the oven. The intruders were baked, browned, and smelled delicious.

"Brownies!" the children exclaimed.

Deadline

The freckled fan stared. "Why would a little green man from Mars pay a pound of gold for one used paperback fantasy novel?"

The alien glanced nervously at his purple chrono. "It's the only example of human slushpulp literature genre that will survive your WWIII awkwardness."

He saucered offplanet hastily.

Hearts

In 1970 I was asked to do a story or article for a British publication, BOOKS AND BOOKMEN, at the Christmas season. As always, I pondered, and came up with a notion that was a cross between essay and story. In fact it's more like a preachment, which I normally don't do. But I refuse to be limited to any special type, so have done about as wide a range of writing as anyone in the genre. *This* was the one published story I overlooked when *Anthonology* was assembled, so it had to wait for this sequel volume.

Hearts

Perhaps there is no greater store of evil in the world than there has been before. But modern technology magnifies its impact and spreads a share to many people who might have been spared in prior centuries. Thus it is that the spirit of Christmas seems deafened by the roar of the jet, blinded by television, suffocated by smog. Charity is subordinated to commercialism, greed and desperation.

In all the town only Amberly was free from evil. He had nothing, he wanted nothing; he was a wanderer, a nonentity.

Yet he felt the oppression of dissatisfaction about him, and he wished that everyone might be blessed with the peace of mind he experienced.

Amberly walked about the town on Christmas Eve, diverting his mind from the chill of the night by concentrating on the problems of others. In one house a child was crying with a stomachache, for he had eaten gluttonously. Amberly took that agony to himself and walked on with one hand holding his midriff while the child went blissfully to sleep.

In another house a husband quarreled bitterly with his wife. Amberly drew in their anger and walked on with bad temper while they kissed and decorated their tree.

He met a man on the street who was morose because his employer had suffered business losses and had provided only token Christmas bonuses. Amberly absorbed that frustration and went on disgruntled while the man found sudden pleasure in his decision to donate the sum to charity.

Three children were playing Hearts in their bedroom, their voices shrill with dismay as the adverse cards appeared. Amberly accepted their ire, and they laughed cheerfully with the pleasure of the game while he felt the pang of negative scores. He was playing his own game of Hearts by amassing the bad while others retained the good. He became more evil with every living heart he purged.

A lonely widow was afraid. Amberly took that fear and left her confident while he nervously avoided shadows.

An old man wept with despair, knowing that his grasping relatives desired his early demise. Amberly brought in that despair together with the avarice of the relatives, and there was a joyous family reunion while he longed for a rich legacy he simultaneously despaired to yield.

A boy cursed his dog, who had chewed a new toy. Amberly punctuated his gait with expletives while they romped.

A young woman preened herself excessively before the mirror. Amberly acquired her vanity and left her sweetly modest.

Each contact degraded Amberly but ennobled the town.

At last only one bit of evil remained, and to that he was drawn. A young man stood in the park, intending suicide. Rejected, he had dosed himself with LSD and stolen a gun. Amberly passed, taking the weapon and its implications. The youth departed whistling: There were other girls, and tonight was Christmas Eve.

Amberly walked on, completely cursed. All about him the people of the town celebrated a more wonderful occasion than they had ever known before: Christmas season free from evil! The goodness that once had competed with ambient evil in each heart now had free rein. Amberly had given the greatest gift of all.

But at what price? He seethed with greed, jealousy and fury. Pain suffused his body, fear tormented his mind, despair gripped his soul. "To hell with Christmas!" he cried, feeling perverse pride in the boldness of expression while despising the attitude it reflected.

Then he remembered the gun. Drug-visions slithered across his wincing perceptions, and a nimbus of evil surrounded the weapon. There remained one sin he had not embraced: the final one. He brought the black empty eye up to meet his tortured living orb and girded himself in cowardice to—

"Joy to the world!" Powerful and pure, the melody embraced him. The people of the town were here, caroling him with all the rapture of their reborn innocence.

The song ended. The man who had donated his bonus to charity opened his Bible and read: "For God so loved the world that he gave his only begotten Son . . ." And Amberly realized that the sins of the world had never been his to expiate. The very name of the holiday identified the One assigned to that task, almost 2000 years before.

Amberly's effort had been a mockery, no more than a macabre game of Hearts. He had tried to assume total evil to spare others, but had only made himself miserable.

The rich happy old man kneeled to place warm new boots on Amberly's feet. The confident widow wrapped a warm shawl about his shivering shoulders. The modest young woman took his arm and led him to the banquet loving couples had prepared. Cheerful children smiled at him. "He got it all," one whispered. "Every single bad card!"

Then the peace of mind he had cherished before was restored in double measure, for this was the rule of the game. But no evil returned to the hearts of the people, for in fact he had not been taking but giving. Evil is a moral vacuum that cannot survive in the presence of good. A gift of this type always multiplies itself.

Perhaps there is no lesser store of evil in the world than there has been before. But its impact seems diminished, for modern technology only serves the will of mankind and spreads some share of good to every heart. Christmas is dominated by generosity, joy and love.

Revise and Invent

As I have mentioned, the theme of this collection is the problem writers have with editors. This is no new attitude on my part, as can be seen by this story, which I put together in 1967. I tried it on seven markets without success. Editors just didn't appreciate it. Well, read it and find out why. Don't be fooled by its format; this is a story, not a letter column. Normally editors return stories with uncommunicative rejection slips, but sometimes they do comment—and that can be mischief too, for the writer who is unwary enough to pay attention. After I had done four versions of a single story for an editor who kept making suggestions for revision, but kept bouncing the result, I wrote "Revise and Invent" and sent it to him—and he bounced it too. I knew he would; I just couldn't resist the temptation.

Revise and Invent

Dear Editor, PACIFIC LITERARY MAGAZINE:

Enclosed is a short story, "Frustration," for your consideration. Any comment you care to make will be sincerely appreciated.

Yours Very Truly,
Jonathan B. Hoskins

Frustration

by J. Benjamin Hoskins

I pushed open the swinging door and stood with my back against it, holding it for Bettye; and she passed through, the cold outwashing of the air-conditioning brushing back her dark hair and molding her elegant dress to her elegant form. We trod the deep soft carpet, marching up to the low thick tasseled cord crossing the hall like a power line, and I stood there with her hand on my arm, waiting, while the gentle music issued from the background and our eyes adjusted to the quiet lighting. And the waiters moved among the tables before, bringing domed platters, and from time to time the conversation ascended above the music: now a word, now a phrase, sensed for a moment, then forgotten, as a fish leaps high before sinking back into the ocean.

And he approached at last, from the far side, a big man in the portly splendor of his uniform, the maitre d'. And the buttons shone and his hair was gray, just so, at the temple, and his bearing was assured and he was a handsome man. And his skin was the color of burnished walnut, so rich against his pale wide lips; darker, much darker, than my skin; and he stood against the cord and he looked at us and he said, "We don't serve Negroes here."

Dear Mr. Hoskins,

Thank you for considering us as a market. While your story shows promise, both your title and your treatment are too obvious and somewhat dated in the light of recent legal decisions. I suggest you change the title and adapt the story to fit something a little closer to your own experience—perhaps an incident in your own house that gave you some special insight into the nature of racial or aesthetic prejudice.

Please be on guard against the overuse of the word "and," particularly at the beginning of a sentence. And be careful of irrelevant metaphor; a fish in water hardly matches the mood of civil-rights conflict.

Sincerely,
Brian Thurgood, Editor

Dear Mr. Thurgood,

Thank you for your comment on "Frustration." I had intended the fish as part of the larger allegorical framework of the story, wherein the conversation rises above the ocean of music but, like a fish, soon falls back; the whole foreshadowing the rising hopes of the protagonist, who also must fall back into frustration. The irony was that another Negro had to be the one to clarify just how deep this ocean of indifference was. But I'm sure that your points were well taken and that the story was too obvious, and have accordingly retitled it "Beauty" (as in "Eye of the Beholder") and changed the setting to a private residence. I hope this meets your approval.

Jon Hoskins

Dear Jonathan,

I'm sorry to inform you that your revised story, "Beauty," is still not suited to our needs. It may be that a well-qualified yardman is sometimes refused employment because of the color of his skin, and certainly the housewife who turns him away after placing the ad is of questionable integrity—but this is not, *per se,* a story. Perhaps it would be better to make the entire episode figurative rather than literal, so that no element of our readership will take offense.

I might also mention in passing that a story without the relief of any dialogue whatever soon becomes tedious in inexpert hands.

Brian Thurgood, Editor

Dear Brian,

I really appreciate your helpful advice. I have rewritten the story to make it figurative and to include dialogue. I hope you like it this time.

Jon

Beauty

The slime rose up to criticize the work of art. "There you sit," it said, "serene and content in your ebony gloss—yet utterly useless. You think you are beautiful, but you are only a molded husk. You are glazed, but you are brittle and shallow. Where is there any softness in you? Where is that fine slippery resiliency that is the heritage of the commonest blob of grease? Where the rippling undulations of fluid motion, the flexibility and warmth of dishwater? You lack the variety of size and shape and color that glorifies the contents of every garbage can. You cannot take flight in the soft air in the free manner known to every particle of dust swept from the floor. You cannot appreciate the refractive art of the dirty window-pane in the sunlight. You can never immortalize your substance by leaving a stain on the wall. And never, never will you bring that worthy satisfaction of a job well done that every human being feels from cleaning up rubbish like me.

"You are not beautiful—you are a monstrosity."

The work of art listened and was ashamed. It fell off the antique table and shattered on the floor. The slime looked on as the housewife swept up the myriad fragments, all shapes and colors and sizes, and dumped them sadly into the waste-basket.

"Now you are beautiful," said the slime, and vanished down the drain.

Dear Jon,

I regret to inform you that your story has become a fantasy, and we do not publish such material. I suggest you try it on one of those oddball magazines that print the latest from H. G. Wells and Samuel Butler.

With best wishes for success elsewhere.

Brian Thurgood, Editor

Dear Editor, PARSEC SCIENCE FICTION:

You were recommended to me as a market for the enclosed story, "Beauty." Any comment will be appreciated.

Yours Very Truly,
Jonathan Hoskins

Dear Jonathan Hoskins,

Some promise here, but suggest you read a copy or three of our magazine before submitting here again. Meanwhile, this particular ms might be more suitable for the slick femme mags. Make it more immediate and personal, involving *men and women,* not jars and gunk, and for God's sake stop lecturing the reader!

Futuristically,
S. F. Parsec, Editor & Pub.

Dear Fiction Editor, HOUSEWIFE:

Enclosed is a short story, "Beauty Revised," for your consideration. Happy to have comment.

Very Truly,
J. B. Hoskins

My Dear Mrs. Hoskins,

This is a very interesting story, I'm sure, but hardly for us. Your portrayal of the protagonist as a rigidly moral, unbending colored man who is shattered by a cruel remark by a voluptuous but depraved white siren seems more appropriate to the confessional market. And "Slimea" is a rather odd name for a woman, don't you think?

Regretfully,
S.L.K. Femme, Fiction Editor

Dear Editor, CROSS-MY-HEART TRUE CONFESSIONS MAGAZINE:

Enclosed is a story.

(Mr.) Hoskins

Dear Contributor:

We at CMHTCM pride ourselves in giving the most careful attention to every manuscript that comes in. Your entry, "Beauty Revised," has possibilities, but there will have to be some rewriting. As you know, we pay an extra penny a word if you do the revision yourself. First, your title is inappropriate; it should express the horror of sin and agony, not beauty. What we need are good, solid, *realistic* stories of human experience. Our handbook on effective plotting is enclosed. You should forget about miscegenation and concentrate on basic human values. Put yourself in your story—first-person viewpoint is an absolute must—and give us your most immediate feelings. You are a man (we do accept some male viewpoint pieces); you meet a typical American girl, not too pretty but compulsively attractive to you; what are your very *first,* real-life impressions?

Next time you submit fiction here, please accompany it

with the signed warranty-of-accuracy form (enclosed) for our files.

Encouragingly,
Story Editor #3

Dear Story Editor #3,

I have revised my story as you recommended and changed the title. Fortunately it is based on a personal experience, or I would not have felt free to sign your affidavit. Do your readers really believe all the stuff you print is *true?* I know it's a sinful world, but—

Fiction Writer Hoskins #1

The Wind of Love

I saw the trees waving outside and knew that a wind was rising. On impulse I stepped out the door, wanting to feel the soft air on my face, to enjoy the oncoming coolness of the evening. I had been working indoors all day, and even a brief change would do me good.

There was just a touch of moisture in the air, not quite a promise of rain. I walked down the street, letting the tensions of the day be blown away in the wind. There was something about an evening like this that made me want to become part of the elements; to drift over the ground like a dry leaf, coming to rest wherever I might.

I saw her standing beside an oak, windblown, smiling gently, holding out a small hand as though to feel the rain. She was not beautiful, but she seemed to be made for this scene; somehow she blended with the mood of the outdoors. I was attracted to her immediately.

"It won't rain," I said, coming to stand beside her. "It usually just spits a little and stops."

She turned to me with a quick smile that brought an unexpected thrill. "I know it," she murmured, and her voice was low and sweet. "I noticed the wind, and I came out to enjoy it. There's something about it that makes me feel so—so *elemental.* It makes me want to sail up into the sky, like a kite, following the breeze. I'm being silly, I know."

I took her hand on impulse. "I feel the same way. It's such a refreshing change."

We stood there, hand in hand, though we had never met before. We shared the wind.

"Do you wonder," she said, turning her deep brown eyes upon me, "do you wonder what happens to a little gust of wind like this? I mean, it blows across us, loves us, now, then it goes on, divides, joins other winds, changes—do you think it remembers us?"

"We remember *it,*" I said, acutely aware of her, so close. "That's what really matters."

Dear Jonathan,

This is better, but you still don't understand about titles. "The Wind of Love" is not a phrase to compel our reader's attention or seduce her imagination. However, we can take care of that editorially. You must also concentrate on plotting. There should be more opposition; the man must overcome some genuine hurdle before he achieves contact with the girl. Only then is the reward worthwhile and satisfying to our readers. Also, there should be some solid *sin* in it. Take care of these details, and give your characters names, and we should have a suitable story. Be sure to enclose your affidavit for the new title.

Story Editor #3

Dear #3,

How's this?

Jon Hoskins, sinner

Seduced by a Busy Signal

I never could get Bea alone. It was that damned phone.
We'd be sitting there in her apartment—she refused to trust
herself to mine—and I'd put my arm around her and she'd put
her head on my shoulder and I'd put my other hand on her
knee and get ready to sin and then the phone would go off. Ten
minutes later I'd get hold of her again and have a whole five
minutes before the instrument rang off the round prema-
turely—again.

I had to put that phone out of commission if I was ever
to put Bea *into* commission.

I called her. "Make yourself pretty," I said. "I'm on my
way."

"Sure, Joe," she said. "Is that all you called about?"

No it wasn't, but I didn't tell her that. After she hung up,
I didn't. I set my receiver on the table, turned up the FM, and
left the music playing into the line.

Bea was beautiful, and I was amorous. But first I lifted
her receiver, heard my music coming over, knew that all was
well, and hung up again.

Maybe she had counted on the phone to chaperon her, as
it always had before. She listened for it as I lifted her skirt and
she cupped her ear as I unbuttoned her blouse, but it never

rang. The only connection that evening was the one I made, and it was positively sinful!

You can get around any hurdle if you put your mind to it, be it mechanical or distaff.

Dear Jon,

I'm afraid we're simply not making connection. He *enjoys* his sin, while our readers insist upon remorse and agony. I don't understand how he put her phone out of commission, and in any event this is technical rather than emotional, which wasn't the kind of hurdle I had in mind. Perhaps one of the "Male" magazines would be interested; they seem to think sex is fun.

Thank you for thinking of us,

#3

PS—I wonder if *that* could be the reason my phone . . . ?

Editor, FIST:

Story enclosed.

J.B.H.

Dear Writer:

Nice try, mac—but FIST likes to sock 'em with real he-man stuff. Show us more *action*.

Editor 007, Slushpile

PS—Watch that stuff on phones. Want to ruin a damn fine system? If my gal ever caught on—

Dear Editor Slushpile,

Enclosed is a revision of "Busy Signal" with he-man action, as you suggested.

J.B.H.

JBH:

Look, mac—having him seduce her at gunpoint is not exactly what I meant by "action." FIST gals are *always* very nubile and very willing. Either put in the sex or try another market, like a mystery mag. And fix it up with a better title, like "Gangbang" or "Stickup"—something with *guts*.

007

PS—Sorry about jumping on you. My gal at the Confess office found out about the phone bit somehow and I'm hard up.

Editor, VIOLENT DETECTIVE MAGAZINE,

Enclosure enclosed.

H

Dear H:

"Stickup" returned herewith. Your opening is good, but the ending is unsatisfying. If he isn't planning to murder the girl, why does he go to all that trouble to jimmy her phone? Here at VIOLENT we aren't too interested in women, anyway. Maybe he should stick up a bank, instead. Only not with a gun, of course—that's passé.

Dick Violent, Editor

Dear Mr. Violent,

Here is the story revised to apply to a bank, no gun, as you recommended.

H

Stickup

It isn't too hard to outsmart a machine. Any machine. All you need to do is figure out its weak spot. You can put a phone out of commission by dialing a number and never hanging up, since only the originating instrument can break the connection in a local call. What is a computer except an overdeveloped phone?

The compu-teller at the bank was supposed to be fool-proof, so there were no guards. I walked into a booth, set up my apparatus, clipped two leads to the alarm wires and pushed the button for service.

The screen came on. DEPOSIT OR WITHDRAWAL? the words flashed, after I gave my account number.

"Withdrawal," I said. "One hundred thousand dollars."

ACCOUNT INSUFFICIENT, it flashed. Sharp, that machine.

"Listen, wirebrain," I said. "I have affixed a 20,000 volt electron bomb to your alarm terminal. Now you either spit out the change in thousand-dollar bills pronto, or I'll set the bomb off and do half a million dollars worth of damage to your circuitry. Activate your alarm and that will trigger it automatically. So which is it going to be—one hundred G to me, or five hundred G to the repair contractor, who's a bigger crook than I am? Remember, you're programmed for economy. You have five nanoseconds to decide."

Sure, they scotched *that* dodge after that, but I was long gone. When I need more dough, I'll figure a new wrinkle.

Dear H:

This is close, but the accent is on cleverness rather than action. Have you tried it on the literary market? They sometimes appreciate cleverness, provided they don't understand it. Use an irrelevant title for them.

D.V.

Dear Mr. Thurgood, PACIFIC LITERARY MAGAZINE:

"Swell Foop" enclosed. No comment necessary.

Yours Very Truly,
Jonathan Hoskins

Dear Mr. Hoskins,

Good to hear from you again. This idea of having a beginning writer be obliged to revise his story so often that it eventually changes completely is intriguing, but hardly credible. I would recommend you try fantastic notions like this on the oddball fantasy market.

Care should be taken on titles. I like this one, but surely it should be "Fell Swoop," and I'm still not certain of its relevance to the story.

Brian Thurgood, Editor

There the story ends, completing its circle. The several parts of it have histories of their own. The title is a parody of "Advise and Consent."

"Frustration" I wrote in 1965 as a comment on what I saw when I moved to the south from the north. Racism exists everywhere, but in the north folk are more likely to be ashamed of it, while in the south they can be proud of it. I tried "Frustration" on NEGRO DIGEST, where it was bounced with a rejection slip. I showed it to a black writer I know, and he made no comment. What do I know about racism, having been brought up in a non-racist environment? It disgusts me.

Beauty, like ugliness, is largely in the eye of the beholder. I started a series of vignettes in 1957 while I was in basic training in the army, about a boy called "Little Pot." This didn't relate to the drug of that name, or the later Cambodian regime, but to the state of his personality, which was sort of un-potty-trained. In 1958 I typed up six of these vignettes, titled "The Stone," "Beauty," "War," "The Behemouth," "The Nihilist" and "The Sisters." I submitted them to F&SF magazine, which bounced them. The first showed how Little Pot, instead of putting a penny to be flattened on the track as the train came by, put a stone, wrecking the train and turning the passengers into steaming meat. As I hinted, Little Pot could be mean. The second you have read. I also used it in a later novel, *Tarot,* as the introduction to Chapter 25. That wasn't its first publication; it appeared in a fanzine back in the early 1960's. "War" had a pun on the infantry: a squad of tough babies who finally got eaten by the marines, which were underwater monsters. Later I drew on that pun for Xanth, with babies growing on an infant-tree. The behemouth was a monster like a behemoth, but with a larger orifice, who seemed threatening but turned out to have a romantic interest in Little Pot's dog. As I recall, the nihilist believed in nothing at all, and vanished when someone asked him whether he believed in himself. The sisters were devastating: Cathy was short for Cathartic, Emmy was short for Emetic, and Asia—oh, that Euthanasia!

"The Wind of Love" I wrote in 1961 or 1962 as an exercise for a correspondence course in writing. I was supposed to start with a blank mind and write a piece showing a certain shade of emotion, so I did. No, I don't feel that I owe my later success to that correspondence course; the folk who ran it meant well but really didn't understand the SF/fantasy genre.

They thought that THE SATURDAY EVENING POST represented the ideal in stories.

The last two vignettes were written for this story. So "Revise and Invent" covered a decade in my writing effort, with several odd bypaths. But it was fun in its way, for me, and I hope for you too.

Baby

In 1989 MORROW asked me to participate in a story contest. No, not to enter, exactly; to judge. The contest was intended for thirteen- or fourteen-year-olds who attended the NEW YORK IS BOOK COUNTRY fair in the fall. I try to oblige my publishers, so I agreed. This was unpaid labor, but as I remark elsewhere, *all* non-novels are essentially unpaid labor for me, even when they are paid. In this case I was to write the beginning of a story, and then select the winning conclusion from the half dozen or so finalists. I did this, and that was that. Somewhere I made a note of the identity of the winner, but I mislaid that note, so I don't remember. I did inform the publisher of the winner, however, and trust that the prize was duly given. One concern of mine is that the first reader of the entries could have overlooked some of the best stories. I've seen that happen elsewhere, and I've seen the prize go to a friend of a sponsor or judge. All I can say is that my part was honest, and I hope the rest was.

One little touch I tried for was to have the birth date of the baby in the story be the same as the date of the Book Fair. But I didn't know that date. So I filled in an approximate one and asked the publisher to correct it to the right one.

So this story is unfinished, deliberately. Let your imagination finish it.

Baby

Acalia was annoyed. "Adoptions?" she demanded. "Hiram, I'm a good free-lance features writer. In fact I'm a good reporter! I want something meaningful."

The editor shrugged. "It's what our readers want. You shouldn't expect to change the world by the stroke of your pen. I'm sure you can make it interesting."

"Just as I've been making fashion shows and debutante parties interesting," she snapped. "You think that because I'm a woman, all I can do is blah female stuff. I want something with teeth in it!"

"Consider it a challenge," he said.

She really had no choice. This was the only newspaper in town, and she couldn't afford to move elsewhere. Fuming, she took the list of contacts and marched out.

But as she got on her way, she pondered the matter of challenge. An article was what the writer made of it. Was there any way she could make this into an item that shook the world? It seemed doubtful, but if it could be done, she was going to do it.

Her preliminary research suggested that these were not conventional adoptions. They were gray-market or even black-market, the origins of the babies shady. Were any of them diseased, or stolen, or were the adoptive parents being held up for huge sums? There just might be something volatile here, if she could get a line on it.

She phoned the first name on the list, explained that she was doing a feature on adoptive babies, and asked to visit for an interview. The man was not eager, but she managed to make it seem that the adoption could be in jeopardy if he didn't agree. Soon she was on her way there.

It was an upper-middle-class subdivision, a good environment for children. The couple was white, and their new baby was a beautiful blue-eyed boy, brimming with vitality. Yes, they admitted reluctantly, they had paid a hefty sum to get this baby, but the papers were all signed and they had been guaranteed no interference from the mother.

By means of careful prying, Acalia got information on the weight, length and date of birth of the baby: seven pounds, six ounces; twenty-one inches; October 15, 1989. She tried to get the name and address of the black-market dealer, but evidently the couple had been warned against that. Their lips became tight, and sealed.

Well, it was a start. But her hope to find a diseased or drug-addicted baby had been dashed; there was nothing like that here. She thanked the people and departed.

The next family was in a "changing" neighborhood, not slum but hardly where anyone would live if he had much choice. The adoptive parents were black, and so was the baby. As before, they were open about the baby statistics and close-mouthed about the actual source. But this was a beautiful and clearly healthy girl, surely worth what they had been able to afford. Still no world-beating story.

The third family was Oriental—and they had a perfect Oriental baby, that matched them so closely there was no casual way to tell he wasn't their natural son. He was healthy and vigorous. Still no story.

Acalia pulled into a fast-food place for a hurried meal in her car. Something was nagging her, and she hoped it was her investigative sixth sense. Was there something about these adoptions that she could make into a real story—one that would put her on the front page instead of the dull features section?

She reviewed her notes on the adoptions. She still had no information on the adoption agency; nobody was talking. But she should be able to ferret that out from court records. There was absolutely nothing physically wrong with those three babies; she had never seen healthier ones. Not even any blemishes. They were all recent, as was to be expected, and all of normal weight and length. Seven pounds six ounces, twenty-one inches, coincidentally, for all three.

Coincidentally? Her sixth sense sounded an alarm. No

investigative reporter believed in coincidence. Feature writers did, maybe, but not the hard-hitting types. How likely was it that three quite different babies had identical birth dates, weights and lengths?

Well, it was possible that the outfit placing them was careless about records, and just listed set figures for any baby, rather than taking the trouble to weigh and measure. Same for the listed date of birth. But now Acalia realized that she had seen a remarkable similarity in those babies. The body types, the facial features—all babies looked somewhat alike of course, but still these were very close. If the white baby were dyed black or yellow, and the eye colors changed, it could have passed for either of the others. Sure, one was a girl, but she fit the same mold. The three were like triplets, differing only superficially.

"I think I'm on to something!" Acalia breathed.

She had a number of other names on her list. If those matched the type . . .

Cloister

In Mayhem 1989 I heard from Lawrence Watt-Evans, a novelist whose work I had admired in the past. I had also encountered him in the fannish press, and admired him there too; he's a liberal of my own stripe. I met him once at a convention too. This time he was turning his hand to editing: Would I contribute a story to his volume titled *Newer York?* Every story was to be about the city of New York.

Now I hate big cities, and New York is one of the biggest. But I try to oblige decent folk. So I agreed to do a story. As you will see, I was unable to give the city much respect.

Cloister

The Abbot heard the heavy thumping of feet long before the monk arrived in the chamber. He set down his quill and waited with resignation, knowing the news was bound to be bad.

"The kings—the queens!" the monk exclaimed as he burst in. "They have formed an evil alliance! They—they—oh, horrors!"

The Abbot stood and walked to the embrasure, gazing

out as he gave the monk time to collect his composure. "The kings and queens do have a certain recurring attraction for each other," he said. "But since they are inveterate sexists and feminists, it seldom comes to much. I really am in some doubt as to how they maintain their populations."

"But this time they have obtained financing from the rich men, and have captured and broken broncs for their mounts," the monk gasped. "They are crossing the East River, and soon will advance on this very monastery!"

"Now what would they want with our impoverished island?" the Abbot asked reasonably. "We are the citadel of literature and learning, the last surviving outpost of civilization as we once knew it. None of them have interest in such things; their horizons are limited to material quests." Still, he peered out the stone slit, worried. The monastery was constructed like a fortress, but the monks were creatures of contemplation and piosity, not warfare. This cloister could not withstand an organized attack.

"They mean to convert it to the manufacture of male hats," the monk said. "It seems there is a profitable market."

"But the Isle of York has no materials with which to make hats," the Abbot protested. "All we have are our vellum manuscripts, our invaluable scrolls of learning—" He broke off, experiencing a surge of sheerest horror. "You don't mean—?"

"They mean to use our vellum for hats," the monk said. "They say there is enough of it to make a thousand hats, which will enable them to turn a sizable illicit profit."

This was worse than he had imagined. The priceless scrolls being sacrificed for man hats on kings and rich men! "We can not suffer this desecration!" the Abbot said firmly.

"But how can we prevent it?" the monk asked rhetorically. "There are a hundred kings under the leadership of Brook and ninety-nine queens led by Lyn, and three rich men led by Miser Staten with bags of gold on their broncs, advancing on our citadel. We have only twenty able-bodied monks, and most of them are pacifists."

How well the Abbot knew it! Now he saw the vanguard marching from the south: a phalanx of armored kings, and another of gaudily garbed queens. The sunlight flashed from their massed crowns, causing the entire line to sparkle. If the doughty monks managed to secure the ramparts against the bold kings, the sexy queens were all too apt to seduce them into capitulation, or the broncs to blow down the doors with their breaking of wind: the so-called bronc's cheer. About the only defense was to blindfold the monks—but then they would not be able to defend against the onslaught of the kings. This was a truly devastating alliance!

"I'm very much afraid the time has come for the ultimate ploy," the Abbot said.

"You don't mean—?"

"The Sphere," the Abbot said grimly.

"But that will change reality as we like to think we know it!" the monk protested.

"It will indeed. But it seems to be the only way we can prevent our enemies from turning our scrolls into hats and our plowshares into swords."

"But it's so risky!"

"Yes. That is why I have not used it in a decade. But the time has come to do what we must do, for the sake of civilization."

The monk nodded, trying to mask his unmonkly fear. "I will notify the others," he said. "We shall pray for your success, and that it will not be too bad this time."

"I appreciate that," the Abbot said. They all knew the stakes, and how great the risk was. Then, before he could lose his nerve, he went to the locked chamber in the highest pinnacle of the cloister. He brought out the great key, unused in ten years, and wedged it into the corroding lock. He half hoped he would not be able to get the door open, but though it squeaked noisily in complaint, it finally yielded.

Within, shrouded by dust, was the dread device. It did not look threatening. It was a translucent sphere about the size of a medicine ball, set on a firm table. Above, beside and before it were three markers, each fixed on a supportive framework. Each marker could be moved with respect to the Sphere. From each extended a line that penetrated the Sphere. One went down, another went across, and the third went deep. Where the three intersected was the vertex of reality.

Who had made this thing the Abbot had no idea. It had been at the cloister as long as anyone knew, and as long as records existed. They assumed that the first Abbot, centuries before, had somehow crafted it, with due help from the Eternal, and left it to be used only in dire necessity. Certainly it was the reason the cloister had survived so long, while literacy and civilization faded in the rest of the world. When destruction of the cloister, or degradation of its mission seemed inevitable, the Sphere had been there to save them. There was no violence and no subterfuge; it was the ultimate pacifistic defense.

What it did was set the mortal sphere of existence. It was the device that determined which aspect of reality, of all that existed, was physical. Within it was the universe, in all its possibilities, and where the three lines crossed, the current reality was defined.

A decade before, barbarians had marched on the cloister, seeking to ravish and loot it. The Abbot had saved it by using the Sphere to shift to an aspect of reality that rendered the barbarians into horses. They had lost their intelligence, such as it was, and settled down to graze in their territory of broncs, representing no further hazard. Prior threats had shifted avaricious invaders to rich men, who had then lost their interest in the poor spoils the cloister offered. Similarly, on other occasions before the Abbot's time, the kings and queens had come about, their overweening ambitions satisfied by making them *all* royal. None cared about learning, but that had been a net advantage, for they saw nothing appealing in the stored scrolls of the cloister.

But now, with this horrible notion of making a profit from the substance of the scrolls, the threat was back, and once again the mortal sphere would have to be shifted. The Abbot wished he had more time, for this was no light matter.

The wrong setting could make their situation much worse. The Sphere had no effect on the cloister itself, only on the surrounding world, but that surrounding realm was treacherous. Each time reality shifted, it was necessary to go out with extreme caution to make new contacts, for the monks were not fully self-supporting and had to deal with the secular realm for sustenance. That was no pleasant effort.

But it had to be done, and without delay. Once the kings breached the walls, it would be too late, because then the shift of reality would not affect them, and they would be able to proceed without hindrance about their regressive business.

The Abbot nerved himself and touched the top marker. There was an eerie quaver in the surroundings as he did; though the immediate reality did not change, the mere touch of the Sphere shifted the external reality, and that sent a sympathetic shudder through the region. This marker determined, as nearly as he had been able to ascertain, the political framework; by moving it, he could ensure that York would dominate the region. So he shifted it to a new York setting, that should be stronger than the old York. That should mean that the kings and queens and rich men would still be there, but would honor allegiance to York. Indeed, the glow marking the vertex expanded greatly: that suggested enormous secular power. The Abbot didn't want to be greedy, but was tired of the constant problems resulting from weakness and poverty.

But any change in reality caused other changes. He saw by the dimming of the point that the level of literacy and learning had declined. That was no good; it was time to have the very highest level. He moved the side marker until the point glowed like a miniature star. The cloister was now the very center of the literary cosmos, as well as being politically powerful.

But the color was bad. What use to achieve power and learning, if the realm lost its soul? So he adjusted the front marker, whose line penetrated through the very depth of the Sphere, to recover the soul: the essence of this region, its true character. In a moment the color became so intense it was almost iridescent: The character of this new York was far more evident than the old one had been.

It was done. The Abbot stepped away from the Sphere and departed the chamber, carefully locking it behind him. He hoped never to have to do this again. Because the real challenge was not in moving the markers, but in dealing with the new reality beyond. What would he find outside, now?

He went to the nearest embrasure and peered out—and was astonished. The kings and queens had become gaudily dressed but seemingly harmless men and women, wandering around, peering at the gardens and terraces like so many tourists. What were they doing?

In the course of the next few hours the monks went out to survey the world of new York, and discovered that the settings were accurate: It was the capital not only of the five local territories, but of the whole world. Most of the rich men had left their section, but it was still called Richmons, or Richmond. The broncs had returned to human form, and called their region Bronx. The kings had assumed peasant garb and called their region Brooklyn, after an evident union between King Brook and Queen Lyn, but the queens at least had hung on to the original name for their portion. Whether this retained the character of the area was problematical, but the Abbot was prepared to concede that character was measured in things other than superficial appearance. As for learning: this isle now supported the greatest assemblage of scribes the world knew, and it exported texts at a phenomenal rate. So the vertex was true.

But.

The things he *hadn't* defined had changed so radically as to bend his mind. For one thing, the population: It seemed that when he increased the political power, he had done it by multiplying the residents by a thousandfold. Now the entire isle of (New) York was crowded with people, and so were the adjacent regions. The lovely open fields and dense forests were gone. The roads were jammed with metal vehicles, so that motion was almost impossible. The pollution of their fires made the air almost unbreathable, and their wastes made the clear waters of the rivers and sea opaque. It was horrible!

Worse, it seemed that the plot to turn vellum into hats had been successful, for the isle had been renamed man-hat-on, or Manhattan. The cloister remained unchanged, true; it was now titled The Cloisters, and was considered a tourist attraction. But its function was gone; it was no longer the ultimate repository of learning. That had been pre-empted by the larger literary and commercial establishment at the south part of the isle. Meanwhile, the tourists flocked in, especially their females, in their unmentionable clothing, turning the heads of even the saintliest monks—it was a time for desperate prayer! Who could guess what further degradations awaited to be discovered?

The Abbot pondered. Had he made a mistake? Should he return immediately to the dread Sphere and change the settings again? This might result in improvement—or an even worse situation. What should he do?

Meanwhile, oblivious to the threat to reality as they thought they knew it, the kings, queens, rich men, broncs and hatters went about their business. Had they but known . . .

Love 40

![black rectangle decoration]

In 1991 I was solicited for a story for a new British magazine, FAR POINT. I make an honest effort to oblige such requests, though I really do hate to take time off from my novels. So I checked to see if I had any loose notions, and I did have one, so I wrote it up. I don't regard "Love 40" as the greatest of stories, just the best I could come up with on short notice. I always do the best I can, but conditions make the result vary. Would it have been accepted if it had been submitted by an unknown author? I hope so, but I can't be sure. I never liked the system when I couldn't sell my stories because I was unknown, and I don't like it now that I am known, but it's the only game in town. So I hope you enjoy the story, and I hope it helps establish a market that you can sell to yourself, if that's your ambition.

Love 40

Galen hardly noticed the Oriental girl in the next court. He was concentrating on the tennis balls coming at him from the machine. It was set to feed a variety of balls, so that he could get his exercise the fun way. The girl was evidently setting up for something similar.

Actually, he wasn't paying much attention to the tennis balls either. He was hardly a tennis player, or even a reasonable duffer. He was a special investigator. Several people had mysteriously changed their lives after staying at this resort, and the resort administration had hired him to find out whether anything sinister was going on. Because many extremely wealthy foreign tourists stopped here, and the very hint of danger or scandal could cost the resort heavily.

So Galen, during his vacation from the police force, was not only earning a very nice spot fee, but was being treated to the kind of luxury living that millionaires expected. He was methodically exploring every one of the facilities, constantly watching for anything sinister or even out of the ordinary. He luxuriated in the Jacuzzi, had an expert massage, exercised on the most modern equipment, played a round of golf, feasted morning noon and evening, danced with the most exquisitely garbed and amenable girls and watched a wider assortment of TV than he had known existed, including some he had thought to be illegal. He was coming to realize that laws did not have the same bearing on the wealthy as on ordinary folk. Now he was trying one of the lesser facilities, because as yet he had found nothing to account for the management's unease.

He wasn't doing well. The machine was keeping score on his responses, and the score read LOVE 40. That meant that he was supposedly the server, and was about to be skunked on the game.

There was a flash. Galen paused, missing his shot. What had happened?

The girl in the next court paused too. Galen looked at her, and found her looking at him. This time his shock was of recognition. Not of her, exactly, for he had never seen her before this session. But of their relationship. This was the woman he loved.

They walked together and embraced. Then they kissed. It was the sweetest kiss Galen had known.

They drew their faces apart and gazed at each other. The girl looked amazed and alarmed, but she did not try to move away from him. Her pupils were large despite the brightness of the day, and her jaw slack. It was the gaze of sheer adoration.

"I, uh, do you speak English?" he asked.

"Yes," she replied. "I love you."

"And I love you. But I don't know you. I don't understand this."

"This is very bad," she said. "I must go before my father sees."

"Yes. I'm sure we have nothing in common."

"Nothing," she agreed.

Then they kissed again. She was the most precious thing he could imagine.

After a moment they tried to separate again, and could not. "Maybe we'd better introduce ourselves," he said. "I am Galen Holt, here on temporary business. I go back to Massachusetts next week."

"I am—in your language I call myself Sue," she said. "Next week I return to Japan with my family."

"Then we'll never see each other again."

"Never."

"I've never done anything this weird before," Galen said. "I have a girlfriend back home. I don't hit on strangers."

"I have never been close to a man of your race before," she said. "This is a great scandal. I must go immediately."

They kissed a third time. It was infinitely wonderful.

"Your place or mine?" he asked, failing to make a joke of it.

"You have a room to yourself?" she asked, and saw his nod. "Then it must be there."

"You know this is absolutely crazy." But they were already walking off the courts, forgetting the rackets and balls.

Then a man was calling. Sue jumped. "It is my father! We must get far away from each other."

"Yes."

But they did not follow through. They stopped and kissed once more.

Sue's father arrived. He was well dressed and formidable.

Galen wanted to be anywhere else, but he could not let go of Sue.

Under the man's glare, Galen and Sue made a valiant effort to separate. They drew a few inches apart. It felt like the end of all joy. Then they flung themselves together again.

Sue's father, realizing that something very strange was occurring, addressed Galen in English. "What is this spell you have cast on my daughter?"

Galen turned his head to the man without letting Sue go. "I don't know, sir. We were just practicing tennis shots in adjacent courts, and suddenly it happened. I love her."

Then he made a connection. This astonishing development—could it be related to his investigation? The people could have been changed two at a time. There were an equal number of men and women affected, though he hadn't thought of it that way before. Could sudden, overwhelming love account for it? There had been one suicide, two disappearances, one rape and two abrupt resignations from high places. All coming without warning or explanation. Galen had been alert for some kind of criminal involvement, but maybe he had been focusing on the wrong thing.

Yet instant love—how was it possible, let alone reasonable? He could appreciate how a man might see a lovely young woman in a tennis outfit, and be smitten by her body, and try to seduce her. Perhaps even to rape her. But that was only one case of six. Maybe if she rejected his advances and he was depressive, he could commit suicide. That might account for a second case. Or if she returned his interest, but they were married to others, then they might run away together. Thus the two disappearances. Or if he were important in government, and started an affair with a woman he met here, but couldn't keep out of the notice of the press, he might resign so he could pursue his illicit love in private.

It was coming together. Instant love *could* account for what had been happening. But *how* did it happen? He had not even been paying attention to Sue, or she to him, when suddenly they had found each other to be compellingly attractive.

It couldn't be purely physical, for though Galen was healthy, he was no Adonis in body and was strictly average in face. As for Sue—well, it was hard to be objective, because he loved her, but all Orientals *did* look remarkably similar to him, and she was slightly thickset and not exactly of starlet aspect. He had never entertained the slightest notion of dating one. This wasn't bigotry, just culture; his ignorance of the ways of Japan was monumental. As for her personality—he had yet to discover what it was. This was truly blind love.

Meanwhile Sue was speaking rapidly to her father in Japanese, evidently supporting Galen's ridiculous story. She clung desperately close to Galen.

The man assessed the situation. He was evidently conscious of being in a foreign land, and he did not want to generate an international incident. But he was not about to let his daughter get into trouble with a stranger. He wanted a quick and polite termination of the incident.

"What exactly were you doing when it happened?" he asked gruffly.

Sue spoke more Japanese, pointing to her court. Galen agreed, pointing to his.

A Japanese woman came out, evidently Sue's mother. The man spoke to her. She went unquestioningly to the court where Sue had practiced. Then the man went to Galen's court. Following instructions, they picked up the rackets, and turned on the machines. The balls started flinging out.

There was a flash. Simultaneously the man and woman paused, looking surprised. Something had happened to them.

That flash! There had been one just before Galen discovered Sue. A flash from the ball-hurling machine. He had forgotten it, in the surge of his emotion. The Japanese, more objective than he, had done what he should have done, and investigated the exact circumstances of the conversion.

The two walked quickly together and embraced. Sue stared; evidently she had never seen her parents do that. Then she took advantage of the distraction to turn to Galen and kiss him again. Galen had heard that Orientals did not display passion in public. So much for that.

The older folk separated. "It is a love device," the man said. "It has made us love each other as we did soon after our marriage. This is what happened to you."

A love device! Something that focused on the man in one court, and the woman in another, and zapped their emotions. It had made his "Love 40" score become halfway literal. This could indeed account for the resort's mystery. Because Galen was ready to dump his career and elope with Sue, and he knew that she felt the same.

But that was foolhardy. They were superbly ill-matched. They would never have gotten together, except for this random zapping. His common sense informed him that what they needed was not togetherness, but an antidote.

He faced Sue. He tried to tell her of his conclusion. Instead he kissed her.

Meanwhile the older couple went to one of the ball machines. Efficiently they dismantled it. "As we suspected," the man said. "A device has been added."

Galen realized that they were doing his job. "We'd better get over there," he told Sue. "I—I love you, but there's something I have to tell you."

"And something I must tell you," she agreed.

The man had removed the extra device, which looked like an elaborate camera. As Galen approached, he handed it over. "Hide this, while we get the other."

"But I have to tell you, I'm with the police. This is evidence. We can't tamper with it."

The man gave him a straight look. "The police will reassign you, and you will never see Sue again. Do you desire this?"

"No!" Sue cried, clinging to him. She was merely echoing his own sentiment.

Galen held the device, while the older couple worked on the one in the other court. He was helpless to interfere, because he knew that his report would indeed destroy his romance. The Japanese family evidently had something better in mind.

"We are not police, we are business," Sue murmured. "We intercepted reports of something odd, and came to investigate. We have been looking for several days. Then we realized that you too were looking, so I was assigned to keep an eye on you. I think you did not notice me, before."

"I sure didn't!" he said, amazed. She must be very good at being inconspicuous.

"A thing like this—it could be excellent business," she continued. "Because surely there is much market for love." She turned her eyes up to him. "But I did not expect to be caught in it myself. I did not realize at first that we had found what we sought."

"Maybe the thing can be reset," he said. "To reverse love. So we can be free of this nonsense."

"My father will have it analyzed," she said. "If there is a way, he will find it. Then, as you say, we can be free."

"But meanwhile—" he started.

"Meanwhile—" she echoed.

They kissed. It was as if they could not survive for more than a minute or two without it.

The man approached with the other device. "Come to our suite," he said. "We know that is private."

Galen followed, holding the one device in his left hand, his right arm around Sue's waist. "You must understand, I never intended—"

"We understand." Obviously they did, for they were walking with their arms linked.

In the suite, the man got serious. "We want three things from you, Mr. Holt. We want you to bury your police report, so that we can take this device directly to Japan for analysis. We want you to locate the one who made this device, so we can hire him. And we want you to join our company, and keep its secrets. We can make this worth your while."

Galen had heard that Orientals could take forever to get to the point. Evidently when in America, they played by

American rules. "I don't know," he said. "I would lose my job, if I didn't report."

"We will quadruple your present salary, guaranteed for life, indexed to inflation, with generous bonuses."

That was persuasive. But Galen hesitated. "I don't like leaving my job undone. This device has made some real mischief, and could make more."

"We are removing the device, so there will be no more incidents. The resort will be satisfied that the problem has been handled. Indeed, you have already fulfilled your obligation in that respect."

Galen remained doubtful. "I don't know anything about Japan."

"You can work in America. It is your loyalty we want, not your location."

Galen realized that he was in danger of being swept off his feet. It was tempting. Yet he temporized. "And it might take some time to locate whoever made this thing. I don't know how well I could function, apart from Sue. Until we get the antidote."

"She is actually an employee, not our daughter. She will remain with you for the duration."

Galen looked at Sue. She smiled. That was what he needed. He made one more effort to resist, knowing it would be instantly shot down. "There will be complicated paperwork—I mean, I can't just say I quit the police and am working for someone I met on a tennis court."

"We will handle it. There are ways."

Galen considered, and realized that it was a good deal—the best he was ever likely to be offered. "Okay."

They shook hands. Then Sue fetched her things and carried them to Galen's room. They tarried there for an intense half hour before feeling ready to get back to work, and they still didn't know anything about each other's minds.

The older couple vanished from the scene, with the two devices. They would be in Japan before the resort management realized they were gone.

Galen and Sue set up a watch on the two tennis courts. They found a supply shed where they could hide, and took turns peering out the slitlike window. Sooner or later, the proprietor of those devices should come to check on them. Then the two of them would follow him.

It was a dull watch, but a pleasant time. While Galen watched, Sue rested against him, rubbed his back, massaged his shoulders, and kissed the back of his neck. While Sue watched, he hugged her, stroked her hair, and ran his hands across places that he should have lost interest in after their session in the hotel room. Their love might be artificial, but it was thorough; all they wanted was more of each other.

As dusk loomed, a technician came to check the equipment. When he looked at the first ball-hurler, he froze. Quickly he checked the other. Then he hurried away.

"That's our man," Galen whispered.

They piled out, tucking in their clothing as they went. They tracked the man to his car, and noted the license tag. But they also followed him, in Galen's car. It wasn't difficult, because he seemed distracted. That was understandable; he had just discovered that someone had stolen his special devices. Did he think it was the resort management? Was he going to clear out before he got arrested?

"Best to handle this immediately," Galen said. "Before he can take his stuff and disappear to another state or country." Sue nodded agreement, and squeezed his arm.

Galen went up to the front door, while Sue circled to the back, just in case. When the man answered, Galen introduced himself. "I helped take your love devices," he said. "I have a deal to offer you, if you're the one who made them."

The man let him in. "You're not a cop?"

"I am a cop, but that's not why I'm here. A Japanese company is taking your two boxes to Japan to analyze and reproduce. They figure to make a considerable profit marketing those things. They want to hire you too. Or whoever knows how to make them."

The man walked back to a small makeshift laboratory

and machine shop. "I make them, but they're not for sale," he said. "I'm testing them, to see how well they work, before I get rich selling the secret." He opened a trunk and brought out a device similar to those on the tennis courts. "I've got just one more, but it's enough."

"I don't think you have a choice," Galen said. "Several people have been harmed by them, and you are liable for that. I got put into love with a Japanese woman, and now I'm working for her company. The Japanese will pay you well, and they already have two boxes to copy if you don't cooperate. So you might as well deal with them."

The man laughed. "Think I'm an idiot? Those machines are set to self-destruct the moment anyone tries to get into them. You're lucky you didn't get your head blown off when you took them out of the ball-throwers. They won't be any good to anybody. I'm the only one who knows the secret, and I stumbled on it by such sheer blind chance that no one else will ever duplicate it. I set those two out at the resort so I could see how well they worked with one emotion. Now I know they work perfectly. They should work just as well on the other settings."

"Other settings?" Galen asked, feeling a chill.

"They're emotion tuners. They can lock in any emotion. I can make two people love each other, or hate each other, or forget each other. Or anything else. I'll make others fiercely loyal to me alone, and then I'll give them more tuners so they can use them on the leaders of the world and make them swear fealty to me. I'll be king of the world!"

"That's a megalomaniac dream," Galen said.

The man pointed the device at Galen. "You are about to change your attitude." He adjusted a setting.

Galen's chill intensified. He knew how well the device worked! "You're going to make me loyal to you?"

"No, I don't know you. I'm not ready for followers yet. I'm just going to make you forget everything. This one's set on amnesia. I'll dump you off somewhere, and by the time they figure out what happened to you, I'll be long gone with my equipment and notes. I've got everything packed, here." He nudged the open trunk with one foot. "I was going to leave the moment anything happened, and now it's happened. I'll be gone within the hour."

Galen realized that it was possible. Those devices were far more versatile than he had assumed. Not just love, but all the emotions, and amnesia too! The man could eliminate anyone who tried to interfere with him, and convert those he chose. By what fluke he had stumbled on the secret Galen might never know, but it obviously hadn't given the man a mature perspective. He wanted to rule the world, and didn't care how much mischief he made in the process.

Was there any way to escape? He doubted it. All the man had to do was click the device on, and he could do that before Galen managed to move more than a couple of feet.

Galen knew he was done for. In that moment he suffered a revelation. *This had to be stopped!* But he was afraid he wasn't going to be able to stop it.

Then a shape appeared in the far doorway, behind the man. Sue!

"Stop him before he zaps me!" Galen cried to her.

The man ignored him, probably thinking it was a ruse. He lifted his free hand to the top of the device.

Sue hurled herself across the room. She grabbed the device from the man's hands and moved on to the front of the room beside Galen. "I couldn't let him hurt you, my love," she gasped.

"I'm grateful for that!" he said, taking the box from her. He pointed it at the man and touched the button on the top. There was a flash.

The man looked around. "Where am I?" he asked plaintively. "Who am I?"

"You're in the condition you had in mind for me," Galen said. Then he threw the device at the trunk on the floor.

The man had not been bluffing about the self-destruct mechanism. The device exploded, setting fire to the papers in the trunk. In a moment there was a hearty little blaze.

Galen turned to Sue. "I love you, and it tears me up to make you unhappy. But whatever that device is, it can't be trusted to any living person. Not the one who made it, not me, not your employers. So I have destroyed it, and the notes to make it, and wiped the memory of the only one who knows how to make it. It's gone. Now hate me if you have to; I did what I felt I had to do." He stopped, waiting for her fury.

"I had come to the same conclusion," Sue said. "I heard him talking, and realized that it was much worse than I feared. I thought I would have to use the device on you, before I could destroy it." She paused. "But my employer will not understand. I dare not return to Japan. I must hide. Do you think you can help me?"

He took her in his arms. "You know this artificial love is bound to wear out in a year or two. We probably have nothing to hold us together. We're just two people who happened to get zapped at the same time."

"Then perhaps we should make the most of our limited time together," she said, smiling.

They had, perhaps, just saved the world from emotional slavery. But a stranger passing at that moment would have been hard put to distinguish them from any other couple in the first intense flood of romantic love.

Maybe, Galen thought, their love would last after they did get to know each other. Maybe for forty years. After all, it had started at love 40.

Kylo

■

One of my stray fascinations is with dinosaurs. I've done a dinosaur novel, *Orn,* and similar creatures have appeared elsewhere in my fiction. One minor offshoot of my research for the novel was "Kylo," which I completed Jamboree 1, 1967. It was bounced by F&SF, ORBIT, GOOD HOUSEKEEPING, PLAYBOY, SATURDAY EVENING POST, REDBOOK, COSMOPOLITAN, MCCALL'S, and BEYOND. In short, I tried the fantasy, male, female and general markets, with no success. If you wonder why some of those magazines aren't with us today, maybe it's because they weren't interested in what I had to offer. That's plausible, isn't it? But a decade or two later a "small" magazine asked me for something, and I proffered "Kylo," and it was published in PANDORA IN 1988. It is a slightly different story; I do all kinds.

Kylo

I hadn't seen the Grossets in two years, and Selma was blithely filling my ear with local gossip that was, frankly, of little present interest to me. I tried to avoid glancing too often at my watch as I wondered when Ian would get home. Something banged at the back door. "Oops," Selma said, bouncing up so quickly her graying curls jiggled. "I forgot to feed Kylo. Just a minute." She went out, and I could hear her solicitous murmurs in the yard.

Now I could dwell upon the time. It was four-thirty—probably another hour before Ian finished his day at the accounting office. I should have anticipated this before exposing myself to his undoubtedly pleasant but vociferous wife.

"You keep a pet now?" I inquired as she returned, resigning myself to an interminable account of some dutifully unique hound.

"Oh, no, Kylo isn't ours. We're boarding her for a few days while old Butterfeldt is in the hospital. It's quite a bit of trouble, really, but Ian said . . ." and she continued with mundane details of neighbors and illness and obligations that slipped my mind at about the speed of sound. "It isn't that Kylo is bad-tempered or anything like that, but taking her for a walk every day is tedious, to say the least."

Not, I thought darkly, more tedious than hearing about it. "You mean you have a local leash law? Most people I know just let their dogs run loose to squat on someone else's lawn, law or no law."

"Dogs?" she asked, perplexed.

"Kylo. Remember?" I wondered whether she was growing absent-minded. She looked shocked. "Kylo isn't a dog!"

It occurred to me then that the sound at the door had had considerably more authority than one would normally expect from canine scratchings. It had been a definite thump as of solid bone. "Do you mean to say you're boarding a horse? In the suburbs? Why don't you ride him—I mean, her—around the block, in that case?"

"Ride her!" she exclaimed indignantly. "Kylo isn't a horse. She's a dinosaur!"

I smiled at her vehemence.

"No, I mean it," she said, nettled. "A dinosaur. Ankylosaurus—Ian says technically it's Paleoscincus, because of the tail—one of the extinct armored reptiles. She—"

"Sure, Selma," I said, hardly paying attention to her fantasy about the animal. She *was* getting old!

"She gets balky sometimes, and she's so big."

"Suppose you let me walk her for you today," I said, now rather curious, as well as glad for the pretext for a break.

Her relief was almost too evident. "Oh, *would* you? She's really quite harmless, but she does need her exercise. Maybe Butterfeldt will come home tomorrow, and we can take her back to him."

She led the way to the rear. "Now, she knows what 'stop' means, so you won't have trouble running into traffic. But when she stalls, sometimes the only thing you can do is kick her in the side. Don't worry; you can't hurt her. That carapace is tough. And it won't matter that you're a stranger. She's not too bright that way; anyone can lead her."

Carapace? Pure hyperbole, surely!

"Sure," I said amiably.

We turned the corner.

I stiffened and grabbed at the wall for support. A monster lay in the yard! A reptile a good fifteen feet long with terrible pointed teeth sticking out the sides. It reminded me a little of an alligator, but the short beaked snout and solid elephantine feet set it apart from any water creature. And yes, it had a carapace, like a huge turtle shell. The woman had been speaking literally!

Selma walked up and reached around its mail-scaled neck to fasten the leash. "Mr. Arnold is going to take you for a walk, Kylo," she said sweetly.

I found my voice. "That—that's a—"

"Dinosaur," she agreed. "A medium-sized Ankylosaurus." She handed the end of the leash to me with a somewhat smug quirk of a smile. "Once around the block will do."

My fingers convulsed about the stout handle. "It—that thing is harmless?"

"Certainly. Kylo is a herbivore. Just don't bang against her spines." Had I not known better, I could have sworn there was a gleam of malice in her eye. I realized I should have masked my boredom with her company better.

She returned her attention to the creature. "Come on, Kylo. Get up. Time for your postprandial stroll."

Kylo was obviously not the smartest of pets, but she finally got the message and heaved herself to her feet. The difference was hardly perceptible. There now appeared to be an inch or two of daylight under her ponderous flat belly. She stood about four feet high and slightly more wide. Her six-inch spikes projected from low flanks, about fifteen on a side, forming an impressive barricade. The overlapping scales of head and neck seemed impregnable. Even the tapering tail was armored to the tip. Woe betide the obnoxious mutt that tried to take a chomp of her!

"Come, Kylo," I said somewhat gruffly, bracing myself for the embarrassment of being ignored. To my surprise she came. Once en route, she had a respectable pace: a good three miles an hour. I walked beside her at the limit of the leash, hoping not to encounter anyone who knew me.

We passed the house and turned onto the street. Kylo seemed to know the way, or at least to comprehend that the pavement was for traveling.

Gradually I felt less foolish, because of the bulking mass of the creature I accompanied. After all, who would laugh at fifteen feet of solid, long-extinct reptile?

A man was polishing his car a few houses down. I fixed my eyes straight forward as if oblivious to my surroundings. But he heard the dinosaur's heavy tread and looked up. He smiled.

"Hello there, Kylo. Stay clear of my roses."

Kylo eyed the roses. "Nuh-uh!" I said sharply. Her nose angled forward again, to my relief.

At the corner an oncoming car braked. The driver leaned out to wave us pedestrians by. "Corners are hard for Kylo," he explained. "Wouldn't want an accident."

A neighborhood grocery store stood across the street on the back side of the block. The proprietor beckoned. I shrugged and tugged at the leash, and the reptile obligingly ambled across to the store.

The man brought out a cardboard box. "Some of this stuff is getting old," he explained. "It won't keep over the weekend." He drew out a wilted head of lettuce and fed it to Kylo, who took it into her mouth entire and chewed it twice before gulping it down. Half a dozen bruised tomatoes and a soft watermelon went the same way.

"Make sure she gets a few rocks to go along with that," he told me. "She needs them for her digestion."

"She eats *rocks?*"

He nodded seriously.

Farther along two eight-year-olds walked up, petted Kylo's head, and climbed carefully aboard her carapace. They paid no attention to me, and so I kept quiet. They had obviously done this before, and the dinosaur didn't mind.

In fact, nobody paid much attention. Kylo, apart from a couple of balks near tempting shrubbery, gave me no trouble. She was leash-trained, and not phenomenally hungry after the meal at the house and the groceries at the store. We completed the circuit without untoward event.

My old friend Ian appeared shortly after I turned Kylo loose in the yard, but the greetings were perfunctory.

"Butterfeldt died," he said. "It was much more serious than he let on."

They had not been close; Butterfeldt had been only a neighbor, and not of long standing. The pressing concern was Kylo. "We can't keep her," Selma said. "She's just too much for us to handle on a regular basis, and there's no telling how long she will live. We don't even know what vet she goes to. The bill for vegetables—" She turned to me. "She can't eat grass, you know. It's too tough for her digestion. Just vegetables and flowers and fruits. She likes bread, too, but she can eat so much!"

"No grass? Surely if she can digest rocks—" I began.

"That's different. She doesn't *digest* them; they just help to grind up the food inside. Birds do the same thing."

I shut up, feeling stupid. I should have made the connection when the grocer told me.

"We'll have to call the SPCA," Ian said unhappily.

I was shocked. "You mean—?"

"No, I *don't* mean," he said, irritated. "They don't put away animals unless there's no alternative. Kylo's perfectly gentle, once you understand her, and she *is* unique. I'm sure they'll be able to find a good home for her."

It was that simple. I had to go home, and my business kept me there, but I saw the ad in the city newspaper, a few days later:

PET OF THE WEEK: "Kylo," affectionate Ankylosaur, leash-trained, suitable for children. Extinct 65,000,000 years but in good health. Prefers head lettuce. Unique. Call after 5:30 P.M.

They even ran her picture. I swear her beak had a sad-eyed cast. Those pictures always do. I'm sure she found a home, for the ad was never repeated. I'm glad. But somehow I have this nagging feeling that I have missed something important. Have I?

Plague of Allos

In 1985 I received a brochure from the ElfQuest folk. I had met Richard Pini at a convention in 1983, and my daughter Cheryl, then thirteen and a dedicated ElfQuest fan, was thrilled to actually talk with the proprietor of that series. We have a picture of her about to burst, because she had taken a mouthful of a soda and he said something to make her laugh. We had remained in touch, expecting to do business in due course, as indeed we later did with their graphic adaptation of Xanth #13 *Isle of View,* in which Jenny Elf from the World of Two Moons comes to the Land of Xanth. But this brochure was about a different project, BLOOD OF TEN CHIEFS. It was to be ten stories set in the ElfQuest realm, each covering one of the ancestral chiefs. Would I like to participate?

Well, I pondered. There was a time when I was eager for invitations like this, but that time is long past. The thing is, payment for a story is measured in cents per word, while for a novel I can earn dollars per word. Since I like the novels I do, and I like being well paid, simple economics converted me from a story writer to a novel writer, and I have had more novels published than stories. So I no longer write stories for money. I do get paid for them, but that isn't my motivation, since every story I do represents a net loss of income for me, as does every collaboration. But I did want to remain in the good graces of the ElfQuest folk, and Cheryl would love to have me rise in the literary realm enough to appear in an ElfQuest volume, so I agreed.

I told them to give me whatever Chief no one else wanted. That turned out to be Prey Pacer, the third in the line. So when I finished writing my novel *Being A Green Mother* I got to it, and early in 1986 wrote my story of Prey Pacer and his challenges both romantic and adventurous. I had Cheryl give me pointers about the ElfQuest realm. But in one case she steered me wrong. Were there rabbits there? I asked, and she said no. So I made a similar creature, a ravvit. Later I learned that there *were* rabbits there. But it seemed that the ElfQuest folk liked my notion, because thereafter ravvits showed up elsewhere among the elves.

I named my characters descriptively, and sometimes it seemed I went wrong there too. Thus Hoverhair became Wreath in the published edition. But since this is my volume, I'm rendering this in the original version, flawed as it may be.

One more point: I am a vegetarian, which means I eat no meat, fish or fowl, and I try to avoid anything that causes animals pain in the acquisition, such as leather. But I do not impose my personal foibles on my readers, regardless of what critics claim. On the World of Two Moons blood flows frequently, so it does also in this story.

BLOOD OF TEN CHIEFS was a success, and went on to other volumes, but I did not contribute because my time just got more and more jammed. It was nice being part of that world once, though.

Plague of Allos

The great wolf lay as if asleep, so that even when a random leaf tumbled across his nose no whisker twitched. His fur was as brown as blown sand, his paws as gray as weathered stones; when he lay still, as now, he tended to fade into the landscape. Instead it was his elf-friend Prune Pit who moved, and rather clumsily too. There seemed to be no chance for a successful ravvit stalk. Yet the elf seemed confident; his sling was poised, a solid pit in the pouch.

His arm moved. The pit flung forward to strike in a thick patch of grass. Sure enough: A fat ravvit leaped out, startled by the near miss.

The elf jumped to the prey's right, herding it toward the still wolf. The ravvit veered left.

Now! the elf cried in thought, sending not so much a word as a target region: a spot in the air not far to the side of the wolf's nose.

The ravvit leaped, coming to that spot just as the wolf's jaws closed.

In a moment it was over; the prey hung from the wolf's mouth, dead. Another hunt had been concluded successfully.

"Let's go home, Halfhowl," Prune Pit said, satisfied. "There isn't another suitable animal in the vicinity." He sent another spot location, and leaped at it; the wolf made a swift dive, putting his back just beneath that spot as the elf arrived. Prune Pit mounted so efficiently that it seemed as though they had rehearsed that maneuver many times. Actually they had not; the elf's sending made rehearsal unnecessary.

Prune Pit was the son of Rahnee the She-Wolf, but there was no evidence of this in his aspect. He was neither handsome nor large, and his brown hair fell down across his eyes in chronic tangles. His skill with his chosen weapon was mediocre; he normally missed his target, as he had just now. He had to carry a good supply of ammunition because of this. Prune pits were lighter than stones, and their regular shapes made it easier for him, but still it was evident that he lacked the physical coordination ever to be truly effective. Worse, his sending was defective; he could not properly tune into other elves, and consequently was forever getting things garbled. He was not simpleminded, but sometimes seemed so. The other elves of the tribe were of course circumspect about their attitude, but it was true that if any member of the tribe could be said to be held in contempt, that member was Prune Pit. Rahnee had never expressed disappointment in him, but surely she had felt it.

Yet it was also true that in this time of the hunting drought, he alone had maintained his ratio of kills. This was because his telepathy was attuned to animals rather than to his own kind. Halfhowl had been the first wolf to recognize this, and had chosen Prune Pit to be his rider. Theirs was the closest bond between elf and wolf, and this was part of the reason their hunts were almost inevitably successful. Halfhowl never had to listen for Prune Pit's directive, either physical or verbal; he knew it as fast as the elf did. He was always there when the elf wanted him, and there was no subservience in this, it was as though the desire to be there had originated with the wolf. Often that might be true; it did not matter. What mattered was that the two never miskeyed; they always acted with such perfect coordination that the other elves and wolves could only watch with muted envy.

The other part of the reason for their success was Prune Pit's identification with the prey. He could tell the prey's next move at the same time as the prey did, for animals did not think ahead in the way elves did. From a distance this made no difference; there was no catching the prey anyway. But in close action, the prey's specific dodge became critical. In the hunt just completed, Prune Pit had in effect linked the minds of ravvit and wolf, allowing the two bodies to coincide.

The others of the tribe had chosen to believe that Prune Pit was mostly lucky; it was hard for them to accept the notion that this elf who could hardly send to his own kind could be superior with other kinds. Thus Prune Pit's status was higher among the wolves than among the elves. It seemed likely that he would in time turn to animal-healing as his life's work.

There was confusion as they drew near the holt. Something had happened—and Prune Pit felt a surge of dread. Another elf would have known instantly what the problem was, but the vague dread was all that Prune Pit could receive. It involved his mother, known as the she-wolf.

Rahnee had led a party out to explore the nature of the allos, the big saurians who seemed to be swarming into this region. The allos were huge, vicious reptiles, not as efficient predators as the wolves, but their increasing numbers were making them a nuisance. When the horde swept through a region, hardly any other species of creature survived. The allos were normally solitary hunters, and their relative clumsiness enabled them to prey mainly on the old, the infirm and the unlucky. Now, their numbers increased perhaps a hundred-fold, they required no subtlety of approach; they saturated the range, snapping up everything that moved. Migratory prey had all but disappeared, if its migration took it through the infested regions.

It was obvious that blind, ravening hunger would bring the allos to the region of the holt, for here the hunting had until recently been good. Now it was not—because of the depredations of the allos—and it was likely to get much worse. What would the reptiles hunt, after the last legitimate prey was gone? The answer just might be: elves.

So Rahnee had gone out to assess the menace—and now there was a commotion, and no sign of her wolf, Silvertooth.

Softfoot hurried to intercept him. ":Your mother—" she cried. "Silvertooth is terribly injured, and—"

Then he knew. Rahnee was dead, and the tribe was without its chief.

It was worse than that. Rahnee's party had included the best hunters in the tribe—and most of them were dead too. There was no obvious prospect for new leadership. Rahnee's lifemate Zarhan was loyal and good, but he had no interest in taking her place. Prune Pit, her son, seemed to follow his father's temperament. He had never imagined challenging her for leadership, and would have felt disloyal to try for it now that she was dead. Even had he not felt this way, he would have known that no elf would follow a leader who was defective in sending; how could the tribe coordinate in times of crisis? He did not grieve for Rahnee as a son might, for they had not been really close after he grew up. But her loss was tragic for the tribe and he wanted to steal no part of her glory. There had to be a leader, for the dread allos were swarming closer, and in a few days would be here.

In the confusion of the horror of the disaster, one voice emerged with clarity. This was Hoverhair, the loveliest of the younger female elves, the object of much male interest. She was brave, beautiful and cold; her fair hair floated above her like a lattice of snow. It was said that her heart was formed of extremely pretty ice. She had never, to Prune Pit's knowledge, done anything for anyone other than because of calculated self-interest. She was a fine huntress, adept with the bow, but had no pretensions toward leadership; it seemed that that would have been too much work to suit her. When she encountered a male routinely, her inclination was to inhale, smile, and give her magnificent cloud of hair a careful toss, causing him to catch his breath and lick his lips, while his heart accelerated. Her own heart never fluttered, however. In short, she was a flirt, not a leader. She had been looking for some time for a companion, but had wanted to be absolutely sure she had the best match. That meant Recognition—and it hadn't come. Perhaps, Prune Pit thought, that was just as well.

"Why don't we choose as chief the one who can stop the menace of the allos?" she inquired briefly. "Because if we don't stop them, soon they will wipe out all the prey in our forest, and then we'll starve."

This made so much sense that the others were amazed. Why hadn't any of them thought of it? There was a murmur of agreement.

"So who knows how to stop the allos?" Hoverhair inquired. That was where it went sour. No one had any notion. The allos, according to the description of the survivors of the party who had straggled home, were big, vicious and numerous. No single wolfrider could stand against an allo in combat, and indeed, the holt's best hunters had been savaged as a group. The elves were simply overmatched.

"If we don't get a leader," Hoverhair pointed out, "we shall have to flee our holt."

But no elf stepped forward. If the she-wolf had been unable to stop the menace, how could any of them?

The tribe spent a glum night. Softfoot stayed up late, talking with Prune Pit. "There has to be a way!" she kept saying. She was a warm, understanding person, lovely in her personality rather than her appearance. Her hair was like a fuzzy dark blanket. Her feet had seemed malformed in her childhood; they had in time grown normally, but she was not swift on them, and was a much better rider than runner. She was good with the spear, when on her wolf. She, alone of the tribe, had appreciated Prune Pit's strength, and had not perceived him as mentally stunted. It had not been hard for him to love her, and he had never regretted their association.

Reluctantly, Prune Pit spoke. "I think there might be—but if I'm wrong, it would be even worse than now."

She virtually pounced on him. "A way! What way?"

"You know how I hunt by relating to the prey," he said, "and by putting it in touch with Halfhowl."

"Yes, of course; you have never received proper credit for your skill."

"Well, if I could relate to an allo, then we could hunt allos. That would give us and our wolves suitable prey, and help reduce the numbers of the reptiles, until the normal ratios of animals returned."

Softfoot shook her head. "You couldn't hunt an allo, Prune Pit! They say that a single allo killed Rahnee and two of her hunters and two wolves, and it wasn't even the largest allo! Those monsters have horny scales that make them almost invulnerable to our weapons, and their teeth are horrendous. We can't even recover Rahnee's body from them."

"They are reptiles," he said doggedly, suppressing the thought of his mother's body; there was indeed nothing the elves could do about that. "That means they are slow to move in the cool morning, and not too smart. They can't have armor in their eyes. If we knew how to avoid their teeth and claws, we should be able to score on a weak point. And I do know."

She began to be swayed. "You aren't afraid? An allo is no ravvit, you know; it's a predator."

Prune Pit's mouth was dry. "I'm terrified. But we have to find a way to fight allos, and I think I can."

"Sleep now," Softfoot decided. "If you still think the same way in the morning, we'll talk with someone." This was her way, to consider something, then sleep, and reconsider. It seemed to work well enough. She had done it when they had become lifemates, taking time to be certain. Prune Pit was glad to have her doing it now. If she concluded that his notion was viable, in the morning, then perhaps it was. He had spoken forthrightly enough, but the thought of hunting an allo made his body cold.

"I think we should test it," Softfoot announced in the morning. "But not on an allo."

Prune Pit hadn't thought of that. He liked the notion. "What can we test it on? There isn't any prey near."

"On mock-prey," she said. "One of the wolves, maybe. If you can catch a bit of leather the wolf holds between his teeth, when he knows you are trying to do it and doesn't want you to—"

Prune Pit considered. He had never tried that on a wolf; his effort had always been to cooperate with Halfhowl. Yet Softfoot's reasoning seemed valid: If he could do it with an alert wolf, he could probably do it with an allo. "But what wolf? We need to integrate with our own wolf-friends; that's the key to this. I won't attack an allo alone; I need to coordinate an attack by a hunting party."

"Maybe a volunteer," she suggested.

Prune Pit called to Halfhowl with his mind. As always, he did not send coherent instructions; it was more of a single thought, the concept of a wolf agreeing to do something special. In a moment Halfhowl tuned out; he was inquiring among his kind.

Prune Pit and Softfoot walked out through the forest, waiting to meet with the wolves. The dew was bright on the leaves, and things seemed peaceful. Yet they knew that the ravening horde of allos was moving closer; peace was illusory.

Three wolves cut through the trees toward them. They were Halfhowl, Hardfoot, and Silvertooth. The first two were Prune Pit and Softfoot's wolf-friends, both tawny and somewhat shaggy. But the third—

"You are the volunteer, Silvertooth?" Softfoot inquired, astonished. "But your injuries—"

Silvertooth was Rahnee's wolf-friend, and had dragged herself back to help give the warning after the disaster. She was silver in more than the tooth; her fur was like the light of the moons, seeming almost to glow despite her advanced age. She was limping now, and moved slowly, for she had lost blood. She should have been lying in her den, recovering what strength she could.

Prune Pit touched her mind, and understood. "She feels she has no better use than this, now," he reported, translating the feeling to human terms. "She could not save her elf-friend, and may die herself, but she can help the rest of us oppose this menace."

"That is very generous of her," Softfoot agreed. "Then we can do it now."

But another wolf approached, this one with a rider. "Do what?" Hoverhair asked. "Why is Silvertooth out here?" Her wolf, Curlfur, stopped, and she dismounted. She was, as always, a splendid figure of a woman, even bundled as she was for the morning. "I saw the wolves coming here, and so I followed."

"Prune Pit has a way to stop the allos," Softfoot said. "We're about to test it."

"Oh? What is it?" Hoverhair turned to Prune Pit, gazing directly into his face for the first time.

As their eyes met, something happened. Prune Pit had always known that Hoverhair was beautiful; now her beauty seemed to intensify like the sunrise, striking through to his heart. He stared at her, almost unblinking. "Aiyse," he said, awed. It was her soul-name, a thing she had never told another person.

"No," she whispered, horrified, staring back at him. "Not this!"

"What's the matter?" Softfoot asked, perplexed.

"It's Recognition," Hoverhair said, never breaking her gaze into Prune Pit's face. "I know your soul-name. Owm. I know its meaning. But I never sought this!"

"Neither did I," Prune Pit said. She had, indeed, read his soul-name: that concept-sound that defined his essence, the thing that distinguished him from all other elves. His ability to relate telepathically to animals was defined by that name. "I love Softfoot."

"It can't be!" Softfoot cried with dismay. "This—we have other business!"

"Not any more," Hoverhair said. Then she wrenched her gaze away. "Oh, why did this have to happen now?"

"Maybe we can fight it," Prune Pit said without conviction.

Softfoot regrouped. "Fight it? Easier to fight the allos!" she said angrily. "Recognition is absolute." Then she realized what she was saying, and tears stifled her. Her relationship with Prune Pit had been based on understanding and acceptance and respect, not Recognition. Recognition was the involuntary mating of particular elves, seeming to be a mechanism of the species to ensure offspring that bred true.

"It must be a mistake," Prune Pit said. "I don't love Hoverhair."

"And I don't love you," Hoverhair said. "I never had any interest in you! I don't have any interest now!" For the first time, he was seeing her expressing genuine emotion and of course it was negative.

"Let's be practical," Softfoot said. "Recognition doesn't care whether two people love each other or even whether they like each other. It's just a mating urge. We all agree we don't want a—a longer relationship. Could we perhaps hide it?"

"From whom?" Prune Pit asked. "It's all I can do to keep my hands off her!"

"Try to manage it, though," Hoverhair said grimly.

"From the others," Softfoot said.

"To what point?" Hoverhair asked. It was obvious that this was a phenomenal nuisance to her, despite its validity.

"To the point of getting the mating over with the least disruption of our lives," Softfoot said with difficulty. She would have given anything to have been the one to Recognize Prune Pit, and now had to accept its manifestation in one who didn't want it or him. "Since Recognition can't be resisted, the only way to make it go away is to complete it."

"Complete it?" Prune Pit said with horror.

"I know you love me," Softfoot said. "Why don't you do what you have to do with her, and when it's done, turn your back on it and be with me? I confess it's not my favorite situation, but it does seem the best way through."

Prune Pit looked at Hoverhair. "And never tell the others," he said, finally understanding what Softfoot was offering.

"And never tell the others," Hoverhair said, brightening. Her cold nature seemed unaffected by the Recognition; she was eager to minimize its inconvenience. "Maybe that would work, except that when the baby comes—"

"Any elf would be glad to think he made it—with you," Softfoot pointed out. "Who would suspect Prune Pit?"

"I have not *been* with any elf!" Hoverhair protested.

"They won't believe that," Softfoot said. "They'll assume you have a secret love."

"Meanwhile, we can try to stop the allos," Prune Pit said, uncomfortable with this dialogue.

Hoverhair looked at Softfoot. She was quick enough to recognize the proffered convenience. "When?"

Softfoot shrugged. "Now, if you want."

"I *don't* want! But if it's medicine I must take, the sooner the better, so I can forget it."

"We were going to run our test," Prune Pit said with an edge.

"Let's find a good place for it," Softfoot suggested. Prune Pit was unable to read her exact meaning, but evidently Hoverhair did.

They mounted and rode their wolves to a sparse section of the forest, well clear of the elves' usual haunts. They drew up at a large thicket of brush through which animal paths threaded. "There," Softfoot said brusquely. "I will scout about with the wolves."

"Now, wait—" Prune Pit protested as she rode off.

But Hoverhair took him by the hand. "The faster we get this over with, the better," she said. "If we're lucky, one time will do it. I assure you this is no fun for me."

"Oh." He followed her into the brush. He never would have believed that he could anticipate such an act with such a lovely creature with so little enthusiasm. Hoverhair had no concern at all for his feelings, or for Softfoot's. If she could have gotten bred without being physically present, she certainly would have done it.

But when she opened her leather tunic and smiled at him, he found it impossible not to react despite his awareness of the calculated nature of her actions. Her bosom did not look as if it contained ice; indeed, she was warm all over. Perhaps the Recognition changed her nature, for this one occasion. All the elven conjectures about the loveliness of her body when naked were emphatically confirmed.

"Turn your face away," she said, reminding him abruptly of reality.

He did so, trying to imagine that it was Softfoot he held, but it was no good. He knew it was Hoverhair, and that she was facilitating this chore so that it would take the very minimum time. Such was the compulsion of the Recognition that it made no difference.

Softfoot rode Hardfoot, circling around the thicket. The wolf had been named for his thick claws and heavily callused pads. His tough feet were exactly what she needed, and she had always appreciated this. Perhaps that was why Hardfoot had come to her, to be her wolf-friend. The terrain was ragged, but no more so than her thoughts. She knew she had done something foolish: She had made a decision that could affect the rest of her life, and she had not slept on it. If it turned out wrong, it would be because of that carelessness.

Yet how could it turn out wrong? Recognition could not be opposed. She was no strong telepath, but she had picked up enough to know that what had passed between Prune Pit and Hoverhair was valid. She also believed them both when they said they had neither sought nor wanted it. Recognition did not require its chosen to seek it; it chose on its own basis, trampling under any other concerns. If she had fought it, encouraging her lifemate to flee it, he would have sickened, and his love for her would have suffered. From the moment the Recognition occurred, Prune Pit and Hoverhair were destined to mate. There was nothing else Softfoot *could* do except accept it.

Then where was her error? As she mulled it over, she knew what it was. She had ignored Hoverhair's motives. Oh, of course Hoverhair had no more choice than did Prune Pit. Recognition accepted no motive but its own, as it went single-mindedly after the best combinations for the breed. But Hoverhair had always wanted to better her status, in whatever manner status existed among the elves. If she could have fascinated a chief, so as to be the life-mate of the most influential leader of the tribe, she would have. But there had been no male chief of her generation.

Now, however, Prune Pit might become chief, if his idea for hunting allos worked. If he became chief, he would be suitable material for Hoverhair's interest. Her interest, once aroused, was apt to be devastating. She would, quite simply, take him for her lifemate. Prune Pit had settled for Softfoot partly because it had never occurred to him that a woman like Hoverhair would be interested in him. Indeed, she had not been, and would never have been, but for the Recognition. But what was planned as a strictly temporary tryst was in danger of becoming more than that, and Softfoot could do nothing to prevent it. Hoverhair's beauty, and her total self-interest, and the Recognition, made that clear.

Yet what could Softfoot have done? She was sure she had made a mistake, but she could not see how she could have avoided it. Maybe if she had slept on it, she would have found a way. Now she was stuck; she loved Prune Pit, and would always love him, but perhaps would lose him.

She laid her head against Hardfoot's furry shoulder and let the tears flow. The wolf ran on, completing the scouting without her direct guidance. He was aware of her misery, but did not fathom its source, so he let it be.

Prune Pit and Hoverhair emerged, and mounted their wolves. Physically, they seemed unaffected; it was as if nothing had happened. But mentally everything had changed; the compelling hunger of the Recognition had abated.

Another woman had made love to Softfoot's lifemate, and had done it better than Softfoot had ever been capable of. Cold as Hoverhair was, she was always good at what she put her mind to, and Recognition made it easy. No, there was no way Softfoot could compete—if Hoverhair decided on more than mere mating.

Prune Pit joined Silvertooth, setting his hand on the great wolf's head for the strongest contact, explaining the role required of her. The wolf understood: She would run and dodge and feint, never truly attacking, and her actions would be scored as attacks. She was weak, but this she could do. She accepted a piece of leather; this she would protect with her mock-life.

Now Prune Pit conferred with the others. "You must not try to guide your wolves," he told the two women. "You must use your weapons only as the opportunity arises; it will seem like chance, for you will not know how your wolves will move."

"I don't like that," Hoverhair said. "It will be like riding a strange wolf."

"I know. But my plan is to link the minds of the wolves to the mind of the prey, so that they can maneuver as fast as it thinks. No wolf—and no rider—will be in danger as long as that is the case. Then the riders will be able to strike at will."

"If they don't fall off their mounts!" Hoverhair exclaimed. "I'm glad this isn't a real allo!" She could readily have added that she would have been even happier if she hadn't had to undertake a real mating.

Now they started the test. The three riders on their wolves surrounded the mock-allo, who growled and snapped convincingly, but never let go of the banner. But when Silvertooth lunged, the wolf before her dodged away, while the two others moved in closer. She snapped to the side, but again the target was moving at the same time she did, avoiding her without effort.

Then Prune Pit reached forward just as Silvertooth hesitated, and caught away the banner. It had been almost too easy; it seemed like sheer chance. Had the prey reacted differently—

"Let me be the allo," Hoverhair said, dismounting. "Anything I tag is dead." She took the banner from his hand and held it aloft.

"No, we could not take it from you, without suffering losses," Prune Pit said. "I can not relate well enough to elven minds, only to animals. But the allos are animals."

Hoverhair nodded. "I think it will work," she said. "We must try it with the rest of the tribe."

Prune Pit grimaced. "They will resist the notion. No one likes to have any other person between him and his wolf."

"Not if six of the finest young elves show how well it works," she said confidently. "Then the women will believe too."

"Six young men?"

"I will ask them," she said. "They will not refuse."

* * *

They did not refuse. No male elf refused anything Hoverhair truly wanted, however crazy it might seem. Not even this. The elves were openly skeptical, but the demonstration worked. "Now we must go and tackle an allo," Prune Pit said. "Only when we have proven that we can kill allos without taking losses, will we know that we can handle this crisis." For the numbers of the elves were not great, and had been depleted by the recent disaster; they could not spare any more lives without throwing the viability of the tribe into question.

They rode out the next day, a party of their best remaining hunters. They did not have far to go, for the allos had forged steadily toward the holt. All too soon they encountered the first one.

It was a giant of a reptile. Its hide was knobby rather than scaly, but tougher than any ordinary leather. Its color was faintly reddish, as if heated by the sun. But this was morning; the sun's full heat had not yet come, and the trees shaded the ground. The creature moved somewhat lethargically. Even so, its huge claws and teeth made it formidable. It outmassed the elven party, and it had no fear.

Prune Pit stared at the monster, daunted. The thing was so big, so ugly, so sure of itself! It did not flee them; instead it came purposefully toward them, taking them to be prey. It did not move as fast as the wolves, but no elf afoot would be safe.

Would his system of mind-linkage work on such a monster? Prune Pit quelled his doubt. It had to work!

"Remember," he called. "Let the wolves guide themselves."

The elves nodded. They had seen it work in the rehearsal; they did not feel easy with it, but they knew what to do.

The group of them spread out to surround the allo. Prune Pit reached for the reptile's mind—and was appalled. The thing was a nest of sting-tails, concerned with nothing but hatred and hunger. Hatred for all other creatures, and hunger for their flesh. This was simply an attack entity, with no concern for danger, indeed hardly any awareness of it. Charge, bite, tear! swallow—that was its desire.

The allo leaped for a wolf—but the wolf was already moving out of the way, while three on the other side moved in close, their riders lifting their weapons. A spear plunged toward the monster's ear-region, and an arrow winged toward its eye.

The spear slid off; the ear was armored, and the point was unable to penetrate. The arrow seemed about to make a perfect strike—but the monster's heavily ridged brow squinted, and the arrow bounced off and was lost.

The head whipped back to snap at the three attackers. As before, the three were moving before the head did, retreating, so that the great teeth closed on air. Simultaneously, the wolves on the far side moved in close, and their riders attacked.

A spear sought the monster's nose. But this too was armored, and the teeth caught the spear and crunched it to splinters. The allo bit at anything it could reach, whether flesh or wood. If it ever caught any part of a wolf or elf, that would be the end of that creature.

The allo lurched this way and that, thinking to snap up its tormenters, but they were impossibly elusive. Prune Pit had linked the minds of the wolves to the mind of the reptile, and the wolves had better minds. They reacted more swiftly to the allo's thoughts than it did itself, so that any action it tried was useless. The system was working!

Or was it? The attacks and counters continued, but the allo was taking no significant injuries, and the longer the action proceeded, the more alert the reptile was becoming. It was really a standoff, with neither side able to harm the other. Prune Pit had assumed that once they nullified the reptile's attack, it would be only a matter of time before they killed it. Now he saw that this was not the case.

What good was it to harass the allo, if they couldn't hurt it?

There was a growl from the side. A second allo was coming!

"Withdraw!" Prune Pit cried.

The elves resumed contact with their wolves. The group fled from the allos, outdistancing them. But the field of battle belonged to the reptiles.

They drew up in a glade. The wolves were panting; they had been working hard. The elves were in good order, but they had lost a number of spears and arrows.

Prune Pit was dejected. "The thing is too tough," he said. "Our weapons won't dent it!"

"But it couldn't touch us!" Softfoot exclaimed. "We were like ghosts to it!"

"Ghosts can't hurt real folks," he reminded her. As a general rule, elves did not believe in ghosts; a dead elf was dead, with no apologies. But human beings believed, and so the concept was known, if not respected.

"We just have to find its weak spot," Softfoot said. "If we strike there, then we'll have it!"

The discussion lapsed; there had been no evidence of any weak spot. The allo was protected at every point.

There was a crashing in the brush. Another allo was coming! Hastily the elves mounted, and the wolves fled the glade. If there had been any doubt who controlled the terrain, this removed it. It was becoming increasingly evident why the allos had defeated Rahnee; the elves had never before encountered so tough an enemy.

Prune Pit found himself riding next to Hoverhair. She beckoned him closer. Did she want another mating? This was hardly the time, even if the Recognition was developing its imperative again.

But she had another matter on her mind for the moment. "I think the allo must be soft inside," she said as Prune Pit's ear came close.

He laughed bitterly. "I do not care to go inside it!"

"But if we could attack it from inside—"

"How? Without first encountering its teeth?"

"By setting something inside it," she said. "I notice that it bites at anything it reaches. Suppose it bit a burning ball of tar?"

Prune Pit's mouth dropped open. "The tar pit's not far from here!"

"Yes. Why don't you tell the others?"

"But it's your idea!" he protested. "You should have the credit for it!"

"I want you to have the credit."

"Why?"

"Because if it works, you will be chief."

"Yes! So you could be—"

"I am no leader," she said. "You know that. But you could be."

Prune Pit was not at all certain that she lacked qualities of leadership. Hoverhair had fought well and kept her poise throughout, and now she had an idea that well might turn the tide of battle.

She was also infernally beautiful, and his Recognized.

Her wolf veered away. The dialogue was over.

Prune Pit shrugged. Of course Hoverhair did not want to be seen with him. They had agreed that no one would know of their Recognition. Still, she could have given her notion to another hunter. Why had she wanted him to have the best chance to be chief? He was sure that she had a selfish reason, and it bothered him to be the beneficiary of a gift whose motive he did not understand.

Softfoot rode close. She did not speak; she just glanced at him. He knew she had observed his dialogue with Hoverhair. Surely she misunderstood its nature!

He beckoned her. "She has a notion!" he called as she came closer.

Softfoot made a moue.

"Not that one!" he exclaimed. "She—"

But Softfoot's wolf diverged, and he could not finish. He

had hurt her, without meaning to. If only he could send to his own kind as well as he could to animals!

Well, perhaps his action would clarify it. "To the tar pit!" he cried, gesturing in its direction.

At the tar pit they drew up again. There were no allos here, yet.

"If we gather tarballs, and light them, and feed them to the allos, that should kill them," Prune Pit said.

The elves considered. "How can we feed the monster a tarball?" Dampstar asked. He had come by his name when traveling at night, seeing a star reflected in the river.

"With an arrow," Prune Pit said. He picked up a stick, dipped it in the thick tar, and got a blob on the end. "We must have the tar-arrows ready, and light them when we approach the allos, then shoot them in when the time is right."

"But only the wolves know when the time is right," Soft-foot pointed out. "We can not connect to the mind of the reptile."

"I might do it, if Curlfur warns me," Hoverhair said. She was an excellent shot with her bow. "But I will need some help in setting up my arrows."

Several male elves volunteered immediately to help. Prune Pit was left alone for a moment with Softfoot.

"It was a good notion," she said. "I'm sorry for what I thought."

"But I don't understand why she gave it to me," he said. "She said it was because she could not be chief, but I could. Does that make sense?"

"She wants her child to be the offspring of a chief," Softfoot said, biting her lip.

"But if no one knows the father—"

"The blood knows."

He looked at her. "You know I could not resist the Recognition. But my feeling for you—"

She turned away.

"It's *your* child I want to have!" he cried.

"I can not give you what she can."

"How do we know that? Breeding is not limited to Recognition! Maybe—"

She faced him. "I have not denied you," she said. "I would have your child if I could. But it may not be possible. That may be why the Recognition struck. Who knows."

"If only—" he began. But then the elves returned with Hoverhair's arrows, each dipped in tar.

"We must have a firepot, too," Hoverhair said.

They filled a container with the tar, and the elf who had the fire-talent struck flame, lighting it. The tar burned with guttering vigor, throwing up thick smoke. The wolves shied away from it, apprehensive about the fire, but Prune Pit touched their minds and showed how this fire was their friend. Curlfur even consented to carry the firepot, smoking in its harness, so that Hoverhair could have it ready without delay.

It was now midday. Prune Pit hesitated. Was it wise to tackle the allos again now, when they would be most vigorous? Yet if they waited another day, the reptiles could be almost at the holt. It would be better to do it here, where there was still room to retreat.

They rode slowly back to intercept the allos. It did not take long; the horde was in full motion, on its search for what little prey remained.

"We must strike quickly, and retreat," Prune Pit warned them. "We don't know how long it will take the tar to do the job. It doesn't have to be fast, just sure. Now turn over your wolves to me."

The elves did so with better grace than before; though they had not succeeded in killing the allo, they had appreciated the perfect coordination of the wolves, and had understood its necessity.

They rode up to meet the first allo. This one was larger than the one they had tackled in the morning, and faster, because of the heat of day. It screamed and charged them with appalling ferocity, its jaws gaping.

Hoverhair stood her ground. Calmly she touched an

arrow to the firepot, waiting for its gooey tip to blaze up. Then she fitted it to her bow and took aim.

Prune Pit saw that she was going to be overrun, but he couldn't even yell; he had to keep the wolves connected.

Hoverhair fired her arrow. The aim was perfect; the missile shot right into the throat of the monster.

Then Curlfur moved, almost slowly, for Hoverhair was not holding on. He carried her just that minimum required to avoid the charge of the reptile, while wolves to either side crowded close, harassing the creature.

But the allo had abruptly lost interest in the wolves. Smoke was issuing from its nostrils, making it look like the human concept of a dragon. Human beings had a number of odd concepts, which was one reason—hardly the only one!— that elves stayed away from them. It swallowed—then screamed, as the burning material coursed down its throat.

The agony hit Prune Pit like a savage storm. He was burning inside! Quickly he tuned out—and suddenly the wolves were on their own, the connection broken.

But the job had been done. The allo whipped about, trying to free itself of the pain. It rolled on the ground, its tail thrashing wildly.

The commotion alerted another allo. It charged in, intent on the first. Without hesitation it bit, needing no inducement other than helplessness. The elves watched, horrified yet fascinated by the savagery.

"Kill one, distract one," Softfoot murmured.

"But we have no meat for our wolves," an elf pointed out. "We need a kill we can butcher."

"Well, get it," Prune Pit said. "Now we know how to kill the allos."

They closed on the feeding reptile. It growled, warning them off, but did not stop feeding. Hoverhair readied another arrow.

Prune Pit linked the minds of the wolves with that of the second allo. They circled close. The allo growled again and made a feint, opening its mouth wide—and Hoverhair dipped her arrow and fired it.

She scored on the inside of the mouth. Now the allo roared, trying to spit out the fiery barb, but only burned its tongue. The tar was stuck in its mouth, blazing.

Unfortunately, this new commotion attracted several other allos. They came in a monstrous wave, big ones and small ones, smelling the blood. The elves had to flee.

"There are so many!" Softfoot exclaimed. "Every time we kill one, more come!"

Prune Pit nodded. The problem was so much more complicated than he had supposed it could be! He had thought that when they killed one allo, that would be the turning point. Instead, the problem had grown with each success.

Hoverhair rode close again. "You know why you're having so much trouble?" she asked. "It's because you're not thinking like a chief."

"I'm not a chief!" he replied.

"You showed how to deal with the allos," she reminded him. "That makes you chief. But it will never work unless you believe it yourself."

"But I can't just declare myself chief!" he protested.

"Why not?"

"They would laugh!"

"If you don't, they will die, as the allos overrun our holt."

He was very much afraid she was right. He had taken on this mission because of the need; he had not thought beyond it. Now he appreciated the greater need: for a continuing leadership, that could handle problems as they came, whatever they might be.

Still, he did not feel competent, because he couldn't solve the problem of the numbers of allos. What good was it to slay one, or two, or three, or ten, if more always came?

He mulled that over as they rode, outdistancing the reptiles. He felt ashamed, because so much of his thinking had been done for him by the woman who didn't want to share his life, Hoverhair. A chief didn't let others do his thinking! For that matter, what chief had a name like Prune Pit?

Then he suffered a major realization.

Stop at the next good resting place, he thought to the wolves. That was the elven version; the actual message was simply a vision of a nice spot, with wolves relaxing.

When they stopped, Prune Pit called out to them to gather around. "We agreed that whoever solved the problem of the allos would be chief," he said. "I have shown how to solve it, so I am declaring myself chief. I admit that the problem is not over yet, but I will dedicate myself to dealing with it. I am the only one who can unify the minds of the wolves with the mind of the prey, and that is what we need to do this job."

He paused, but there was no reaction. They were waiting to hear him out before drawing their conclusions.

"To signify this determination, I am taking a new name," he said. "I enable the wolves to link with the prey, to pace it, moving before it can move. Therefore I will call myself Prey Pacer, and that will be my name as long as I am chief."

Still they did not speak. He hoped he was not making himself ludicrous. The key element of his assumption was coming up.

"But I do not know all the answers to all the problems. I never expected to be chief, before my mother died, and have had no practice in it. I know I will make mistakes if I try to decide everything myself. So my decision is—to make no significant decision without first getting the best advice I can. For example, I don't know how to stop the allos from taking meat of whichever ones we kill. Does anyone here know?"

They considered. "Why don't we kill one and butcher it?" Dampstar asked.

"That sounds good to me," Prey Pacer said. "Does anyone have an objection?"

"Yes," Hoverhair said. "Those reptiles track by the smell of blood as much as anything else. They could collect under that tree and never leave."

"But then we have a way to stop them!" Softfoot pointed out. "We can hang flesh in several trees, and the whole horde will stop right there."

The elves pursed their lips, thinking about that.

"Well, either they'll stay by the tree, or they won't," Prey Pacer said. "If they stay, they won't bother us elsewhere. If not, we have a cache we can return to. I think it's an excellent suggestion, and I'll do it if a better one doesn't come along. Thank you, Dampstar."

Dampstar grinned with pride, just as if a real chief had complimented him.

Hoverhair nodded, gazing at Prey Pacer with new appraisal. He was making it work.

But Softfoot was looking at Hoverhair. What was passing through her mind? She must be suspicious that Hoverhair was reconsidering about keeping the secret, and might decide after all to be the lifemate of a chief. He was suspicious of that too—and knew that as much as he loved Softfoot, he would not be able to deny Hoverhair if she decided to take him. That single mating with her—already he felt the yearning returning. Perhaps it was only the Recognition, asserting its hunger to generate the baby it had chosen. But perhaps it was his own fickle male nature, vulnerable to beauty no matter what his mind said.

There was a roar. Another allo had come across them, and was charging in.

The elves leaped for their wolves. But Hoverhair reached for an arrow first, dipping it in the firepot. She took aim at the monster bearing down on her.

Prey Pacer, astride Halfhowl, looked back, abruptly realizing that she had not mounted. He had never witnessed an act of greater courage! But it was foolish courage, because she had no way to escape the reptile in time. Already the allo's huge head was orienting on her. Sweeping down as the terrible jaws opened. Curlfur remained close to her, but could not make her mount before she was ready.

Hoverhair fired into that open mouth. The flaming arrow

went right into the throat. The allo choked, but its momentum was such that even as it stumbled, it was coming down to crush the woman. It was far too late for Prey Pacer to do anything, even if he had been able to act.

Then a shape shot by, passing almost under the falling monster. It was a wolf and rider, leaping to intercept Hoverhair. The rider launched from the wolf, pushing off to tackle Hoverhair and shove her out of the way as the allo's head and neck whomped down at her.

The monster struck the ground. Hoverhair stumbled clear, safe by the narrowest margin. But her rescuer had not made it; her legs were pinned under the fallen allo.

Then Prey Pacer realized who it was. Softfoot lay there, unconscious.

Prey Pacer was the first to reach them. "Why did she do it?" he gasped, horrified.

Hoverhair swallowed. She was not so cold as to overlook the narrowness of her escape. "Because she loves you," she said, awed.

"But you are her rival!"

"And she was protecting your child—whoever carried it," Hoverhair added. "I think I could not have done that."

Softfoot groaned. "She's alive!" Prey Pacer exclaimed.

"But will be lame, I fear," Hoverhair said. "She never was apt on her feet, and now will be worse. She will need a lot of attention." She gazed down at Softfoot, and a tear rolled down her cheek. It seemed that her cold heart had at last been touched. Then, as the other elves arrived, she raised her voice. "Get sticks! Lever this monster off the chief's lifemate! She saved my life!"

Then Prey Pacer knew that no matter who bore his child, no one would try to separate him from Softfoot. One woman had acted with measureless courage, and brought down an allo single-handed. The other had acted with similar courage, and with measureless generosity, and won the respect and gratitude of two who would not forget.

* * *

Prey Pacer was indeed chief, and was known as the most superlative of elven hunters despite his seeming inadequacies of weapon and of sending. It took time, but he succeeded in abating the menace of the allos, and they retreated to their former obscurity. He sired not one but two children. The first was Hoverhair's daughter, to be named Skyfire, inheriting the beauty and nerve of her mother. The second was Softfoot's son, to be named Two-Spear, trained in his mother's weapon. But for a long time, only the second was known as Prey Pacer's offspring, until the secret no longer mattered.

Think of the Reader

In 1989 the editor of THE WRITER, a magazine devoted to the interests of writers, asked me to contribute an article. It's a good magazine; I recommend it to those who are seriously hopeful writers.

Now there is a paramount rule that every editor will tell you: Never try to write for an unfamiliar market. Read several issues of a magazine before you try to submit anything to it, or you are bound to fail.

Like many rules, this is only for those who don't know better. I hadn't seen an issue of THE WRITER for twenty years. So I wrote an article, sent it off, and it was accepted and published, and included in the annual volume, THE WRITER'S HANDBOOK. You see, I hadn't seen the magazine, but I did know how to write. Also, I had seen the prior year's annual, so I did have a notion what they wanted. I wasn't flying blind. But I was flying my own course. As I say in the article: "The writer who passively accepts the dictates of the experts is unlikely to become expert himself." But of course I was dealing with an editor, and if you don't know how editors are by this time, it isn't because I haven't tried to educate you. So what do you think happened? Right: She cut that sentence. This is the original, unexpurgated version.

I mention in this article something that was fresh at the time: my correspondence with Jenny, who was in a coma at the time I first wrote to her. She was to become my leading correspondent. Indeed, keep an eye out for *Letters to Jenny,* from this publisher. She does illustrate my point about writing. I care about you my readers, and you care about me, and that is a precious connection. May it always be so.

Think of the Reader

I am known as a writer of popular fantasy and science fiction, though my output is not limited to that. Thus my view is that of a genre writer who is trying to understand more general principles.

Back when I was struggling to break in to print, I took a correspondence course in writing. The proprietors knew a great deal about writing, but little about science fiction. No matter, they said; the fundamentals of good writing apply to all genres, and they could help me. They were half right: The fundamentals do apply, but you do have to know the genre—any genre—in order to write successfully for it. Their ignorance of science fiction made much of their material useless to me. They could not accept the notion that I, an unpublished writer, could be privy to a fundamental they weren't, and in their unconscious arrogance they failed me.

I studied my market on my own, and in the end I made it on my own. From this I derive a principle: There is virtue in being ornery. The writer who passively accepts the dictates of the experts is unlikely to become expert himself. I continue to be ornery, and continue to score in ways the critics seem unable to fathom, as the tone of this essay suggests.

A writer *should* study his market, and study general principles; both are essential. He should also forge his own way, contributing such limited originality as the market will tolerate. There is plenty of excellent instruction elsewhere on such things. I am concerned with a more subtle yet vital aspect of writing than most: the writer's liaison with the reader. This can make or break a piece of writing, yet few seem to grasp its significance. This is one of my many differences with critics, so I will use them as a straw man to help make my point.

I picture a gathering of the elite of the genre, who are there to determine the critic's choice of the best works of science fiction and fantasy of all time. That is, the List that will be graven on granite for the edification of the lesser aspirants. In the genre these would be Delany's *Dhalgren,* Aldiss' *Report on Probability A,* and Hoban's *Riddley Walker,* and the finest writer of all time would be J. G. Ballard despite his one failure with *Empire of the Sun.*

Have you read any of these? Have you even heard of them? No, except that you did like the motion picture based on the last? Well, the critics have an answer for you: You are an ignorant lout whose library card and book store privileges should be suspended until your tastes improve.

Yet any ordinary person who tries to read such books will wonder just what world such critics live in. The answer is, of course, a different world. They are like the poet Shelley's Ozymandias, whose colossal ruin lies in the barren sand. "Look on my works, ye mighty, and despair." Yet his works are completely forgotten.

I am in the world of commercial writing, which means it is readable and enjoyable, and the only accolade it is likely to receive from critics is a mock award for WHO KILLED SCIENCE FICTION? (I was in a five-way tie for runner-up on that one last year, but there's hope for the future.)

But I maintain that the essence of literature lies in its assimilation by the ordinary folk, and that readability is the first, not the last criterion for its merit. Therefore I address the subject of writing, regardless of genre, from this perspective. What makes it readable? To hell with formal rules of writing; they are guidelines in the absence of talent, and should be honored only so long as they do not interfere. If it's clear and interesting and relates to the needs of the reader, it will score. I like to tell audiences that they may love or hate what I write, but they will be moved by it. Then I prove it. The only person to fall asleep during one of my recent readings was a senior editor. Well, there are limits, and even I can't squeeze much blood from a stone. I am successful in part because I make connections with my readers that bypass the editors as well as the critics.

How do I do it? Well, there are little tricks, and one big secret. All of them are so simple that it's a wonder they aren't practiced by every writer. But they are not, and indeed critics condemn them and editors try to excise them from my manuscripts. I have had many an internecine battle with editors, and finally left a major publisher because of this. I understand I am known as a difficult writer to work with, though no editor says it to my face. I can't imagine why!

All the tricks can be subsumed under one guideline: *Think of the reader.* Do it at every stage. Every paragraph, every word. If you are writing fantasy, don't use a word like "subsumed," because the reader won't understand it. It's a lovely word, but unless your readership consists of intellectuals or folk interested in precise usage—such as those who are presumed to read a magazine like this one—forgo your private pleasure and speak more plainly. "All the tricks add up to this." I can with ease overreach the horizons of my readers, but I do my damnedest not to. Any writer who thinks he's smart when he baffles his readers, whether by using foreign phrases or obscure terminology, is the opposite.

When you have reference to a character or situation that has been absent from your recent text, refresh the matter for your reader, so that he won't have to leaf back interminably to find out what you're talking about. Don't say "The List is foolish." Huh? What list? Say "The List of the critics' top genre novels I parodied above is foolish." Editors seem to hate this; they blue-pencil it out as redundancy. But it enables the reader to check in with your concept without pausing, and that's what counts. Never let your reader stumble; lead him by the hand—and do it without patronizing him.

When you introduce a new character, don't just throw

him at the reader unprepared. Have him introduced by a familiar character, if you possibly can. In my forthcoming mainstream novel *Firefly* I start with one character, who later meets another, and then I follow the other character. That one meets a third, and I follow the third. In the course of 150,000 words, the only character the reader meets cold is the first one. Thus the reader can proceed smoothly throughout, never tripping. It was a job to arrange some of the handoffs, but that *is* my job as writer: to do the busy-work for the reader. Some of the concepts in this novel are mind-stretching, but the little tricks smooth the way.

When I do a series—and I've done ten so far—I try to make each novel stand by itself, so that the reader who comes to it new does not have to struggle with an ongoing and confusing situation. Yes, this means repeating and summarizing some material, and it is a challenge to do that without boring those who have read the prior novels. But it means, for example, that a reader can start with my tenth Xanth novel and read backwards toward the first, and enjoy them all. Xanth has many readers, and this is part of the reason: it is easy to get into, and it does not demand more than the reader cares to give. Perhaps no other series shows a greater dichotomy between the contempt of critics and the devotion of readers. I do know my market, and it is not the critics. I suspect the same is true for most commercial writers.

Science fiction is fantastic stuff. Little of it is truly believable, and less is meant to be. It represents a flight of fancy for the mind, far removed from the dullness of mundane affairs. Yet even there, human values are paramount. There needs to be respect for every situation and every character, no matter how far out. Every thing is real on its own terms, and every one is alive, even when the thing is as outrageous as a night mare who is a female horse bearing dreams and one is the Incarnation of Death itself, complete with scythe. Can a robot have feelings? Yes, and they are similar to those of a human being. For in the tacit symbolism of the genre as I practice it, a humanoid robot may be a man whose color, religion or language differs from those of the culture into which he is thrust, and his feelings are those any of us would experience if similarly thrust. The essence of the genre is human, even when it is alien.

As I write this article, I am in an ongoing situation that illustrates the way that even the most fantastic and/or humorous fiction can relate to serious life. A twelve-year-old girl walking home from school was struck by a drunk driver, and spent three months in a coma, barely responsive to any outside stimulus. At her mother's behest I wrote her a letter, for she was one of my readers. I talked about the magic land of Xanth, and the sister realm of ElfQuest by another author, and the value of children to those who love them, and I joked about the loathsome shot the nurse would give the Monster Under the Bed if she saw him. I spoke of the character with her name who would be in a future Xanth novel, an elf girl or maybe an ogre girl.

The child's mother read the letter to her, and it brought a great widening of her eyes, and her first smile since the accident. She became responsive, though able to move only her eyes, one big toe, and her fingers. She started to indicate YES or NO to verbal questions by looking to placards with those words printed on them. She made her preference emphatically clear: an elf girl, not an ogre girl!

It is my hope that she is now on the way to recovery, though there is of course a long way to go. It was fantasy that made the connection to reality, her response to my interest and my teasing. I think that fantasy needs no more justification than this. I, as writer, was able to relate to her, my reader, and she responded to me. The rest will be mostly in the province of medicine, but the human spark was vital to the turning point.

And here is the secret I am working toward: Writing and reading are one on one, writer to reader and back again, and the rest of the universe doesn't matter. The writer must know his readers, not the details of their lives, which are myriad, but their hearts and dreams. He must relate. He must care.

When I write to you, it is as if we are in a privacy booth, and we are sharing things that neither of us would confess elsewhere. We love, we hurt, we laugh, we fear, we cry, we wonder, we are embarrassed—together. We *feel*, linked. We share our joy and our shame, and yes I feel your tears on my face as you feel mine on yours. We may be of different sexes and other generations, or we may match—but we relate to each other more intimately than any two others, dream to dream, our emotions mixed and tangled—for that time while the book that is our connection is open. When it closes we are cut off from each other, and we are strangers again, and we regret that, but we remember our sharing, and we cherish it. We were true friends, for a while. How precious was that while!

PIERS ANTHONY
THE GRANDE MASTER

☐	53114-0	ANTHONOLOGY	$3.50 Canada $3.95
☐	53098-5	BUT WHAT OF EARTH?	$4.95 Canada $5.95
☐	50915-3	CHIMAERA'S COPPER	$4.95 Canada $5.95
☐	51384-3	DRAGON'S GOLD	$3.95 Canada $4.95
☐	51916-7	THE ESP WORM 　　with Robert E. Margroff	$3.95 Canada $4.95
☐	52088-2	GHOST	$3.99 Canada $4.99
☐	51348-7	HASAN	$3.99 Canada $4.99
☐	51982-5	MOUVAR'S MAGIC 　　with Robert E. Margroff	$4.99 Canada $5.99
☐	51177-8	ORC'S OPAL 　　with Robert E. Margroff	$4.99 Canada $5.99